The Sweet Bye-and-Good-Bye

"Paradise isn't the sleepy little farm town it used to be," I agreed.

"But people still don't want me around," said Savannah.

"It's not easy to come back," I admitted. "I wasn't exactly welcomed, either."

Savannah let out a reedy laugh. "They'd probably keel over dead if I moved back. They can hardly stand to be in the same room with me."

Reminding her that she'd earned her reputation wouldn't accomplish anything, so I went for a less confrontational response. "People are curious, especially about why you've entered the contest. Obviously, you don't need the prize money. Some people wonder if there's another reason."

Savannah laughed as if the thought of being mysterious delighted her. With her long, dark hair and striking coloring, she looked beautiful even in the dim glow of the streetlamp. Not surprisingly, I felt like a lump of clay beside her—but, then, I always had.

"You know how it is. You'll be big news for a few days, and then they'll find something new to talk about."

"As long as I don't give them something new to sink their teeth into, right?"

Candy Shop Mysteries by Sammi Carter

CANDY APPLE DEAD

CHOCOLATE DIPPED DEATH

A Candy Shop Mystery

Chocolate Dipped Death

Sammi Carter

BERKLEY PRIME CRIME, NEW YORK

THE BERKLEY PUBLISHING GROUP
Published by the Penguin Group
Penguin Group (USA) Inc.
375 Hudson Street, New York, New York 10014, USA
Penguin Group (Canada), 90 Eglinton Avenue East, Suite 700, Toronto, Ontario M4P 2Y3, Canada (a division of Pearson Penguin Canada Inc.)
Penguin Books Ltd., 80 Strand, London WC2R 0RL, England
Penguin Group Ireland, 25 St. Stephen's Green, Dublin 2, Ireland (a division of Penguin Books Ltd.)
Penguin Group (Australia), 250 Camberwell Road, Camberwell, Victoria 3124, Australia (a division of Pearson Australia Group Pty. Ltd.)
Penguin Books India Pvt. Ltd., 11 Community Centre, Panchsheel Park, New Delhi—110 017, India
Penguin Group (NZ), Cnr. Airborne and Rosedale Roads, Albany, Auckland 1310, New Zealand (a division of Pearson New Zealand Ltd.)
Penguin Books (South Africa) (Pty.) Ltd., 24 Sturdee Avenue, Rosebank, Johannesburg 2196, South Africa

Penguin Books Ltd., Registered Offices: 80 Strand, London WC2R 0RL, England

CHOCOLATE DIPPED DEATH

A Berkley Prime Crime Book / published by arrangement with the author

PRINTING HISTORY
Berkley Prime Crime mass-market edition / March 2006

Cover art by Jeff Crosby.
Cover design by Steve Ferlauto.
Interior text design by Kristin del Rosario.

For information, address: The Berkley Publishing Group,
a division of Penguin Group (USA) Inc.,
375 Hudson Street, New York, New York 10014.

ISBN: 0-425-20894-X

BERKLEY® PRIME CRIME
Berkley Prime Crime Books are published by The Berkley Publishing Group,
a division of Penguin Group (USA) Inc.,
375 Hudson Street, New York, New York 10014.
The name BERKLEY PRIME CRIME and the BERKLEY PRIME CRIME design are trademarks belonging to Penguin Group (USA) Inc.

PRINTED IN THE UNITED STATES OF AMERICA

10 9 8 7 6 5 4 3 2 1

To the Women of the Weekend . . .
Jo Ann, Vanessa, and Paige

Chapter 1

"I can't *believe* she had the nerve to show up." My cousin Karen kept her eyes riveted on the dark-haired woman across the room and shoved an empty tray in my general direction. It teetered precariously on the edge of the table and would have fallen if I hadn't snatched it away from her. "What is she doing here, anyway?"

I slid the tray onto a shelf beneath the flowing white tablecloth that hid extra containers of candy, score sheets, programs, and the other necessary but unattractive supplies for running a three-day candy-making competition. I'd been up since five that morning and running nonstop all day as I dealt with a litany of questions, complaints, and problems. I was in no mood for trouble now.

Somehow we'd managed to turn the drab second-floor meeting room of Divinity into a thing of beauty. Swaths of flowing fabric draped the walls. Crisp white cloths covered tables in the judging and staging areas. Silver trays loaded with specialty candies nestled among pine boughs and the burgundy velvet bows Karen and I had stayed awake most of one night to make. I was proud of what we'd achieved.

Even the weather was cooperating. Snow falling outside the windows added just the right touch on a January night. I just hoped no one snooped around behind the scenes where piles of raw wood and construction equipment had been left behind by my brother and his friends after they rebuilt the stairs to my third-floor apartment.

The look on Karen's face made nervous tension knot between my shoulders and shot a big fat hole in my satisfaction with a job well done. This might be the Tenth Annual Confectionary Competition for Divinity, the candy store I'd inherited a few months earlier, but it was the first time around the block for me. I was nervous as a cat and desperate for the weekend to go well. Karen was my only help, the one person who could provide the continuity and history the contest needed. I needed her to stay focused.

I gazed around the room, checking the judges, heads together as they debated their final decision, then moving on to the contestants, who waited anxiously for the announcement. The winner of tonight's round would be one-third of the way toward scoring the grand prize on the final night: five hundred dollars in prize money and a month in the featured candy spot at Divinity, not to mention a lovely engraved plaque. It wasn't the largest or most prestigious prize in the world, but the ladies who entered the contest every year competed for it fiercely.

Satisfied that everything was going well, I tried to divert Karen's attention away from the woman she'd been glaring at all night. "Does everyone know what time to be here tomorrow?"

"Of course." Karen brushed an auburn curl from her forehead, but it fell right back into place. "I told everybody—even people I shouldn't have."

There was no mistaking who she meant, but I ignored the bait and arranged a few pieces of almond bark on a silver tray. "Good. Just as long as every one of the contestants knows, I'm happy."

"Well, I'm not." Karen shoved her hands into the pocket of her apron and planted herself directly in front of me. Karen's a few years younger than my own thirty-nine, and she's never been afraid of a fight. She's also skinny as a rail—something I think is unnatural on a candymaker. "You shouldn't have let Savannah Vance enter the contest, Abby. There's going to be trouble."

I'd gone to high school with Savannah way back when. She'd been Vance then, but her married name was Horne, and she'd made it very clear that she wanted me to use it. I'll admit she's never been my favorite person. But twenty years have passed since we knew each other, so I gave a casual shrug and looked away. "Her registration fee is as good as anyone else's."

"Yeah. Right." Karen laughed through her nose and narrowed her eyes. "Savannah doesn't compete. She just takes whatever she wants. She's up to no good, Abby. Mark my words."

"Let's not borrow trouble, okay?" I smiled and turned away to continue my inventory. To my relief, most of the silver candy trays were still reasonably full, and the candy bouquets I'd settled in strategic spots, hoping to convince people that they were an acceptable alternative to traditional flowers on special occasions, seemed to be generating some interest.

So far, so good.

When I turned back, it was painfully obvious that Karen wasn't going to give up, so I reluctantly dragged myself back to the conversation. "Maybe Savannah was like that in school," I said, "but that was twenty years ago. People change."

Karen ran a judgmental glance across Savannah's tall, willowy figure and scooped a peppermint crunch from the candy dish at her side. "No they don't. Especially not people like her."

It wasn't like Karen to be so negative. "How can you be so sure?" I asked. "You haven't even seen her in how long?"

"Not long enough."

"And you told me yourself that you didn't even speak to her last time she was in town."

Karen's brows knit in a deep scowl. "So what's your point?"

"That maybe she's doing exactly what she told us she's doing. Maybe she came to see her sister and settle her mother's estate, and maybe she just wants a diversion while she's in town. Can we please stay focused on what's important here?"

"This *is* important," Karen said with a curl of her lip. "It's the middle of ski season. There are plenty of other diversions Savannah could find if that's what she wanted."

Her bitterness surprised me. "What do you have against Savannah, anyway?"

Karen rolled her gaze toward me. "You want the whole list, or just the top ten things?"

"One would do."

"Okay. Fine. I don't like her because she's selfish. She always has been. No matter what's going on, no matter who else is involved, it's *always* all about her. What could she possibly want from this competition?"

"How about recognition?"

"As the best candymaker in Paradise? Don't make me laugh."

Savannah swept past us, then past Evie Rice on her way to the judging table. Neither of us missed the venomous look on Evie's face as Savannah placed her dish in front of the judging panel. "Did you see that?" Karen whispered. "If looks could kill, nobody would have to worry about Savannah Horne."

"That's not funny," I whispered back. I shoved a tray full of peanut clusters into Karen's empty hands and tried to put a stop to the conversation. "Take that over to table three, and then check with the judges to make sure they have everything they need. And no more about Savannah Horne. I have enough to worry about this weekend. If Savannah wants something besides a plaque at the end of the competition, I don't want to know about it."

"You only say that because you don't have a husband," Karen muttered. "If Roger was here with you, you'd be worried."

Her comment froze me in my tracks. So *that* was it? Karen thought Savannah was still interested in Sergio after all these years? Thank goodness it was nothing more serious than that.

There's no tactful way to tell a woman that her husband isn't the stud he used to be, so I didn't even try. "I'm sure I would be worried if Roger were here. He wasn't exactly the faithful type, remember? That's why we're divorced." She started to speak, but I cut her off. "Look, I know you have reasons to dislike Savannah. I'm sure a lot of people do. But none of that has anything to do with tonight's competition."

When Karen scowled doubtfully, I nodded toward Miles Horne, who watched from the other side of the room. He was a tall man with broad shoulders, thick legs, and a naturally grim expression.

He wore an impeccably tailored suit and a pair of polished leather loafers, and he dangled the keys to his BMW from one finger—either thoughtlessly comfortable with his own affluence, or making sure the rest of us saw how well Savannah had done for herself. "She's married," I said, "and she seems happy. So please, just let it go, okay? Help me get through this weekend, and you can go back to hating her on Monday morning."

Karen's lips curved into a grudging smile. "By then, it might be too late."

I locked eyes with her. "Sergio loves you, Karen. He may have wandered that one time before you were even dating seriously, but you have nothing to worry about now." I paused to let that sink in, then tried once more to draw her attention to what really mattered. "Don't forget to check on the judges. They'll be announcing tonight's finalists in a few minutes, and I want to make sure everything goes smoothly."

Karen actually looked as if she might refuse, but before she could, a shrill cry went up from the other side of the room. The buzz of excited voices rose, and folks standing nearby surged toward the sound. I met Karen's shocked gaze a split second before we both sprang into action.

Praying that no one had been hurt, I slipped out from behind the serving table just as a wild-eyed Rachel Summers, owner of the candle shop a few doors away, burst through the crowd and waved Karen and me over. "You'd better get in there," she warned as we closed the distance between us. "I swear one of those women is going to kill the other."

"Who is it?" I asked.

"Savannah and Evie," Rachel said, sharing a knowing glance with Karen. "Who else? I knew there'd be trouble the minute I saw Savannah walk through that door. You never should have let her register, Abby. She's going to ruin everything."

I was beginning to think she and Karen were right, but how could I have known? Most people don't drag childhood rivalries with them into middle age. At least, I don't think they do. Savannah and Evie were certainly putting that assumption to the test.

They'd been rivals in almost everything since junior high, and maybe even earlier than that. I distinctly remember them going nose-to-nose over which one got to do their seventh-grade research paper on France. And who could ever forget the war over first violin position in eighth-grade orchestra? Apparently, their rivalry was still going strong two decades later, and Divinity was about to become just another in a long line of battlegrounds.

Determined to regain control of the evening, I pasted on a smile and waded through the crowd. Savannah is tall, full-bosomed, and curvaceous in a way that appeals to men. She's probably a few pounds heavier than she was back in high school, but the extra inches haven't dulled her appeal. She still wears her dark hair long and loose, her blouses low and tight. Even in the middle of January, she was showing an ample amount of cleavage, and you had only to look at the sparkle in the eyes of men around her to know they'd noticed.

I didn't want to encourage Karen by admitting my own feelings, but Savannah has always been more trouble than she's worth. The fact that she'd driven all the way from Gunnison to compete for a prize she couldn't possibly want was typical Savannah. I didn't blame Evie for challenging her. I just wished that she'd choose somewhere else to do it.

I found Evie red as a fireball, breathing heavily, and waving a pink scoring sheet under the judges' noses. She stands barely five feet tall, and her blond hair hasn't begun to show even a hint of gray. She's maintained her teenage cheerleader figure by religious use of a membership at the Paradise Health Club, but she's always been a more wholesome type than Savannah. Evie's the kind of girl boys took home to meet their mothers. Savannah's the kind they hid in the backseats of their cars.

One of the judges looked up as I approached, and the clear relief on her face brought Evie around to pounce on me. "Something has to be done about this," she shouted, as she wagged the scoring sheet at me. "It's a travesty."

"You're making a fool out of yourself," Savannah

grumbled before I could get a word out. "Why can't you just accept the fact that the judges prefer my entry to yours?"

All three judges sat stone-still behind the judging table. Beverly Lembeck, the judge whose round face had most recently been threatened by the scorecard, rose to her feet and glowered at Evie. "This is most unprofessional—" she said, but the rest of her protest was lost in another wail from Evie.

Under the watchful gaze of his wife, Henry Stokes—judge number two and owner of the Edelweiss Bakery—struggled not to look at Savannah's cleavage. Marshall Ames, the third judge and owner of Gigi, a French restaurant on the corner of Twelve Peaks and Poison Creek, couldn't tear his eyes away.

Far from the dignified contest Aunt Grace had always conducted, I had a three-ring circus on my hands.

"I certainly hope you don't condone this kind of behavior from your contestants," Beverly said, dodging Evie and coming to stand in front of me. Locks of graying hair hung in limp curls against her flushed cheeks, and the effort of getting around the table had her breathing hard. "All decisions of the judges are *supposed* to be final."

"And they are," I assured her. I caught a glimpse of the smug I-told-you-so on Karen's face and felt the tension in my neck knot even tighter. Struggling to appear in control, I turned to Evie. "What seems to be the problem?"

She whipped around so fast I worried she might fall off the soles of her platform shoes. Her eyes gleamed as she shoved the score sheet in front of my face—far too close for my almost-forty-year-old eyes to focus. "Have you seen this?"

"No, and I can't see it now, either." I tried without success to nudge her hand away. "I take it you have a complaint?"

"She wants you to rearrange the scores from tonight's competition to suit her." Savannah and her breasts moved closer. "Apparently, she's having trouble believing that I scored higher than she did."

Years of pent-up fury flashed in Evie's violet eyes. "Only because *you* ignored the requirement to use an original recipe." She pivoted back to me, still lashing about with the scorecard. "She downloaded her recipe from the Good Cooks Network website, Abby. She should be disqualified. This isn't the first time she's done something like this, either."

Savannah's mouth thinned, and her eyes narrowed. "I'd be careful if I were you," she warned. "An accusation like that could get you in trouble."

Evie didn't seem to care. She squared her shoulders and straightened to her full height, which put the top of her head roughly even with Savannah's shoulders. "I'm not worried. It will be easy enough to prove. I warned you that your nasty little habits would come back to bite you one of these days."

I could feel the crowd closing in around us, angling to get a better view, trying harder to hear what the two women were saying. I was going to have to do something fast, or the whole weekend would be ruined.

"Evie—" I began.

Savannah cut me off. "Are you accusing me of cheating?" I don't think anyone missed the sudden flush of color in her cheeks.

Or the triumphant smile that crossed Evie's face. "I'm saying straight-out that you've cheated *again*. But this is the last time, Savannah. Do you hear me? I swear to God, this time I'm going to stop you." She gestured roughly toward her second-place red ribbon and the two-pound box of candy she'd just been awarded. "I didn't almost kill myself making that fudge for *that*."

No, but she'd expect anyone else to be content with it.

"Do something, Abby," she demanded. "I'm counting on you to make this right."

I backed a step away, wanting to put some distance between myself and her anger and also hoping to prevent anyone from thinking that I was taking sides. "Evie," I said quietly, "I don't—"

"You don't what? Don't believe me?"

"I didn't say that," I assured her. "I just think it might be best to discuss this somewhere else." I glanced over my shoulder at the rapidly gathering crowd. "Privately."

"Why? Everyone here knows what Savannah's like. There's probably not a soul in this room she hasn't hurt."

That was going a bit over the top, and I worried about Savannah's husband's reaction, but if Miles heard the vicious accusation, he gave no sign.

"Why don't we try to stay focused on tonight's contest?" I suggested. "Let's not drag the past into the discussion."

Tall, blond, and surprisingly handsome considering what a nerd he'd been in high school, Marshall Ames left the judges' table and came to stand beside Savannah. "Don't you think you're being unnecessarily harsh, Evie?"

"Why don't you let her fight her own battles?" Evie snarled, leveling Marshall with a look of disdain. "I told you, I can prove what I'm saying."

"Impossible," Savannah said with a laugh. "If there's a recipe for Kentucky Colonels on some website, I certainly didn't copy it. This recipe has been in my family for generations."

The nervous ball of energy in my stomach grew stronger, and I tried again to take the argument away from the public eye, but Savannah straightened majestically and cast a royal glance around the crowd. "Don't listen to her, Abby. Tonight's scores were fair, and I, for one, refuse to give in to Evie's raging paranoia." She caught her husband's eye and beckoned him toward her. "Why don't one of you take poor Evie out for a drink? I'm sure a little alcohol will make it all better. It usually does for her. I'll see the rest of you tomorrow night."

She turned away, hitching her purse strap onto her shoulder and dismissing Evie's protests at the same time.

Maybe I should have stopped her, but I just wanted the argument to be over. At least this gave me a chance to look into Evie's allegations without the whole town peering over my shoulder. If I was lucky, I could clear the whole mess up before tomorrow night's segment of the competition.

I couldn't know it as I watched Savannah stalk out the door, but things were about to get a whole lot worse.

Chapter 2

An hour later, I settled the last dirty plates and empty cups on Aunt Grace's huge silver tray and started carefully down the steps into the kitchen. As I stopped to turn out the light with my elbow, I spied Evie's red ribbon and the gold-edged box of candy she'd left behind. Guess she wasn't kidding when she said the prize wasn't good enough.

Irritation stung the muscles in my neck, and pain burned in the small of my back. Even after nine months, I wasn't used to working on my feet all day. How Aunt Grace had stood behind the shop counter for more than forty years without needing surgery was a mystery I'd probably never solve.

But this wasn't the first difference in the two of us I'd run across. Aunt Grace had definitely been made of sterner stuff. She'd been strong enough to buck the system in the sixties to open the store in the first place. Back then, when banks almost never loaned money to women (especially those without a man to back them), Aunt Grace applied for the loan on her own, got it, and never looked back. To the best of my knowledge, she'd never lost control of a situation like the one we'd had tonight. The fact that I was working cleanup detail alone proved just how inept I was at soothing ruffled feathers.

Sighing with frustration, I hoisted the tray high and slowly descended the stairs, feeling for each step before trusting my weight since I couldn't see around the mound of garbage and dirty dishes. I was so engrossed, I didn't realize that I wasn't alone until I reached ground level and a deep voice asked, "Need help?"

I let out a startled yelp and wheeled around to find a man standing in the shadows of the two refrigerators we keep in our candy kitchen. My heart slammed against my rib cage, and I croaked, "Who's there?"

A figure wearing dark jeans and a black turtleneck sweater moved into the light, but when I saw the sheaf of honey-blond hair and horn-rimmed glasses, I laughed with relief. "You scared the daylights out of me, Marshall. What are you doing here?"

He closed the distance between us and took the tray out of my hands before I completely registered what he was doing. "Sorry. I was clearing the snow from my windshield when I saw Karen and Evie leaving. I thought I'd better come back and see if you needed help." He ran a glance over the pile of dirty dishes and grinned at me. "Looks like I was right. You'll be here all night if you have to clean up by yourself."

His concern surprised me. Marshall and I might have been in the same class in school, but we'd never really been friends. He'd always been too bookish and quiet for me, and I'd probably been too much a tomboy for him. Until tonight, I'd seen him only a couple of times since my return to Paradise, and both times for only a few minutes. Never long enough to talk or get acquainted.

"I'm fine," I assured him. "I asked Karen to take Evie somewhere and calm her down."

"She's still upset about tonight's results?"

"That's putting it mildly." I moved past him to clear a spot for the tray among the boxes of toffee and stacks of saltwater taffy we'd made for the following night. "Evie's absolutely convinced that Savannah cheated somehow."

"Don't let Evie make you paranoid," Marshall said as he followed me across the kitchen. "She's . . . different."

"She's also determined to challenge the decision you three reached tonight."

"She's desperate. We all know that. The only way she *won't* challenge our decision is if we let her win." Marshall wedged the tray onto the counter and gathered a handful of silverware from amid the trash. "I don't care what she says, Abby, we weren't wrong. I know she worked hard, but her entry wasn't the best one out there tonight."

For some reason, just hearing him say that made me feel a little better. "Do the other judges feel the same way?"

He shrugged. "I'm sure they do. You know what a stickler Beverly is, and Henry's no pushover. He's been judging this contest since the first year, and he's furious with Evie for making such a stink. The only question is, what will it do to your contest if Savannah actually wins on Sunday night?"

The heater kicked on, and I savored the welcome rush of warm air on my feet. "What do you mean?"

"Just that Savannah Horne's not the most popular person who ever lived in Paradise. If she wins, Evie won't be the only person who's upset."

"If she's the best, she deserves to win."

"I'm not sure everyone else will see it that way."

I inched closer to the heat vent and studied his expression carefully. "Are you suggesting that I fix the contest?"

Marshall shook his head. "Of course not. I just want to make sure you're prepared, that's all. You lived away for a long time, but memories last a long time around here. People can be slow to forgive—especially someone who shows no remorse."

I squirted soap into the sink and turned on the hot water. "Savannah's been gone as long as I have," I reminded him. "People can't be hanging on to memories that are *that* old."

He lifted one shoulder. "Like I said, people can be slow to forgive. Savannah hurt a lot of people when we were kids."

"She made some people angry," I agreed, "but I don't think she did anything *that* awful—unless you know something I don't."

Marshall's lip curved as he stacked dishes next to the sink. "No. I didn't really know her all that well back then. I'm just going by how people act when her name is mentioned. You saw how they were tonight. Karen. Rachel. Evie. I think her husband was the only friend she had in that entire room. If people think you've taken her side, it could cost you." He planted both hands on the counter and sweetened his smile. "It's just a friendly warning from one business owner to another, that's all."

I didn't know how to take his "friendly" warning, so I laughed it off. "Well, I'm not going to panic yet. This was only the first night of judging. Everything could change tomorrow."

Marshall leaned against the counter and folded his arms across his chest. "Maybe. But her entry tonight was surprisingly good. I don't think any of us thought Savannah could cook like that. She didn't seem all that interested in the domestic arts back in school."

I laughed in spite of myself. "No, she didn't. But she's had plenty of time to learn. People *can* change, you know."

Something hard and cold flickered in his eyes. "Not people like Savannah Vance."

"Horne," I corrected automatically. I shut off the water and plunged my hands into the warm suds. "You're the second person tonight who's said that. But why do you feel that way? I thought you didn't know her."

"I don't, but I know of her."

"So what makes Savannah different from the rest of the world?"

"Think about it, Abby. Why *should* she change? Her way of doing things has always worked pretty well for her. She's always gotten everything she wants." Marshall scratched at something on the countertop with his fingernail, then mopped it up with a damp rag. "She and Miles are obviously doing well. He was educated at Harvard, you know. And they're moving to New York as soon as they leave here. He's been offered a top position with a Fortune 500 company, so it's not as if Savannah needs the cash."

Judging from the little I'd seen of Miles Horne, that was no doubt true, but the conversation was starting to make me uneasy. "Just tell me one thing," I said. "Do you think Evie was right? Do you think Savannah cheated?"

"Honestly?" Slow as molasses, Marshall shook his head. "I don't know. Savannah's always taken care of Savannah, that's all I know. If she wants something, she'll move heaven and earth to get it."

"Yeah, but what could she possibly want *here*? A plaque with her name on it? A blue ribbon? A few hundred dollars in prize money? I can't imagine she considers any of that worth her time."

"Maybe she just wants another chance to show us all that she's the best."

"Maybe," I agreed reluctantly. "But if that's the case, I wish she'd find some other way to do it." I was worried enough about keeping Divinity in the black.

Marshall tossed the cloth onto the counter and came to stand in front of me. "Just do yourself a favor, okay? Keep an eye on Savannah tomorrow. If she does have an ulterior motive, maybe you'll be able to figure out what it is."

I nodded and managed a thin smile. "Yeah. Sure. And thanks for the help. I appreciate it."

"Not a problem. I was happy to do it." He crossed to the door and let himself outside on a blast of cold winter air. I watched through the window until he disappeared around the corner, wondering why I'd never gotten to know him before. Except for his life at the restaurant, I didn't even know what he'd been doing since high school. Had he ever married? Did he have children? I really should know the answers.

He wasn't the only person I'd lost touch with over the years. I could count on one hand the number of times I'd come back to Paradise during my marriage to Roger. He hadn't wanted me tied to my past, and I'd given in without argument. I could justify my actions a dozen different ways, but the truth is, I'd let him dominate me. It's not a mistake I'll make again.

Every one of my relationships had suffered during my absence. My nieces and nephews barely knew me, old friends had grown distant, and cousins who'd once been as close as siblings had trouble trusting me.

I guess that was only fair. Sometimes I had trouble trusting myself.

The third-floor apartment I call home is not a large space, nor is it particularly beautiful. It's decorated with a jumble of furniture handed down from various relatives and mingled together in no particular style. Some—my ex-husband, for example—might even say the apartment is ugly, but it suits me just fine.

I'm not going to lie to you, though. It's a whole lot worse since my roommate moved in. I'm never sure what I'll find when I open the door. That night I found half a roll of shredded toilet paper, one bra, an apple core, a half-eaten giant jawbreaker stuck to the welcome mat, and the toilet brush on the kitchen floor. In the living room, I found three empty toilet paper rolls (ends chewed), the splintered remains of a basket, three paperbacks (corners chewed), stuffing from some unidentifiable source, and one rawhide bone—untouched.

One of these days, when I find a little spare time, I really have to take Max in for obedience training. He hadn't been nearly so destructive when he was living and working with his former owner, but Brandon had taken Max to work with him every day at his clothing store. It's a little harder to do that when you work in the food industry. Health inspectors tend to frown on having dogs and their fur in the kitchen.

The jingle of dog tags warned me to brace myself as Max loped out of the bedroom and launched himself at me. At least the deep depression he'd suffered right after Brandon's death was a thing of the past. He's always happy to see me when I come home and reasonably well-behaved when I'm around, so I hold out hope that the rest will come.

I spent a few minutes scratching Max and assuring him that he's the best dog in the world, listening to my messages, and changing out of the clothes I'd been wearing all day. Finally comfortable in jeans and my favorite old sweater, I stuffed my feet into boots, slipped into my coat, and clipped Max's leash to his collar.

Grabbing keys and wallet, I led Max down my new stairs and said a silent thank-you to my brother Wyatt for helping me restore them. Getting in and out of the apartment from outside was no problem in good weather, but sprinkle two feet of snow on the stairs, and it's a different story.

Max got to work almost as soon as we stepped outside, sniffing for just the right place to relieve himself, and dragging me along the ice-covered sidewalks with him.

Soft white clouds enveloped his head as warm, moist breath mingled with the cold air. Shivering, I said a silent prayer that this wouldn't be one of those nights where he couldn't settle on a spot. "All right, boy," I urged between chattering teeth, "Let's get busy. There's leftover pizza waiting for me upstairs."

He snuffled loudly, but he didn't lift his nose from the sidewalk. I took that as a good sign, and followed him along the narrow parking strip that separates Divinity from Picture Perfect, our closest neighbor on the uphill side of the street.

The lights were still on, and the urge to talk with Dooley Jorgensen about that night's fiasco tugged at me almost as hard as Max was pulling on his leash. Dooley had been a great friend to Aunt Grace, and he'd taken me under his wing now that she was gone. Whenever I needed someone to listen, Dooley was there. No matter what the problem, he either commiserated or helped me figure out a solution. Usually both.

But Max needed attention first, so I huddled deeper into my coat and followed the dog to the front of the store. Parked cars and SUVs, most of which sported ski racks, lined both sides of the street. Crowds of people strolled along the ice-crusted sidewalks on their way to or from dinner or drinks, and a steady stream of drivers hoping to find a parking space inched through town going uphill.

Prospector is a two-way street until the snow flies. Then it, like most of the other streets in the narrow part of the valley, change to one-way traffic to accommodate the snow left behind by the plows. That doesn't slow us down at all.

This is one of the things I love about Paradise. It's a small town by almost anyone's standards, but we get enough tourist traffic to keep things from getting boring. There are plenty of old friends to provide roots, but always an opportunity to meet someone new. And there's rarely a time, day or night, when you can walk outside in Paradise and feel alone.

Now that I was out and surrounded by the rich scents of meals being prepared in nearby restaurants, leftover pizza didn't sound nearly so appealing. I'd much rather have a steaming plate of Romano's penne pasta with pine nuts and sun dried tomatoes, or even better, steak with sauce Bordelaise from Gigi.

My mouth was watering as I followed Max around an amorous couple who looked as if they'd just left the ski slopes. I started past another, huddled deep in conversation within the recessed doorway of Rachel Summers's candle shop, but something caught Max's attention, and he ground to a halt.

One of the best things about Paradise is the way everyone watches out for everyone else, so it was pure instinct that made me give the couple a quick once-over to make sure they weren't trying to break in. They seemed innocent enough, probably just taking refuge from the cold. I started to turn away, but a stray bit of conversation blew across the sidewalk on a gust of wind.

"I don't care *what* you do, Miles. Don't you understand that? Now that I know—" Either she stopped speaking, or she lowered her voice so I couldn't hear, but I recognized Savannah immediately. I was still standing there, gawping, when she pushed away from him and snapped, "Don't you get it? It doesn't matter anymore."

Curiosity went to war with discretion—and won. At least until I remembered how I'd felt when someone witnessed one of my arguments with Roger. Feeling like a voyeur, I tugged on Max's leash and headed downhill again, but I only made it a few feet before Savannah called after me.

"Abby? Is that you?"

I turned back, unsure whether to acknowledge that I'd seen them arguing or pretend I hadn't. When I realized that Miles was already striding away uphill, I decided that honesty was the best policy. "Sorry about that," I said with a rueful grin. "I had no idea that was you two."

Savannah waved away my apology, and her lips curved into a smile, but even in the dim light I could tell that shadows filled her eyes.

I glanced at Miles's retreating back and asked, "Is everything all right?"

Savannah nodded. "Yes. It's just one of those things. You know how it is."

Unfortunately I did. Roger and I had had a million squabbles while we were married. At the time, I'd considered most of them nuisance arguments. Now I wondered how much they'd contributed to Roger's affair and our eventual divorce. But second-guessing myself wouldn't change the past, and I try to avoid dragging my ex-husband, his new girlfriend, or their baby into my new life whenever possible. Shaking off the memories, I started walking again. "He seems like a nice guy."

"Miles?"

"That *was* him, wasn't it?"

"Yes. Yes, it was. And you're right. I guess he does make a good first impression." Before I could decide what to say to that, Savannah seemed to shrug off whatever mood she was in and changed the subject. "I'm surprised you're speaking to me. I thought I was the local pariah."

Agreeing with her seemed harsh, so I smiled and said, "I don't know about that."

"Come on, Abby, you can be honest with me. Evie was so upset with me tonight, she nearly choked on her own tongue—and I know she's not the only one."

I thought about Karen, still furious about something that happened two decades ago, and decided Marshall was right. "People around here have long memories."

"Always have." Savannah swept a lock of her glorious chocolate hair over her shoulder and let her gaze travel slowly down the street. "I'd say that nothing ever changes around here, but that's not exactly true, is it?"

"No, it's not. Paradise isn't the sleepy little farm town it used to be."

"But people still don't want me around."

"It's not easy to come back," I admitted. "I wasn't exactly welcomed with open arms, either. There are still people who wonder what I'm doing here."

Savannah let out a reedy laugh. "They'd probably keel over dead if I moved back. They can hardly stand to be in the same room with me."

Reminding her that she'd earned her reputation wouldn't accomplish anything, so I went for a less confrontational response. "People are curious. They wonder what brings you back after so many years, and the people at Divinity tonight are wondering why you've entered the contest. Obviously, you don't need the prize money."

We reached the corner, and she stopped walking. She turned up the collar of her coat to cover her ears and dredged up a smile. "I came back to clear up my mother's estate. I thought everybody knew that."

"Well, of course, everyone's heard the official explanation, but some people do wonder if there's another reason."

Savannah laughed as if the thought of being mysterious delighted her. With her long, dark hair and striking coloring, she looked beautiful even in the dim glow of the streetlamp. Not surprisingly, I felt like a lump of clay beside her—but then, I always had. "I guess things *don't* change around here, do they? Don't these people have better things to do than worry about me?"

I led Max into the intersection behind an SUV laden with half a dozen pairs of skis. "You know how it is. You'll be big news for a few days, and then they'll find something new to talk about."

"As long as I don't give them something new to sink

their teeth into, right?" Savannah's expression sobered, and she stuffed her hands into the pockets of her coat. "I'm curious, Abby. What on earth made you decide to come back? Weren't you living in California?"

I nodded. "Sacramento."

"I could have sworn I heard you were a lawyer."

"I was. Corporate law."

"And now you're back in Paradise making candy." She slid an amused glance at me. "I just know there's a story there."

Not one I wanted to share. She seemed different tonight, but I wasn't foolish enough to trust her. I gave her the simplified version. "I went through a divorce, and then Aunt Grace died, so I decided to stay."

"Do you miss it? Life in the city, I mean."

"Not really," I said, and I was a little surprised to realize that I meant it.

"And most of the folks around here have just accepted you back, no questions asked?"

I felt an odd sense of loyalty toward the people of Paradise, so I sugarcoated the truth just a little. "I wouldn't go quite that far, but for the most part, yeah. Like I said, there are a few people watching to see if I make good, and probably a few more who are waiting to see if I'm really going to stick around, but with everybody else it's like I never left."

Max finally found an acceptable tree and lifted his leg. I told myself it wasn't a commentary on the lie I'd just told.

Shivering in a chill gust of wind, Savannah swept a glance along the street in front of us. "For you, that's probably just fine, but being treated as if I never left isn't really much of an incentive for me."

No, it wouldn't be, but that's not the part of her comment that interested me most. "Does that mean you're thinking about coming back to Paradise?"

Something darted through her eyes, but it was gone before I could identify it. "Me? Come back here? I doubt I'd last very long if I did."

"I thought you and Miles were moving to New York—or is that just a rumor?"

Savannah quirked a half smile at me. "Well, the rumor mill certainly isn't broken. Where did you hear that?"

"I don't remember." It wasn't exactly loyalty to Marshall that kept me quiet, but people *are* slow to forgive, myself included. "It's not true, then?"

Savannah looked away without answering and remained silent for a long time. "The jury's still out, I guess. I'd rather stay in Gunnison, close to family. Or even here."

I'd been wondering why a man who'd been educated at Harvard was working in Gunnison, Colorado. Now I had my answer. Savannah liked it there. I must have looked shocked because she laughed. "Does that surprise you?"

"Actually, yes. It does."

"You're lucky, Abby. I doubt people would forgive someone like me."

She sounded almost wistful, and I felt an unexpected twinge of pity for her. "I'm sure they would if they knew you'd changed. Why wouldn't they?"

"Let's face it. I didn't exactly endear myself to people when I lived here."

"Nobody's perfect."

"Least of all me, I know. I think Evie would be happy if I fell off the face of the earth. Karen, too."

"Evie's emotional," I agreed, "but she's not completely unreasonable. And Karen—well, I'm sure that if you talked with her, she'd realize that you're not the girl you used to be and the two of you could move on."

Savannah cut me off with a sharp laugh. "Oh, Abby, it's a nice thought, but you know it's not ever going to happen. Karen would sooner kill me than look at me." As if she realized she'd crossed a line, she waved a hand in the air between us and glanced up the hill. "Ignore me, okay? I'm just in a mood."

A mood I'd never seen before, and I'll confess I didn't know what to do with it. I heard myself ask, "Do you want to go somewhere? Maybe have a drink, or dinner?"

She studied me for a long moment, then shook her head. "Thanks, but I need to get back to the hotel and get some sleep. I'll be all right by tomorrow, I'm sure. Setup starts at four, right?"

I nodded. "And judging begins at seven."

"Okay then." She smiled and turned away, but she only went a couple of steps before she looked back again. "Abby?"

"Yeah?"

"Thanks."

I tried not to let her see my surprise. "For what?"

"For talking to me as if I wasn't Savannah Vance."

I didn't know what to say to that, so I muttered something inane and turned Max toward home. But I had trouble putting Savannah out of my mind. The strange thing was, I actually liked her in that oddly vulnerable mood. I wished more people could see her like that, but I was realistic enough to know that probably wouldn't happen.

I just wish I'd known how right I was. Maybe I could have made a difference.

Chapter 3

I fell asleep the minute my head hit the pillow and slept hard until Max's cold, wet nose planted firmly in the crook of my arm brought me back to the land of the living. I try to be sensitive to my dog's needs, but I was still so tired I hurt and far from ready for another walk outside.

Groaning softly, I pulled my arm away and snuggled deeper into the covers. "Ten more minutes," I mumbled. "That's a good boy."

Max whined softly and planted one hefty paw on my bed just as someone set up a ruckus outside my front door. The pounding came first, followed by a frantic female voice shouting, "Abby? Abby! Where are you? Open up. It's freezing out here."

Karen?

I bolted upright, panicked to think that I'd overslept. Shivering in the sudden chill, I stumbled into the living room, whacked my shoulder into a wall, and bruised my shin on the coffee table before I woke up enough to realize that it was still dark outside.

I ground to a halt and tried to focus on the glowing red numbers on my VCR clock. What time was it, anyway? Was somebody actually outside, or was I just having a bad dream?

"If you don't open the door," Karen shouted, "I'll just let myself in through the shop."

I guess that answered my question. Max plopped down in front of the door and wagged his little stump tail as if a visit from Karen at two thirty in the morning was a good thing. Obviously, he and I needed to have a talk.

I made a mental note to install a dead bolt on the back door, maneuvered carefully around the coffee table, and opened the door a crack. "Karen? Is that you?"

She shoved the door open the rest of the way and strode inside, dragging a suitcase with her. "I'm going to kill her, Abby. I swear on all that's holy, I'm going to kill her."

I was still too sleepy to think straight, so I made myself ask, "Who are you talking about?"

"Savannah Vance, who else?"

I groaned aloud, sank onto the couch, and turned on one dim lamp. "Why? What happened now?"

The lamp was a bad idea. Karen's hair looked as if she'd been caught in a whirlwind, and her eyes were red and puffy from crying. She sniffed loudly and plopped onto the other end of the couch. "Exactly what I told you would happen. She went after Sergio. I *told* you she would."

I shook my head in confusion. "Hold on. Say that again? She did *what*?"

"Went after Sergio."

I was almost fully awake now, but she wasn't making any sense. Savannah had been on her way back to the hotel, hadn't she? I pushed hair out of my eyes so I could see Karen better. "Are you sure?"

"Do I look like I'm not?"

"But how? Where? *When?*"

"The same way she always does. Tonight. At O'Schuck's."

O'Schuck's is an upscale nightclub around the corner and down two blocks, so Savannah would have had no trouble getting there, but I was having a hard time putting everything together in my head. "Are you sure? Maybe it's just a vicious rumor."

"I wish!" Karen spotted half a loaf of chocolate tea bread on my kitchen counter and snagged it. She sat on the couch, curled her feet up under her, and tore off a piece. "Evie and I walked in and found them, all cozied up together and laughing—" She broke off with a shudder and crammed another bite into her mouth. "I can't stay with him," she mumbled around the bread. "I absolutely *refuse* to sleep in the same bed with him."

The fumes of whatever she'd been drinking hovered in the air between us, and her eyes had a vague, unfocused look. I wondered if she'd done the bulk of her drinking before she met up with Sergio and Savannah, or after. "Are you *sure* that's what Sergio was doing?"

Karen glared at me. A crumb dropped from the side of her mouth onto the couch. "I know what I saw."

"I'm sure you do," I said quickly. "It's just that—well, I know how much Sergio loves you, and I have a hard time believing he'd throw it all away like this. Maybe you should tell me what you saw—exactly."

Karen pulled her knees up to her chest and dropped her forehead onto the shelf they made. "Just what I told you," she muttered into the denim of her jeans. "Sergio and that . . . that . . ." Her head shot up. "That *woman* were sitting together *this* close. He was looking at her with that look—you know the one I mean."

I reached across the cushions and tore off a piece of bread for myself. The only difference between Karen and me is that Karen won't be wearing the bread around her hips next week.

"God only knows what I would have found if I'd been ten minutes later," she said, her voice thick with emotion.

Her pain was raw and palpable, and it wasn't alone. All the hurt and outrage I'd felt over Roger's affair was there, shoring it up.

I reached across the cushion again, this time to link my fingers with hers. "You don't think Sergio would have . . . you know?"

Karen's hazel eyes darkened. "Had sex with her? Absolutely. You know how men get when they're around Savannah. It's like they can't even think."

"Yeah, but—" I cut myself off before I could defend her. Maybe she'd fooled me, too. Maybe everything she'd said tonight on the street had been an act, designed to win sympathy. If so, it had worked like a charm. Feeling foolish, I nodded toward the suitcase. "So you left him? For good?"

"I don't know yet. I'm so angry I can hardly see straight. I can't even bear to look at him right now."

"What about the kids?"

"They're home. He can take care of them for a while. Let's see how much time he has for getting friendly with an old girlfriend while he's washing dirty underwear and running kids to karate class."

I wondered just how much laundry and carpooling Sergio would actually do, but I didn't dare raise the question aloud. He was in enough trouble as it was. "So where are you going?"

The corners of Karen's mouth turned down. "Going?"

"You've left home, and you're carrying around a suitcase. You must have something planned."

"Well, of course I do. I'm staying here with you."

"Here?" I uncurled quickly. "*Here?* But—"

"You don't want me?"

I knew I must look horrified, and I didn't want to add to her pain, so I shook my head and dug up a smile. "I didn't say that. It's just that this place is so small—"

"It's not *that* small. This sofa still makes out into a bed, doesn't it?"

"Well, yes, but—"

"Okay then. There's plenty of room for the two of us here. Mandy and I lived here for a couple of years before Sergio and I got married, remember? We got along just fine."

Yeah, but—but this wasn't Aunt Grace's "community" property anymore. It was mine, and I wasn't sure Karen and I could coexist peacefully in such close quarters. Since my divorce, I'd learned to value this space of my own. I just didn't know how to say that without sounding selfish or greedy.

Besides, what kind of horrible person would tell her own cousin that she had to leave at two thirty in the morning? In the dead of winter? Sloshed to the gills? Then again, what kind of cousin showed up at two thirty in the morning?

A desperate one.

I couldn't turn her away. Not tonight, anyway. Swallowing all the reasons for saying no, I scrambled from the couch to gather a pillow and blanket. By the time I came back, Karen had changed into a long flannel nightgown, and she was tugging on the couch, trying to unfold the mattress.

"I hope it's not too lumpy," I said as I reached down to help. "It's a pretty old mattress."

She gave another heave, and the bed opened. I wasn't prepared and nearly lost my balance. "You'll have to get a new one soon," Karen said, reaching out a hand to steady me.

Almost before I could regain my balance, Karen toppled onto her side and let out a deep, satisfied moan. She was definitely settled in. I stuffed the pillow under her head and spread the blanket over her, hoping for the sake of our relationship that she didn't plan to stay long. Or that I could stay sane if she did.

I was nowhere near ready to wake up when the phone rang the next morning. Inching open one eye to make sure it was light outside, I rolled onto my side and dragged the comforter over my head to block out the sound.

It didn't work. After six irritating rings, I gave up and swam out from beneath the covers. Even through sleep-blurred eyes, I registered that it was six thirty in the morning—way too early to expect coherent conversation, especially after less than four hours' sleep.

On the other hand, maybe it was Sergio looking for his missing wife. That thought got me lunging for the receiver. "Wait! Don't hang up. I'm here."

"Abby?"

I froze, my torso half off the mattress, and tried to place the unfamiliar voice. "Yes?"

"Miles Horne here. I hope I didn't wake you."

Was he serious? I struggled upright against the headboard, pulling the comforter with me. "You're calling me at six thirty and wondering if you woke me?"

"I know. I'm sorry. I wanted to catch you before you got busy."

"This is Paradise, Miles, not New York. What did you need?"

"I'd like to talk with you first thing this morning—both Savannah and I would."

"It's not about the contest, is it? Because I really shouldn't talk to any of the contestants alone."

"Understood, but Savannah's terribly upset over the accusations that woman made against her. She hardly slept a wink all night."

It probably wasn't the contest that kept her awake, but

I decided not to say so. Somebody else could clue Miles in on his wife's late-night activities. "I'm sorry to hear that, but I still—"

Miles cut me off impatiently. "Don't you think Savannah deserves a chance to defend herself?"

"Well, of course she does. I'm just not sure that defending herself is going to be necessary. I'm hoping that Evie's had a good night's sleep and plenty of time to rethink her position."

"Do you really think that's going to happen?"

I sat on the edge of the bed and felt around with my foot for my slippers. Max was used to Karen, but I didn't know if letting her sleep here would upset his routine. If he'd left any deposits on the floor, I'd rather encounter them with a wad of paper towel and a mop than my bare foot. "Evie's not an unreasonable woman," I said. "Once she thinks about what happened last night, she'll realize that there's no real evidence that Savannah did anything wrong."

"I hope you're right, but that doesn't change the facts. The fact is, she accused my wife of cheating in front of a large number of people. Whether or not she rethinks her position, my wife's reputation has already been damaged."

"It would take more than a few accusations from Evie Rice to hurt Savannah's reputation," I said. "And I spoke with one of the judges last night. They have no intention of overturning their decision."

"Again, I'm glad, but I think you're missing the point. The point is, that woman owes my wife a public apology, and I intend to see that she delivers."

A public apology? From Evie? Never in a million years. She'd die first. Uneasiness settled in my stomach like a stone. "Was this Savannah's idea?"

"She agrees with me one hundred percent."

I quirked an eyebrow. "About demanding a public apology."

"Absolutely."

Then Savannah had lost her mind, that's all there was to that. Here I was, praying that we could pretend last night had never happened, and Miles was all set to throw everything into turmoil again. "This trouble between Savannah and Evie goes back a long way, Miles. I don't think it's going to be that easy to get Evie to apologize."

"I never said it would be easy, but surely you understand why it has to happen."

"Frankly, no, I don't. Everyone knows that tempers were flaring last night, but it wasn't the first time that's happened."

"So you plan to just sweep the whole thing under the rug?" His tone was sharp and accusing.

I didn't react well to it. "Evie might have been on the rampage last night," I said, letting irritation shave the edges off my tone, too, "but Savannah has done her share over the years to provoke her. If you expect Evie to apologize for last night, she'll expect Savannah to apologize for some of the things she's done. This is difficult enough now. Digging up the past will only make it worse."

"I'm not concerned about the past," Miles said.

"Around here, you'd better be." When he didn't back down, I said, "I *might* be able to arrange a meeting between the two of them—a private meeting. But even that's a stretch."

"Look, Abby, just between you and me, I know that Savannah's not well-liked here in Paradise. I don't know why, but I'd have to be dead to miss the looks on people's faces when she walks into a room. But she *is* my wife, and she *is* trying to make things better. I just don't know how she can do that if people won't even give her a chance."

I thought about the conversation I'd had with Savannah the night before and felt myself thaw slightly. I knew how it felt to be an outsider. If Savannah really did want to make amends, who was I to stand in her way?

"Just talk to us," Miles urged. "Give Savannah a chance to explain. That's all I ask."

I must have hesitated, and that was enough to convince him I was weakening. "We can be there in an hour," he said eagerly. "Savannah's out jogging right now, but she should be back soon. Half an hour at most. I can head over right now if that's okay. I'll just leave her a note to meet me there when she gets back."

I resented being railroaded, but I had to consider the contest and the future of Divinity. Both Evie and Savannah were more than capable of causing trouble for the shop—and for me. The only way out of this was to figure out a compromise they could both live with. Maybe I could convince Miles and Savannah to forgo the public apology if I met with them over coffee. Maybe I could convince Evie to stop crying foul. And hey! After that, maybe I could spin straw into gold.

Impossible as compromise seemed, I had to try. I grimaced at the ratty sweats and oversized T-shirt I'd worn to bed and tried to stall him. "There's no need to rush. The store doesn't open until ten. Just wait for Savannah to get back and then come over together."

"I'd rather come along now, if that's all right." Miles paused, sipped something close to the phone, and set off a strong craving for coffee. "I'd like a few minutes with you before Savannah gets there."

I couldn't imagine why, but I sighed and dug a pair of socks and clean underwear out of my drawer. "All right. Fine." If I wasn't too fussy about my appearance, that would be plenty of time.

After Miles disconnected, I tiptoed to my bedroom door and peered into the living room to see if the phone had woken Karen. Instead of finding my cousin hungover and snoring, I found Max curled up on the sofa bed, his head propped up on Karen's pillow. He lifted his head at the sound of my footsteps, yawned noisily, and flopped back onto the pillow.

I checked the kitchen, the bathroom, and even shouted downstairs into the shop, but Karen's car wasn't in the parking lot, and I couldn't see or hear any sign of her anywhere.

Hoping she'd gone home to work things out with Sergio, I scuffed back down the hall toward my bedroom. I know it sounds incredibly naïve, but for a few minutes there, I actually thought my luck was changing.

Chapter 4

Freshly showered and ready to face the day, I hauled on a clean pair of jeans and my favorite red sweater, then pulled on boots and gloves and led Max down the stairs and outside into the cold. Twenty minutes later, the dog was back in the apartment with a peanut butter doggie pop, and I was standing in the middle of Divinity's candy kitchen.

To fortify myself for the meeting with Savannah and Miles, I decided to whip up a batch of Aunt Grace's Celestial Chocolate French Toast. Even when the world is falling down around you, there's not much that can stay wrong when you have a plate of golden brown toast stuffed with melted chocolate sitting in front of you.

I ground shavings from the specialty chocolate we laid in for special occasions, beat together the eggs, milk, sugar, vanilla, and salt, and then layered chocolate between slices of bread, and left them to soak in the egg mixture while I poured my first cup of coffee.

I spooned in sugar and a dash of creamer, then added two heaping spoonfuls of milk chocolate powder and carried my cup into the shop. Before I could even come up with a strategy for negotiating a compromise, a black BMW pulled up to the curb. Miles Horne stepped out onto the street during a lull in the early morning traffic, glanced around almost nervously, and strode toward the store. He wore a long dress coat over black pants and a black turtleneck, and he moved with that brand of self-confidence that seems to accompany money.

Reluctantly abandoning my coffee, I unlocked the door and let him inside. He slid past me into the empty store and took a quick look around. Making sure we were alone, or just taking stock of his surroundings? I couldn't be sure.

"Thanks for agreeing to talk to me," he said with a smile that wiped away my uncertainty. "I promise not to take long."

I shut the door and locked it again. "I hope you're not here to ask for preferential treatment. If the other contestants find out you've been here, there could be trouble."

"Well, then, we just won't tell them." Grinning at his own response, he nodded toward my cup. "Do you have any more of that? The heater in that rental car is a piece of crap."

"Sure. There's plenty." I slipped behind the counter, poured a cup, and grabbed the sugar, creamer, and chocolate, just in case. When I caught a glimpse of the French toast, still soaking in the baking dish, my stomach rumbled. I hadn't planned on offering the Hornes breakfast, but I wasn't about to let all that glorious food go to waste.

While Miles doctored his coffee, I heated the griddle and got to work. Minutes later, I removed the last golden square from the burner, created a pinwheel of triangle-shaped pieces on a serving plate, dusted the whole thing with confectioners' sugar and chocolate shavings, and carried it to the table.

"I made more than enough," I said when Miles looked

up in surprise. "Help yourself—unless you'd rather wait for Savannah."

He leaned forward, sniffed, and lifted his gaze to meet mine. "Is that chocolate?"

"What else?"

His eyes twinkled, and he levered two thick slices onto an empty plate. He took one experimental bite, grinned like a kid in a . . . well, a candy store, and stretched out his legs in front of him. "That's incredible. Do you serve this here every day?"

I shook my head. "Comfort food. You were in the right place at the right time."

"I'll say. So why are you stuck way up here in the middle of nowhere? You could really do well with a store like this in, say, downtown Manhattan."

"This is where Divinity has always been."

"No law that says it has to stay here, is there?"

"No law," I said, "but an awful lot of tradition."

Miles laughed and forked up another mouthful. "Got it. It was just a suggestion." He fell silent, concentrated on getting the right amount of cream and sugar into his coffee, then finally treated me to a toothy grin. "Perfect. So why don't you tell me what's wrong? You look worried."

"Try confused and not quite awake yet." I sat across from him and moved two slices to my own plate. "I'm not sure what you think I can do for you."

"Maybe nothing. We won't know until we try, eh?" He sipped and set his cup aside. "I'm worried about my wife, Abby. That's the long and the short of it. Savannah has always acted as if she could take or leave Paradise, but now that we're here, she's suddenly consumed with this place and the people in it."

That didn't surprise me as much as it did him. I wolfed down a couple bites of French toast. I would have enjoyed it a lot more if I was relaxed and alone, but it was heavenly even under the circumstances. "I guess the past never really leaves us alone, does it?"

"The question is, will *they* put the past behind them?"

"Some might."

"And some won't."

"I can't say for sure, of course, but why ask me? Savannah and I weren't even friends when she lived here."

He lifted one shoulder and wiped chocolate from the corner of his mouth. "I don't know. You seem approachable, I guess. I figure you probably know the stories."

I paused with my fork halfway to my mouth. "What stories?"

"About Savannah. Why people hate her."

This was why he wanted to see me alone? *Not a chance, buddy.* "What has she told you?"

"Not much."

"And you want me to fill in the blanks? I don't think so."

"Why not?"

Because you don't tell a man that his wife once slept with half the football team, or that she tried to seduce a married teacher, or that everyone suspected her of starting the rumors that got Evie Rice kicked off the cheerleading squad. Not if you have a brain in your head. I shrugged and said, "Because they're Savannah's stories to tell."

"And I'm her husband."

"If she wanted you to know, she would have told you."

Miles abandoned his plate and scooted his chair closer to mine. For half a second I thought he intended to grab my hands. He didn't, but I shifted away anyway.

"She's hurting," he said, "and I don't know why. I can't help her unless I do."

Nice sentiment, but I still wasn't interested. "I'm not sure there's a whole lot you can do. Whatever trouble Savannah has with people here in Paradise, it's up to her to fix."

With a heavy sigh, Miles sat back in his chair and waved one hand expansively. "Look, I'm not trying to rush in on my white steed and fix her world. I just want to know the best way to support her. At least tell me about Delta. I mean, they're sisters, for heaven's sake, but they act like strangers when they're together. What's that all about?"

I wish I knew. "I think you'd better ask Savannah or Delta about that."

"I have. Neither one will tell me."

All the more reason for me to keep my big mouth shut. I started to say so, but he cut me off again.

"*Please*, Abby. I'm not asking for all the gory details, but it would help so much to have *some* idea of what's going on between the two of them."

I shook my head and stood to put some distance between us. "I'm sorry, but I'm not even sure *I* know the answer to your question. I lived away nearly as long as Savannah has."

"Which is another reason I chose you." He smiled and leaned forward, elbows on the table. "You know what it's like to leave here and then come back. You understand what Savannah is going through. I don't know who else would."

Small towns are wonderful places, but if the doors are shut against you, they're shut firmly. I understood what Miles was asking, but spilling secrets people didn't want shared would almost certainly undo all my hard work—permanently.

I tried to look regretful. "Nobody really knows what goes on inside a family except the people involved. I'm sorry Savannah and Delta don't want to tell you, but there's really nothing I can say."

"Nothing?"

I shook my head and broke eye contact. "No. I'm sorry."

"So I'm wasting my time?"

"You are if that's what you came for."

"Well, hell. You can't blame a guy for trying, huh?" He sopped up a trail of chocolate, wolfed down two more pieces of toast, then sat back with a satisfied groan. "Just what I needed. Thanks." He glanced at his watch, and his smile drooped. "Is it really eight o'clock already?"

I nodded. *Time flies when you're . . . whatever.* "Yes, why?"

"Savannah should be here by now."

"Maybe she's still getting ready."

He shook his head firmly. "No. She wouldn't run this long." He pulled out a cell phone, punched numbers, and waited for an answer. After a minute or two, he disconnected and scowled at the phone in his hand. "That's odd. There's no answer."

"She's probably just someplace where she can't pick up a signal. Service is spotty up here in the mountains."

Miles nodded and put the phone away, but worry etched lines above his nose and around his mouth. "Something's wrong. She should be here by now. Talking with you, working out that apology from Evie was too important to her."

I stood and began to gather dishes. "About that—"

"You think I'm pushy, don't you?"

"I think you're a concerned husband."

"Yeah? If only she'd appreciate it, huh?" Laughing at his own joke, he stood and shrugged into his coat. "Look, forget about all of this. It wasn't fair to put you in the middle, and I shouldn't have asked."

He looked so worried, I tried to console him somehow. "I'm sure Savannah will answer your questions when she's ready." I might even have said more, but I caught movement in the corner of my eye and realized that Karen was outside. Unless there had been a miracle in the past six hours, Miles was the last person Karen should see right now. "Try not to worry too much. I know things looked bad last night, but everything's going to be different today." I unlocked the door and yanked it open, keeping a careful smile on my face so he wouldn't guess how much I wanted to get rid of him.

He looked skeptical. "I hope you're right. I don't want Savannah upset any more than she is already."

"None of us do." I heard the back door rattle and felt the hairs on my neck stand up. "I need to . . . I think I left the stove on," I said, giving him a none-too-gentle shove toward the street. "I'll see you this afternoon. And don't worry. Everything will be all right. I'm sure of it."

He stared at me as if he'd never seen anyone so rude—and maybe he hadn't. I didn't wait around for him to comment but bolted for the back door, still hoping to prevent a disaster. I heard the bell jingle as the door closed, let out a sigh of relief, and tried not to think about what I'd just done.

I'd promised that everything would be all right, but I'd never been less sure of anything in my life.

Karen seemed a little unsteady as she came into the kitchen, and her hair was only a little less wild than it had been at two thirty that morning. Her eyes were red-rimmed and shadowed deeply, as if she'd smudged cocoa powder under them. She wore the clothes she'd been wearing when she showed up at my door, but she didn't have a coat. I was pretty sure she hadn't been to see Sergio, or she'd have taken more care with her appearance. Or maybe she *had* gone to see him and she'd found something that upset her. I almost didn't want to ask.

I made myself ask anyway. "What are you doing running around without a coat? It's freezing out there."

Karen looked down at her sweater as if she hadn't noticed that her coat was missing.

"Karen? Are you all right?"

She looked at me sharply, then nodded. "Me? Sure. Why?"

"I don't mean to be rude or anything, but you look horrible. Where did you go, and what time did you leave? I didn't even hear the door open."

Karen tugged her apron from its hook and slipped it over her head as if she expected to wait on customers looking like Medusa on a bad hair day. "I went for a walk. No big deal."

"You went for a walk at six o'clock in the morning?"

She leveled me with a look. "Is that a crime?"

"No. It's just that you usually don't go out for leisurely strolls before the sun comes up. Where did you go?"

Karen picked up several boxes of toffee, then stopped and stared at them as if she didn't know what they were. "Just out," she said when she realized I was waiting for an answer. "I needed to think."

"I thought maybe you'd gone to see Sergio."

She shook her head. "I wanted to, but I didn't dare. What if *she* was there?"

Understandable. Sometimes you just don't want to know. "I don't think she was," I said. "I talked to Miles Horne this morning. He said that Savannah didn't sleep well last night, and she's out jogging now."

I felt a tickle of worry when I remembered the fear in Miles's expression, but the relief in Karen's wiped it away. An actual spark of life brightened her eyes. "Are you sure?"

"That's what he said, and he had no reason to lie to me."

Suddenly shaky, Karen put down the boxes and dropped onto a chair at the table. "How did you find out? Did you call him or something?"

"He called me. He and Savannah wanted a public apology from Evie."

Karen blurted a laugh. "Are you serious?"

"That's what he said."

"And you agreed?"

"Not exactly. I thought maybe I could convince them to change their minds, but it turned out that he really wanted somebody to tell him what Savannah was like when she lived here."

Karen's lips curved into a tremulous smile. "And did you?"

"Are you crazy?"

Her smile gained a little strength, but the fingers she dragged through her hair trembled. "Can you believe the nerve of that woman? Demanding an apology from Evie? I'll bet Savannah *did* cheat last night. It would be just like her. I just can't figure out why she would."

"That's the million dollar question," I agreed, sitting down across from her. "At least you can relax, knowing that Sergio didn't spend last night with her. Maybe you should talk to him, Karen. Listen to what he has to say. There might be a perfectly good explanation for what you saw."

Her smile evaporated, and she speared me with a sour look. "Oh, I'm just sure there will be."

"Come on, Karen. You know I'm the last person on earth to defend a cheating spouse, and really I don't know what Savannah is like now. But I do know Sergio, and I can't believe he would cheat on you."

"Well, he gave a fair imitation of it last night."

"Maybe it really was just two old friends sitting at the same table, having a drink and laughing at an old memory."

Her lips thinned. "Yeah, and I can guess which memory, too. I could have killed her, Abby. I really could have."

All that anger made me ache inside. "Don't do this to yourself, Karen. I'll admit that Savannah's just about the last person I'd want to see the man I loved with, but you didn't actually see them doing anything wrong. They were just having a drink in a public place."

"That's how it starts."

"Granted. Sometimes. But you're acting as if you caught them in bed together or something."

Karen's expression froze, and her eyes narrowed. "Oh. I see. You think I'm overreacting."

"It's possible, isn't it?"

"No, it's not." Her voice was as cold as the air outside.

"It is possible, Karen, and I think you owe it to yourself to find out what was really going on."

Karen stood unsteadily, knocking over a stack of toffee boxes. "So *you* find your husband with another woman and the whole world stops spinning. I find *mine* with one, and I'm making things up."

Her reaction threw me. "That's not what I meant!"

"Oh, no. Of course not." Karen took a couple of jerky steps toward the door. "Maybe I didn't run off to the city and make a big, important life for myself. Maybe Aunt Grace didn't leave the store to me. Maybe I'm just a housewife with a part-time job, but that doesn't mean I can't be hurt just as badly as you were."

"Karen, I didn't—"

She slammed out the door before I could even figure out what I wanted to say. I heard her footsteps thundering up the stairs, and a second later, the door to my apartment banged shut hard enough to rattle the windows. I figured she'd gather up her things and take off before I could argue with her, and that was fine with me. I *knew* it was a bad idea for her to stay with me. Was I ever right.

I paced around the kitchen for a little while, rehearsing what I'd say when Karen came downstairs again. Ten minutes passed. Fifteen. After twenty, I got tired of waiting and decided to beard the lion in her own den . . . or at least in mine.

I pounded up the stairs, threw open the door, and

launched into my speech so Karen couldn't cut me off. "Look, I know you're hurt, and I don't blame you. But you couldn't be more wrong about how I feel, and I resent the fact that you just *jumped* to conclusions—"

It took me a few seconds to realize that the only one listening was Max, but at least he had the good manners to stop chewing the toilet brush and pay attention. As for Karen, she lay sprawled facedown on the sofa bed, snoring loud enough to wake the dead.

Chapter 5

For the rest of the morning I did my best to forget Evie, Savannah, Karen, and the contest. I finished a large bouquet of cinnamon disk roses, scheduled for delivery that afternoon, filled a handful of smaller orders, and packaged three to go out in the mail. We do a pretty good mail-order business, mostly shipping candy to people who used to live in Paradise. I didn't have any as loyal as the legendary Cole Porter who, back in the jazz age, had nine pounds of fudge shipped to him every month from his hometown confectionary, but I was hoping to get there someday.

With the mail ready, I loaded a batch of apple pie taffy onto the puller and rang up several more sales before I finally gave up waiting for Karen to show up and called in backup. It was Saturday, so I started with my A-list. That proved to be a waste of time. My twin nieces, Dana and Danielle, already had plans, my sister-in-law Elizabeth was in bed with a cold, and my mother would never make it up the mountain from Denver before closing.

The longer Karen stayed away, the more angry I became. She was being childish and petty, and she'd chosen to deliberately misunderstand what I'd said. Even if she walked through the door *that minute* and begged me to forgive her, I wasn't sure I would.

I made about twenty calls before I managed to convince my cousin Bea to help out for a few hours. She had a few things to say about the late notice, and she demanded an exorbitant hourly wage, but beggars can't be choosers. Bea is the oldest daughter of my father's oldest brother, a force to be reckoned with under any circumstances. She's organized and punctual. She's also tall, slim, a natural blonde, and . . . well, bossy.

She showed up a few minutes before eleven and promptly took over. "So what's going on with Karen?" she demanded as she slipped a gold-edged Divinity apron over her clothes. "Where is she?"

I'd managed to evade the question over the telephone, but it was a whole lot harder with Bea standing less than two feet away. "She's tied up this morning," I lied. "Something came up with one of the kids."

Bea stared me down. "Really? I just saw the kids. They all looked fine, but Karen wasn't with them."

"Oh?" I tossed off a casual shrug and turned away. "Well, maybe I misunderstood then."

"Sergio says she never came home last night."

"He did?"

"Apparently, she accused him of cheating on her and took off in a huff. *And* she'd been drinking."

Like I said, news travels fast in Paradise. I was too curious to resist. "What else did he say?"

"Only that she was staying here with you until she pulled her head out. So where is she?"

"Upstairs, sleeping it off. I was hoping Sergio wouldn't have to find out."

Bea laughed and set to work straightening the display of old-fashioned favorites we order from a supplier on the

East Coast. Necco Wafers, Big Cherry, Zotz, Lemon Heads, Chick-O-Stick, Dots, and Crows, a dozen old-fashioned candy bars all crowded together on a glass table with retro lunch boxes from the fifties and sixties. It was a fun display, and one that garnered a lot of attention from our customers.

"Listen," Bea said as she pushed, pulled, prodded, and dusted, "Karen gets emotional. Sergio knows that. This isn't the first time she's come unglued, and it won't be the last."

"So Sergio's not worried?"

Bea shook her head. "She'll stay away for a day or two, then she'll wander on home and act as if nothing ever happened. It's what she does to assert her independence."

I had a hard time believing that, but I was hardly an expert on my family and their habits. "Does she always accuse Sergio of cheating on her?"

The little half smile on Bea's face slipped. "No. That's new." She finished with the retro table and moved to the next display without missing a beat. "I wouldn't worry about it too much, though. I keep saying she should just tell Sergio she needs time away when the kids and the house start to feel like too much, but I don't think she even realizes what's happening until it's too late."

"We're talking about the same Karen?" The woman Bea described wasn't the cousin *I* knew, but then, neither was the Karen who'd calmly threatened to commit murder.

"They have their system," Bea said, "and I guess it works for them. Who's to say?"

Not me, that's for sure. "What does Sergio do when she comes back?"

Bea picked pieces of taffy from the wrong baskets and put them where they belonged. "I don't know. Probably nothing." She stepped back to survey her handiwork, then shot a look at me. "What's wrong?"

Too late, I realized I'd been scowling. It didn't take a genius to see that Bea was familiar with the routine at Divinity, and I wondered if *she* was harboring bad feelings toward me. But I had deliveries to make, a room to set up, and contestants scheduled to arrive in less than five hours, so I shelved my questions with my other family issues and smiled as I turned away. "Nothing. It's just been a long day."

Bea watched me for a few seconds, then shrugged and went back to work. I got busy putting together the baskets of taffy I planned to put out for that night's guests.

Aunt Grace's Divine Saltwater Taffy has been a staple at Divinity since the day the store opened its doors. In the beginning, she sold only a handful of flavors. Now, we offer more than a hundred and fifty—everything from amaretto to wintergreen.

Despite its name, there's really not much salt or even a lot of water in taffy. Legend has it that back in 1883, a man named David Bradley owned a candy shop on the boardwalk of Atlantic City. One night a huge wave hit and soaked his entire inventory in seawater. He'd jokingly called the candy "saltwater" taffy after that, and I guess the name stuck.

When I was a kid, I spent hours watching the old-fashioned rotating hooks stretch the thick, glistening candy ribbons in the shop's front window. I'd loved helping Aunt Grace cut the candy into bite-sized pieces after enough air had been worked in to make the color and texture just right, and I'd felt so important, wrapping each piece quickly so they would keep their shape.

Without a doubt, though, my best memories were wrapped up in the December evenings when Aunt Grace let the cousins make taffy by hand. We'd waited breathlessly while the corn syrup, sugar, water, and cornstarch boiled, and bickered good-naturedly among ourselves over how we wanted to pair up when it was our turn to work. We'd watched, wide-eyed and eager, while Aunt Grace turned the taffy out onto the greased counter and we'd slathered butter on our hands while Grace cut the huge mound of candy into sections just large enough for two kids to handle.

When the candy was finally cool enough, she'd added flavor and coloring, then turned us loose on the thick, shimmering mounds. It must have been pandemonium, with all of us vying for our favorite flavors and whining when our arms got tired, but I believe that Aunt Grace loved those evenings as much as we did.

I pulled a variety of flavors onto the long workbench overlooking the sales floor—chocolate, strawberry, banana, grape, cherry, cinnamon, orange, peppermint, wild huckleberry, and berry blast. Each flavor had a memory attached, and I could have lost myself in them without any effort at all, but remembering how great Aunt Grace had been only made me realize how far short I fell.

Like Aunt Grace, I had no children of my own, but I did have nieces and nephews. Unlike Aunt Grace, I'd spent most of my life on the fringes of their world, too busy with my life as a corporate attorney and Roger's wife to make myself a regular part of their world. I'd been more like Savannah Vance—*Horne*—than Grace Shaw, and I didn't like knowing that.

Well, that was then and this is now, I told myself firmly. Dana and Danielle might be teenagers, but that didn't mean it was too late to improve my relationship with them. And Wyatt's boys were even younger. Brody was eleven. Caleb, eight. I still had time. I just had to be smart enough to use it.

It was midmorning before I found time to take a break. Leaving Bea in charge, I hurried upstairs, made sure Karen was still breathing, then hooked Max to his leash and led him outside. Last night's storm had blanketed the city in eight inches of soft, white powder. Today's cloudless sky left brilliant sunlight winking off the snowdrifts all along Prospector Street. The air was crisp and almost cold enough to make my lungs hurt as Max and I hurried along the sidewalk. This was the kind of weather that drew tourists out in droves, and the city had on its best face to welcome them.

Max stopped in front of the store to investigate something buried under the snow, and I stole a glance at the store's front window. I'd been doing my best to keep up with Aunt Grace's traditional seasonal display windows made entirely of candy and other edible substances. Just last week, I'd replaced December's miniature Christmas village with a sledding snowman molded from tempered white chocolate riding down a cotton candy hill on a bright red chocolate sleigh.

My snowman's chocolate arms waved in gleeful abandon as the sled careened down its imaginary slope. Tiny threads of monofilament ran from ceiling to strategic points on his stocking cap, a carefully constructed mosaic made from broken pieces of red and green hard candy, and the flying ends of his candy-cane scarf.

Without a doubt, Aunt Grace's windows had been both more artistic and more intricate than mine, but my efforts weren't half bad. Give me another twenty or thirty years, and I might even restore Divinity to its former glory.

I was just turning around again when Miles Horne's black BMW roared up the street and screeched to a halt, blocking traffic. The driver of the Suburban behind it had to slam on his brakes and narrowly avoided rear-ending the BMW, but Miles didn't seem to notice as he shot out of the car, leaving his door wide open. Oblivious to the angry shouts of the drivers all around him, Miles headed straight for me.

What now?

I wasn't in the mood for more questions, and I made up

my mind to tell him so, but he surprised me by asking something else entirely. "Have you seen her?"

"Who?"

"Savannah. Has she been here?"

"No. Why?"

He turned away before I finished speaking and covered his mouth with one hand.

"Miles? Is something wrong?"

"I can't find her," he said, his voice low. "I've looked everywhere."

I tried to calm him down. "Have you tried calling again?"

"Only about twenty times. There's no answer. She left the hotel at five thirty this morning. I haven't seen her since."

I had a bad feeling, but I didn't want to make Miles worry even more, so I did my best to look and sound reassuring. "Try not to panic," I said evenly. "There are probably a hundred places she could be."

"And I've checked in every one of them." Someone honked, and another driver rolled down his window and shouted for Miles to move his car. Miles waved them both off, took a couple of jerky steps, and dragged his hand across his face again. "Delta hasn't seen her," he said. "Nobody on the hotel staff has seen her, and she hasn't been to that coffee shop she likes so much. What if something's happened to her?"

"I'm sure she's just fine. Have you driven along the route she takes when she runs? Maybe she twisted an ankle or pulled a muscle and can't get back to the hotel."

He turned a set of agony-filled eyes in my direction. "I've looked everywhere I can, but I don't know my way around that well, and she doesn't take the same route every day. She likes variety."

"Well, I'm sure she's perfectly all right. Why don't you move your car so people can get through? Pull in next to my Jetta there," I suggested, pointing out the lot between Divinity and Picture Perfect. "I'll meet you back there as soon as Max is finished, and we'll figure out where she is."

Miles glanced toward his car as if he hadn't noticed it sitting there and gave the disgruntled drivers a distracted wave. "Sure. Okay. I'd appreciate the help." He stepped back into the street, then looked back one more time. "You really think she's okay?"

"Of course she is," I said. "She'll turn up before you know it.

I was wrong. Savannah didn't turn up, and by one o'clock, Miles was visibly shaken. He phoned the police, but the officer on duty said there was nothing they could do until she'd been missing seventy-two hours. I didn't think I'd survive another sixty-plus hours with Miles pacing back and forth inside the store, so I did the only thing I could under the circumstances. I picked up the phone and called Jawarski.

Pine Jawarski is a detective with the Paradise Police Department. We met while he was investigating the murder of a friend, and I was trying to keep my brother out of jail. We've had dinner together a couple of times since then, but that's as far as our "relationship" has progressed.

Don't get me wrong; he's a good guy. At least, he seems to be. Sometimes when we're together, I think there's something going on between us, but he's not any more ready to find out what that something is than I am. We usually let our awareness of each other flop around in the space between us and ignore it as much as possible.

Jawarski answered on the second ring, and I have to admit that the pleasure I heard in his bass voice did a little something to me. "Abby! What are you doing calling me in the middle of a workday? Don't tell me you finally decided to take me up on my challenge."

He's been trying since Christmas to get me on the slopes again, but it's been too many years since I hurled myself down the face of a mountain, and I was never that good at it anyway. Laughing softly, I moved into the kitchen so Miles wouldn't hear me. "Not on your life, Jawarski. Or mine."

"So you say today, but be warned: I don't plan to give up."

"And I don't plan to cave in. If I hold out long enough, the season will be over, and I'll be off the hook."

"Only until next year."

That smelled of permanence, and that made me uncomfortable, so I cut the chitchat short. "Actually, Jawarski, this is a professional call. We have a situation here, and I could use your help."

He switched gears immediately. "What's going on? More trouble with the contest?"

"You heard about that?"

"Hasn't everybody? Is that what's wrong?"

"In a roundabout way, I guess. One of our contestants seems to have gone missing. Her husband is here, and he's really upset. She left their hotel room this morning at five thirty, and he hasn't seen her since. The police say there's nothing they can do until she's been missing for seventy-two hours."

"Unless there are mitigating circumstances, they're right." At least Jawarski sounded regretful. "I assume this lady's over eighteen?"

I nodded. "She's my age."

"And she's mentally sound?"

"Yes, depending on who you ask."

"What's that supposed to mean?"

"Nothing. Bad joke. Yes, she's mentally sound."

"Any reason to think she's in danger?"

I caught myself hesitating and shook my head firmly. "No. Nothing like that."

"And she's not a danger to herself?"

"Not that I'm aware of, but can't the patrol officers at least keep an eye out for her?"

"She's an adult, Abby. She could be off with friends or taking in a movie, or up on the slopes. We've got a town full of musicians spilled over from the festival in Aspen, and all of 'em just looking for trouble. We'd need a better reason than you've given me to get involved."

I could feel Miles watching me hopefully, but I didn't let myself make eye contact. He'd read the answer in my eyes, but I wasn't giving up yet. "What if I told you that the missing woman is the one Evie Rice accused of cheating last night?"

"Is she?" Jawarski sounded a little more interested at that. "So are you saying you think Evie did something to her?"

"No! Of course not. But Savannah isn't particularly well-liked by anybody, so I don't think she's off visiting friends. I think maybe she's been hurt. A sprained ankle or something."

"There are a thousand other places she could be," Jawarski said again. "Maybe she's getting a little something on the side, and her husband doesn't know about it. Happens all the time, you know that."

My gaze strayed to the stairs to my apartment. If that's where she was, she *would* be in danger when Karen woke up. Maybe I didn't want Jawarski to find her, after all. "So there's nothing you can do?"

"Not yet. If she doesn't show up in a couple of days, give me a call. We'll pull out all the stops."

I nodded. "Sure. Thanks. Got any ideas what I can tell her husband? He's going to wear a hole in my floor, pacing back and forth all day."

"If he's that worried, tell him to go out and look for her himself. He could save himself a giant headache and the taxpayers a hefty chunk of change."

Jawarski was right, I thought when I disconnected, but Miles had already exhausted his resources, and he still didn't know where his wife was. I turned around to find him watching me, a mixture of hope and wariness on his face. "Well?"

I shook my head. "There's nothing he can do."

The hope drained out of his expression right in front of my eyes. "This is ridiculous. A woman is missing!"

"She's an adult, Miles. She could be off shopping or—"

"Not without money."

"She doesn't have any with her?"

He shook his head miserably. "Her wallet with all her credit cards is still in our room. This is going to kill me, but I guess there's nothing I can do but wait."

There were a thousand places Savannah could be, I told myself as I tried to focus on work again. But she'd been missing for more than seven hours already. Even if she had been laid up with a twisted ankle, after seven hours in this cold she'd have more than just a sprain to deal with. "What we need," I said, thinking aloud, "is a search party."

Disheartened, Miles sank into a chair and propped his chin in his hand. "That would be great, but I don't know anyone in this town."

"No, but I do, and Bea knows even more people than I do. I'm sure between the two of us we can round up some help."

"Do you really think so?"

"Absolutely. And under the circumstances, I think we should postpone tonight's segment of the contest. If we're all looking for Savannah, there won't be time to set up."

Miles shook his head firmly. "I don't want you to do that."

"You can't postpone," Bea said. "The contestants have been working all day to get ready."

"I understand, but it's already one o'clock, and one of

our contestants is missing. I think finding Savannah and making sure she's all right is a little more important than sticking to our schedule."

Miles sighed with relief, and his eyes grew suspiciously bright. He turned away, embarrassed. "Thank you, Abby. You have no idea how much I appreciate this."

He didn't need to tell me, I could see it in his expression. I touched his shoulder gently. "Just try not to worry. We'll find her. I promise."

It was the second promise I'd made in less than twenty-four hours, and the second time I'd been wrong. One of these days, I was going to have to learn to keep my mouth shut.

Chapter 6

I divided the list of contestants with Bea, and within half an hour, we'd postponed that night's event and rounded up a handful of volunteers to search for Savannah. I decided not to phone Evie, though. She needed special handling.

Leaving Bea in charge of the store (and of Miles), I loaded Max into the Jetta and headed into the suburbs.

I found Evie's house in one of Paradise's oldest residential neighborhoods, a small two-story house painted pale blue with yellow trim. Someone had made an effort to clear the walks, but chunks of ice buried in the snow made the journey from driveway to front door treacherous.

Evie answered the door almost before I could knock. The wide, wild look in her violet eyes and the deep scowl tugging at the corners of her mouth told me I was too late before she even opened her mouth.

"Meena Driggs just called," she said, her tone ripe with accusation. "You can't seriously be thinking of canceling the competition tonight just because Savannah has run off."

"She's missing, Evie."

"You don't really *believe* that do you?"

"You don't?"

"Hell no." Evie ushered me inside, and I spent a minute making Max comfortable in a sunny spot near the door before following Evie into the kitchen where several dozen chocolate turtles cooled on racks next to her famous candy bar pie. Looked like she'd been working all morning.

Blue ribbons from previous wins in Divinity's contest hung proudly on one wall, photographs of Evie's various other accomplishments hung on another. Young Evie in her orchestra seat grinned proudly at the camera. Teenaged Evie in her burgundy and gold cheerleading costume—before the scandal that had gotten her kicked out—held pom-poms high over head. Evie as a young woman held a trophy and stood in front of a prizewinning bouquet at the Summit County Flower Show.

When she saw me studying the pictures, a pleased smile eased the frown on her face. "Megan calls that my wall of fame. I think it inspires her."

"I'm sure it does." I glanced around, trying to find pictures of Evie's daughter, but Evie seemed to be the only family member memorialized here. "Does Megan have a wall?"

Evie pulled two thick mugs from an overhead cupboard. "I'm working on hers in my spare time. I have tons of pictures, but her father is probably the least ambitious person on the planet. He never did approve of acknowledging Megan's accomplishments in any meaningful way."

"He didn't like what you've done here?"

Evie shook her head. "He's the epitome of mediocrity. He hates competition. Thinks it leads to bad things."

Hmmm. Wonder what makes him feel that way? "So he doesn't let Megan compete?"

"He lets her 'join in,' but he only approves of activities where every child, no matter how good or bad they are, gets the same reward. What's the point of that?"

I've never taken competition to the same level Evie does, but I'll admit that I see nothing wrong with encouraging kids to excel. Life's tough enough. Having something you're good at makes a difference. But I do think parents and teachers should draw the line at teaching that it's important to win at any cost. I've seen that in action, and it's not pretty.

I looked away from the wall of fame, sat where Evie indicated I should, and wondered how Evie got anything done in this kitchen. Staring at that many pictures of myself while I worked would creep me out.

In another room, a clock chimed the half hour, and I realized that time was flying past. I tried steering the conversation back on track. "About Savannah—"

The pinch lines around Evie's mouth reappeared. "She's pulling a fast one on you, Abby. Don't let her get away with it."

"I don't think so. She's been gone since five thirty this morning. Her husband is really worried."

"He ought to be relieved." Evie filled the mugs with homemade cocoa and slid one in front of me. Say what you want about Evie, she makes a great cup of cocoa using an old family recipe she refuses to share. "I don't know what she's up to this time, but you're playing right into her hands."

Carrying that much anger around all the time had to hurt. "So where do *you* think she is?"

"Who knows? Who cares? Hiding out in her room, maybe."

"You think Miles is in on the deception?"

Evie rolled her eyes in exasperation. "Well of course he is. Common sense would tell you that."

She hadn't seen how upset Miles was, but I decided to play along. "So what do you think they're up to?"

Evie shook her head slowly. "With Savannah, it could be anything." She sipped her cocoa and scowled at the ring the mug left on her table. "There's one thing that's been bothering me all night, though. I've been trying to figure out what kitchen Savannah's been using to make her candy. Do you know?"

"No, but we don't ask." The question hadn't even crossed my mind.

Pursuing her lips thoughtfully, Evie traced the ring on the table with a finger. "She's staying at the Summit Lodge, right?"

"That's what she told Karen when she checked in for the contest yesterday."

"Well, you just *know* the chefs aren't letting her make candy there."

I nodded and rolled cocoa around on my tongue, hoping that this time maybe I could discern what Evie used. Legend has it that the Aztec emperor Montezuma drank as many as fifty goblets of cocoa every day, only his was thick, dyed red, and flavored with chili peppers. I still couldn't tell what Evie had used, but I was pretty sure chili peppers weren't on the list.

"Maybe she's working at her sister's house," I suggested, reluctantly giving up and swallowing the mouthful.

Evie shook her head again. "Delta would never let her do that. She's too angry. But you know what that means, don't you?"

"No. What?"

"It means Savannah didn't make the candy she entered in the contest last night."

I was getting more than a little tired of the accusations

and, frankly, I thought Evie owed me a hint about her cocoa just for listening to all of them. "You don't know that for sure," I said.

"But she couldn't have made it, Abby. She couldn't. And she'll show up again tonight, carrying around candy that somebody else made, all ready to pass it off as her own."

"You can't just assume that she's doing something underhanded because you don't like her," I said firmly. "And you can't keep accusing her without proof. If she doesn't do something to stop you, her husband will."

Evie's smile grew chilly. "I don't *like* her because she's always doing something underhanded—and usually to me."

Karen might argue that part with her, but I wasn't going to open that particular can of worms. I really didn't care who suffered most at Savannah's hands, I just wanted to protect the integrity of the contest and stop the public bickering. "Look, Evie, I know that you and Savannah have a long history, and I know that you have reasons for feeling the way you do, but she could be in real trouble."

"Trouble she brought on herself."

I pretended not to hear her. "We're putting together a search party at the shop. Most of the other contestants have agreed to help. Will you come?"

Evie laughed and shook her head. "And play into Savannah's latest head game? I can't believe you're even asking."

"I'd ask for her help if you were the one in trouble."

Evie's smile faded. "And she'd turn you down even faster than I have. Don't worry about her. She's fine. I'd bet everything I own on it."

There didn't seem to be anything else to say, so I thanked her and left her glaring at her cocoa mugs. I coaxed Max away from the warm spot on the floor and led him back outside. I'm not usually in touch with psychic energy and New Age vibrations, but the negative energy surrounding Evie was so thick I stood outside for a few minutes gulping clear, clean air before I could make myself get into the car and drive away.

Evie's attitude bothered me as I drove to the other end of town. Snow and traffic made the usual five-minute drive to Silver River Road take more than twenty, but it felt so good to be alone, I really didn't mind.

I circled the block a few times looking for a place to park, then finally squeezed the Jetta into an empty space at the bottom of the hill. Slowly, carefully, I pulled the bouquet of cinnamon roses from the car and set off on foot with Max at my heels. It was impressive, if I do say so myself, with three dozen glistening cinnamon "roses," set off by deep green silk leaves and clusters of baby's breath, all arranged in a crystal vase. A red velvet bow nestled in the center. Curls of ribbon peeked out from behind the greenery. I hoped Dylan and Richie liked it as much as I did.

Like many of the buildings in Paradise, the Silver River Inn has gone through a number of incarnations since it was originally built. It started life as a schoolhouse, but the sprawling brick building has also been a miner's hospital, a library, and an office complex. Four years ago, Richie Bellieu and his partner, Dylan Wagstaff, bought the place. They gutted it the first year and spent the second bringing it to life again, this time as a bed-and-breakfast.

I was gasping for breath by the time Max and I climbed the two flights of stairs from the street, but I caught my breath when we stepped through the heavy wooden door into the hushed and elegant atmosphere inside. I couldn't see anyone in the long hallway leading to the kitchen, so I turned toward the lobby. Only the sound of Max's claws on the polished hardwood floor broke the silence.

Richie and Dylan were working behind the registration desk. While Richie's fingers flew across the keyboard of their computer, Dylan was focused on the open drawer of a file cabinet. The polite smiles they turned toward the door when they heard our footsteps turned into smiles of genuine pleasure when they saw Max. Oh yeah . . . and me.

They've been life partners for at least ten years, but you won't find two more different people if you spend a lifetime looking. Richie, whose naturally dark hair is carefully highlighted and spiked, is flamboyant and filled with enthusiasm for life. In some ways, he's more feminine than I am, but I try not to let that bother me. He was wearing a pair of tight black leather pants and a silk shirt, half of which was leopard print that faded into a turquoise feather design. A matching turquoise beret tilted just so on the top of his head.

Dylan is quiet and far more reserved. He keeps his light hair neatly trimmed and his clothing conservative. While he makes no effort to hide his lifestyle, neither does he go out of his way to advertise it. Maybe he figures that Richie advertises enough for both of them.

With a cry of delight, Richie abandoned the computer and swept out from behind the desk with his arms spread wide. "Max, you handsome thing. I had no idea Abby was going to bring you to see us today." He wrapped his arms around Max's neck and kissed the air noisily. Max's entire back end waggled with excitement, and he managed to land a couple of wet, sloppy dog kisses before Richie could avoid them.

Richie's delight made the worry about Savannah seem unreal somehow. I grinned at Dylan and slid the bouquet onto the counter in front of him. "You're going to lose him to Max one of these days if you're not careful."

Dylan closed the file cabinet and turned a look overflowing with affection on Richie and Max. "Too late. I can't compete." He pulled his gaze away and focused on me. "This is a pleasant surprise. Is Karen sick or something?"

Dylan's not a gossip, but I didn't feel comfortable talking about Karen behind her back. I shook my head and slipped a cookie from the silver tray at my elbow. "I needed a break, and this seemed like a good excuse to take one." Footsteps clattered down the stairs, and a couple of laughing guests spilled outside. I watched their heads disappear as they descended to the street and looked back to find Dylan inspecting the bouquet. "Business must be good," I observed. "Your parking lot is completely full."

"Business is good all over town," Dylan said. "We're full all this week, and we have another big group coming in next week. I'm almost afraid to say this aloud, but it looks as if we might actually have a good year."

There's nothing more deadly in a ski town than a drought. Ski runs without a solid snowpack aren't good for much. Pile up five or six drought years in a row, and you'll see frightened and frantic faces everywhere you look. The six years the Rockies had just endured had dented a lot of bank accounts and bankrupted others. Everyone was glad to see the snow this winter.

"Nobody deserves it more than you two," I told Dylan. "You've put in a lot of work on this place."

He leaned forward and inhaled the cinnamon scent of the bouquet. "You don't know the half of it. Now let's just hope the snow keeps coming."

"I've got my fingers crossed," I assured him.

He moved the bouquet to the center of the L-shaped counter, spent a few seconds adjusting it, then turned back toward me. "I heard you had a little excitement down at Divinity last night."

Richie looked up sharply, gave Max a final pat on the head, and stood to rejoin us. "Did Evie Rich really accuse someone of cheating?"

Max sank onto the hardwood floor and buried his nose in his side, perfectly content not to chew as long as he was with people. "Yes, she really did," I said. "And now the other contestant is missing."

"Missing?" The word erupted from both Richie and Dylan at the same time. Richie leaned on the counter with both elbows and pumped me for more information. "Missing as in . . . *missing*?"

"We don't know yet." I glanced at my watch and grimaced. "We're trying to put together a search party, but it will be dark soon, so I'd better get back. We can use all the help we can get. If you can break away, even for a little while, please do."

Dylan hitched himself onto a desk behind the counter. "Do you think something's happened to her?"

"I don't know." Just the thought made my stomach churn. "All I know is that her husband can't find her," I said, and filled them in on the details.

Richie looked shocked. "Do you think she was kidnapped?"

The thought hadn't even crossed my mind, but now that Richie brought it up, I couldn't rule it out. "She and her husband have money," I said, "so I guess it's possible. I don't think anyone's made an attempt to collect ransom, though. It's more likely she got hurt while she was out jogging."

"And nobody has noticed her in what? Eight hours?"

Nine, but who's counting?

Dylan jumped from the desk and pulled his coat from a hook in the corner. "Can you handle business here while I help look for her, Richie?"

"Go. One of us should help, and you'll be better out there in the woods than I would. Just tell me what I can do to help."

"Make phone calls," I told him, almost weak with gratitude. This kind of bonding together is the best part of living in a small town. During my years away, I'd almost forgotten how great it is to actually know your neighbors. "Send anyone you can round up down to Divinity. We're organizing the search from there."

Richie nodded and reached for the phone. "What about the contest?"

"Postponed until we find Savannah and make sure she's okay."

He pressed the receiver against his chest. "What if she isn't okay?"

That wasn't a possibility I wanted to consider. "She'll be okay," I insisted, "and the contest will be under way again by tomorrow."

Dylan dug gloves from his pockets and worked his hands into them. "I'll bet Evie is royally pissed, huh?"

Again, I decided to be discreet. "She'd rather go ahead tonight, but she understands why we can't."

"But she's not going to help look for the missing lady, though, is she?" Richie asked.

"Well I—I don't know." It's not that I don't trust Richie and Dylan, it's just that I'm still not sure where I fit in Paradise, and talking about my customers to their friends and neighbors doesn't seem like a good idea.

"She won't help," Richie said, bobbing his head in agreement with himself. "She's way too competitive for that. She's one of the most competitive people I know."

I thought about her wall of fame and knew he was right. But that left an uncomfortable sensation rolling around inside me.

Dylan pulled something from his pocket and tossed it into the trash. "How can you say that? You don't even know her that well."

"She's in my yoga class," Richie said firmly. "I spend an hour with that woman twice a week, and I've seen her practically break her neck trying to be number one. *I* sure wouldn't want to be up against her in a contest."

The uneasy feeling grew stronger. "Why not?"

"Because." Richie said, meeting my gaze steadily. "Evie Rice is the kind of person who would stop at nothing if it meant the difference between winning and losing."

And that, I realized with a sinking heart, was exactly what I was afraid of.

Chapter 7

My conversation with Dylan and Richie made me more determined than ever to find Savannah and get her back home safely. I didn't like wondering if she was alive or not, and I *really* didn't like suspecting Evie of something she may or may not have done. It's hard to look someone in the eye under those circumstances. I needed to find Savannah, if only to get my imagination under control.

Miles had told me that he'd already talked to Delta, and maybe there was nothing she could tell me that she hadn't told him, but she was Savannah's sister. She'd be the most likely person to know where Savannah might be.

Last I heard, Delta was working as a manicurist at the Curl Up and Dye, an establishment I tend to avoid, mostly because Paisley Pringle, the parlor's owner, is determined to "fix" my hair. If I have to "fix" my hair at any point in the future, Paisley is the last person on earth I want to be behind the scissors. Her mother comes in a close second.

Not that my hair couldn't benefit from some attention. It's cocoa brown, short, and coarse. Most of the time, it looks like someone hacked at it with a dull knife, but I'm not a fan of Paisley's work. I'm just not eager to see how much worse I can look.

Under the circumstances, however, maybe I could survive long enough to see what Delta could tell me. I drove back into the center of town and parked in the lot next to the salon. I didn't see Paisley's yellow VW bug anywhere, but her mother's teal Cherokee was parked by the back door, and my heart sank. The nut hadn't dropped far from the tree, if you know what I mean.

Reminding myself that the search for Savannah was more important than staying in my comfort zone, I led Max up the sidewalk. Not needing a haircut was just the top item on my list. I also didn't need waxing, buffeting, or polishing, nor did I need any part of my anatomy covered with acrylic. I just wanted to find out if Delta knew where to find Savannah.

Inside, the Curl looks like a throwback to some earlier era. I just have never been able to figure out which one. A small waiting area holds several molded plastic chairs, two coffee tables, countless yellowing issues of hair magazines, and one oversized rock masquerading as a couch.

The walls are a pale, buttery yellow, the hair dryers a ghastly shade of pink, and white eyelet curtains filter the sunlight at the windows. When you're inside the Curl it's easy to forget that Paradise is becoming more of a resort town every year. This is where longtime locals come when they want their hair cut the same way every time and a stylist who knows the exact shade of hair color to mix without having to ask.

Conversation droned between stylists and clients, and one lone customer—a mousy woman with mousy hair—sat in the waiting area flipping idly through a magazine. The odors of hair product, chemical processors, and nail polish made my nose burn and big band swing played softly on the public address system.

I renewed my vow to be in and out in three minutes flat.

At one minute and fifteen seconds, Paisley's mother, Annalisa Kelso, bounced out of the back room wearing a warm, welcoming smile. She's a short, sturdy woman with sturdy brown hair that never changes—a walking advertisement for Paisley's dubious skills. She swept a glance over me, then settled on the woman sitting patiently behind me. "I'm sorry Faith. I didn't hear you come in. Have I kept you waiting long?"

The woman glanced up, and I felt a jolt of recognition. I'd gone to high school with her, but I would never have recognized her if I'd passed her on the street. In high school, Faith had been bright and bubbly—everyone's friend. Within a year of graduation she'd married her high school sweetheart, Noah Bond, who was now a deacon at the Shepherd of the Hills Church. I'm not sure if marrying Noah sapped the life out of her, or if something else was responsible, but all that brightness had definitely evaporated. Even her hair, once the rich color of Bit-O-Honey had become a nondescript dishwater blonde.

Faith closed the magazine and stood, but I don't think she actually made eye contact. "It's fine. I know you're busy."

"I have you down for your usual cut. Did you talk Noah into springing for those highlights this time?"

A weak smile curved Faith's dainty mouth. "Oh heavens no. He likes my hair just the way it is. A cut will be fine."

It was hard to reconcile this quiet woman with the Faith I used to know, and the changes in her made my heart drop. Annalisa must have felt the same way, because she shared a look with me before saying, "I'm afraid I don't have an appointment for you, Abby. Did you call in?"

"No. I don't actually need anything done. I'd like to talk to Delta for a few minutes if she's working today."

Annalisa's lips pursed, and she glanced over her shoulder toward the pedicure station. "Delta's here, but she's running behind. I'd rather you didn't interrupt her."

"It's important," I said. "I promise I won't take long."

As if on cue, Delta emerged from the back room carrying a load of folded towels, and Annalisa's shoulders rose and fell with a put-upon sigh. "Delta, could you come up here for a minute? Abby needs to ask you something."

There is a family resemblance between Savannah and her older sister, but you have to look hard to find it. Delta's short hair is an unremarkable light brown, and the curves that make Savannah seem lush and ripe have turned to fat on Delta. She was wearing a pair of gold-framed glasses low on her nose, and she stared at me over their rims. "Abby? This is a surprise. What can I do for you?"

"I'd like to ask you a couple of questions, if you don't mind. About Savannah."

Her eyes narrowed, but she nodded once and came around the counter toward me. "What's she done now?"

Maybe I don't like Savannah much, but Delta's reaction still made me sad. "I don't know that she's done anything. Miles hasn't seen or heard from her since she left to go jogging early this morning, and he's getting worried."

Faith's eyes grew round. "She's missing?"

"I'm afraid so. Have any of you seen her or talked with her today?"

Faith whispered something that sounded like a prayer.

Delta frowned slightly, exactly as she might have if I'd asked about a stranger. "Today? No. She hasn't been around here."

"I didn't think she's ever been in here, has she?" Annalisa asked.

Delta shook her head. "Not as a customer, anyway. This place isn't exactly her style."

Yeah, well that didn't make her a bad person. "When did you talk to her last?"

Delta tilted her head and gave that some thought. Her chins quivered and folded over each other. "Monday, I think."

"Did she say anything about leaving, or mention somewhere she might go?"

"Not to me, but then, we didn't really talk about things like that. Savannah and I aren't what you might call close."

"So you don't have any idea where she might be?"

Delta shook her head again. "No, but I wouldn't worry. Savannah knows how to take care of herself. She'll turn up. She always does. Now, if you'll excuse me, I'm running behind."

I trailed after her with Max in tow. Annalisa might ask me to leave, but she won't mess with Max. "She came to Paradise to take care of your mother's estate, didn't she? Is there anything else she wanted to do while she's here?"

What little friendliness there'd been in Delta's eyes vanished. She stuffed towels into a cupboard and turned back to face me with barely concealed impatience. "Why are you suddenly so concerned about my sister?"

"We can't find her," I said again. "Her husband is worried. A group of us are trying to help him locate her."

"What does that mean? You've got a search party or something?" She made it sound childish, and when I nodded, she laughed and pulled several bottles and a large purple brush from a nearby closet. "Don't worry about Savannah. She's just off indulging herself, I'm sure."

"Any idea where?"

"No, but I know Savannah. She's always been selfish, and from what I can tell, that husband of hers is about the same. The two of them probably had a fight, and now he's got you jumping through hoops for him. They're both horribly melodramatic, Abby. Don't let yourself get sucked in."

I'd forgotten about the snatch of conversation I'd overheard the night before, and Delta's warning struck a nerve. If she was right, Miles had a lot of explaining to do. "When do you plan to see her next?"

Delta shrugged and started away again. "I don't. She was supposed to stop by yesterday to talk, but she never showed up. Ask me if I was surprised."

I refrained. Delta's matter-of-fact attitude disturbed me. Good or bad, Savannah *was* her sister. "What did you do when she didn't show up?"

"Do?" Delta put down the things she carried and smirked. "Why would I *do* anything?"

"If she promised to stop by and then didn't . . ."

"You're missing my point, Abby. The point is that Savannah not being where she's supposed to be isn't unusual. My sister has never been the most reliable person in the world."

"You didn't try to call her?"

"I saw no reason to. Take my advice. Go back to your store and forget all about this. Savannah's just fine. You'll see. Once she has enough attention she'll reappear like magic."

She might be right, but I had one more question to ask. "Did you know that Savannah's competing in the candy-making competition at Divinity?"

Delta's gaze lifted briefly. "I did hear that. I also heard that she was accused of cheating."

Bad news certainly travels fast. "I'm curious. Do you know where she's making her candy?"

Delta straightened the cord of her electric file and swept two one-dollar bills into her kneehole drawer. "Why would I know?"

"I thought maybe—well, I thought maybe she was using your kitchen."

"Mine?" She laughed and shook her head. "Not likely. Savannah hasn't set foot in that house in twenty years. She's very good at avoiding anything she considers unpleasant, you know. It's her greatest talent. Now I really have to ask you to leave. My two thirty appointment just pulled in."

I wasn't ready to go, but I couldn't force her to let me stay, and I had no idea what more to ask, even if I could. I wanted proof that she actually cared about her sister, that time and distance hadn't killed whatever feeling she'd had for the little girl who'd once trailed around behind her, but even I could see that I wasn't going to get it. In fact, the more questions I asked, the worse I felt.

When I pulled into my parking space next to Divinity a few minutes later, I was both surprised and pleased to find people milling about outside and a mini–command center set up in Divinity's kitchen. Someone had produced a map of the city streets, and Bea buzzed from place to place, coordinating the search, giving orders, and making sure that everyone knew their assigned task. It was a perfect job for her.

Miles sat at the table clutching a cup of coffee in both hands and staring at the melee around him as if he had no idea what was going on. Since the temperature had climbed a few degrees, I tied Max's leash to the bench outside so he could get some fresh air, then made my way through the crowd to Miles.

I sat across from him and touched his hand briefly. He jerked in surprise and his gaze shot to my face. "Abby? When did you get back?"

"Just a few minutes ago. Is there any sign of her?"

He shook his head sadly. "Nothing yet. I don't even know what to do."

"Just hang in there," I said. "There are lots of people looking for her. It's only a matter of time."

He sipped, made a face, and pushed his cup away. "I feel so useless just sitting here. I'd rather be out looking myself, but your cousin thinks I'll be more help answering questions than I would be out on the streets."

"She's probably right. She usually is."

"Yeah? Well, that doesn't make it any easier to just sit here."

"I'm sure it doesn't. Have you called the hospitals to make sure she's not there?"

Miles looked surprised. "You have hospitals here?"

"Well, not *here*, but there's one in Aspen and a medical center in Vail, and plenty of doctors' offices in the vicinity."

His bloodshot eyes clouded. "No, I—I didn't even think."

"Don't worry. I'll check with Bea. She might have done it already. If not, that's something you could do while you wait."

He rubbed his face with one shaky hand. "Yes. Thanks. Yes, I could."

Before I could say anything more, noise erupted in the courtyard outside, and a second later, a wild-eyed Karen burst through the door.

I didn't want her to get anywhere near Miles, so I shot to my feet and tried to head her off.

Unfortunately, she moved faster than I could. She drew up to the table breathing fire and lasering everything that moved with her eyes. "What the hell do you think you're doing, Abby? Why are you helping *her*?"

At least the alcohol on her breath had disappeared. I grabbed her arm and dragged her onto the sales floor, but not before I caught a glimpse of Miles's stunned expression. Poor man. He didn't need Karen's wild accusations on top of all the other worry.

She fought me, but for once I was stronger. I pushed, pulled, and prodded her toward a cubbyhole on the far side of the sales floor, through clusters of volunteer searchers waiting for instructions and the confused customers who browsed around them. There, in the only place I thought we stood a chance at a private conversation, surrounded by the rich scent of huckleberry fudge, hard candies, and lollipops, I finally gave her an answer. "I'm not helping *her*. I'm helping to look for her. There's a difference."

"You don't really believe she's missing, do you? She's probably sitting in a coffee shop down the street watching all of you run around like chickens with your heads cut off."

Both Evie and Delta had suggested the same thing, but it still didn't feel right to me. "Why would she do that, Karen? What could she possibly hope to get out of it?"

Completely exasperated with me, Karen threw both hands in the air and turned partway away. "We're talking about *Savannah*, Abby. Who knows why she does anything?"

A couple of men standing nearby glanced over at us, so I lowered my voice and hoped Karen would do the same. "She's been missing for almost ten hours," I said. "She could be hurt."

"Yeah? Well, you know what? I hope she is. Maybe she'll learn a lesson about messing around with other women's husbands."

"Karen, please—" I glanced behind me to make sure Miles hadn't followed us. "Her husband is in the other room."

"So what? Don't you think he deserves to know what kind of woman he married?"

"Not while we don't even know where she is," I snapped. "And not when we don't even know if it's true."

Karen narrowed her eyes, and her expression grew stony. "So you still don't believe me."

Praying for patience, I kneaded the bridge of my nose and tried again to reason with her. "I believe that you saw Sergio and Savannah having a drink together last night, but you have no proof that they did anything wrong. If you go in there and tell that poor man that his wife was cheating on him because she had one drink in a public place and you're carrying around a twenty-year-old grudge, then you're just being cruel."

Karen's eyes flashed, and she clenched her teeth so hard I was surprised she didn't crack a molar. "I don't think I'm the cruel one around here," she said.

"I'm trying to understand," I said for what felt like the hundredth time.

"Really? Well, you're not doing a very good job, are you?" She shoved past me, surprising me with her strength, plowed through the volunteers, and out onto the street.

I stared after her, trying to figure out which one of us was wrong. She was so determined to believe the worst, but was I going overboard the other direction? Maybe I should go after her and try again, but would she even listen?

"Abby?" Bea called before I could decide what to do. "Could you come here for a minute? I need your help."

I turned reluctantly. "What is it, Bea?"

She smiled at a middle-aged man with ill-fitting clothes and a comb-over. "This gentleman would like to buy a three-pound sampler, but I can't find the three pound boxes. Are you out?"

"No, the boxes are on the top shelf."

"The top—" Bea looked at me as if I'd lost my mind. "But they've always been on the middle shelf, right at eye level."

Irritation left over from the argument with Karen made

my skin itch. I wasn't in the mood to defend my decisions, and I hated that I felt the need to. I'd had it up to *here* with Karen's attitude and, frankly, I was losing patience with both of my cousins. "Divinity isn't a family business, Bea. I don't have to clear every change I make with you and the others."

Her mouth fell open, and her eyes narrowed. "I'm only trying to help."

"And I appreciate it," I assured her. "I just want you to stop chewing me out every time I move a paper clip, okay?"

Ignoring the internal whisper that told me *I* was overreacting, I reached into the cupboard, jerked out a handful of three-pound boxes, and tossed them onto the counter. But as I strode away, I knew it wasn't the conversation with Bea that had me feeling nervous. It was something else.

The whole time I'd been arguing with Karen, something kept trying to get through to me, and I'd managed to ignore it for hours. Much as I hated to admit it, there was one place I hadn't looked for Savannah. It was probably the first place I should have gone, but the more Karen insisted, the more I resisted.

I guess I didn't want to find Savannah with Sergio any more than Karen did, but like it or not, one of us was going to have to look.

Chapter 8

With Bea tied up organizing the search effort (not to mention not speaking to me) and Karen off feeling sorry for herself, I had to stay behind the counter to wait on customers until we finally closed our doors at seven o'clock. Searchers stayed out until well after nine, but it was cold and dark and hard to see, and the volunteers finally drifted home with promises to come back in the morning.

At a few minutes after nine, I watched Dylan drive away with Miles in his car. He'd finally convinced Miles to at least try to sleep, for which I was profoundly grateful. I was aching and tired, battling a throbbing headache, and ready for a good night's sleep myself. I couldn't have stayed awake with Miles for even another hour.

Yawning noisily, I climbed the stairs to my apartment. I wasn't sure I had enough energy to even get undressed. Inside, I found Karen curled up on the couch, surrounded by a pint of pralines-and-cream ice cream, a bag of Oreos, tortilla chips and salsa, and my nearly depleted stash of toffee. Max lay on the bed beside her, a couple of chew toys and his rawhide bone contributing to the disarray. His leash was draped over the back of the couch, which meant Karen had walked him at some point during the day.

My cousin glanced up and away as I came through the door, acknowledging me while making it crystal clear that she didn't want to talk. Too bad. There was a lot that needed to be said.

I sat on the foot of her bed and tried not to notice the way she shifted her feet away so she wouldn't have to touch me. "We have to talk, Karen."

She looked toward me from beneath lowered lids, but her gaze didn't actually connect. "There's nothing to talk about."

"I think there is. It's not that I don't believe you, or that I don't take you seriously . . ."

"Could have fooled me." Her voice was sullen, her face a cold mask.

"I know you were hurt when you found Sergio having a drink with Savannah, but by all accounts Savannah went back to the hotel after that."

"So *he* says."

"Why would he lie?"

She dragged her gaze up to my face, but it was pretty obvious she didn't like what she saw. "I don't know, Abby. Maybe he's embarrassed to admit that she's cheating on him. Maybe he doesn't care. He's got that fancy new job in New York—maybe he's more worried about his reputation than the truth."

I refused to let her get to me, so I shrugged and stretched my aching legs out in front of me. "You could be right. I really don't know him. But he does seem to genuinely love Savannah, and I think he's really worried about her."

"I never said he wasn't worried," Karen said with a stony smile. "I just don't know what he's worried about most." She scooped a spoonful of ice cream into her mouth and closed her eyes. "If you ask me, anybody who'd marry Savannah and stay with her for more than ten minutes has a screw loose."

I laughed. The sound bounced around in my head, but a more companionable silence than we'd shared in a few days fell between us. I waited a while to break it. "Have you talked to Sergio today?"

She didn't open her eyes, but she nodded. "He was at work."

"So Savannah isn't with him?"

"Not now."

"Did you ask whether he'd seen her today?"

"I asked. He *claims* he hasn't."

I honestly didn't know whether to feel relieved or worried. I settled for a little of both. If Sergio was telling the truth, Karen's marriage might actually stand a chance. But Savannah had been missing for more than fourteen hours, and the volunteer searchers had already been through most of the downtown area and the streets and businesses around Savannah's hotel with no sign of her. That made it hard to feel truly relieved.

I reached for the toffee tin, broke the corner from one piece, and slipped it into my mouth. "So what are you going to do?"

"About Sergio?" Karen shook her head and absently scratched Max's head. "I don't know. I can't decide anything tonight."

"So you're staying here again tonight?"

Her eyes inched open. "Do you have a problem with that?"

My mother always raised me to tell the truth, and there's not much I hate worse than a lie—but nothing could have compelled me to answer that question truthfully. I dug up a smile from somewhere, forced my aching legs to stand, and carefully shook my pounding head. "No, of course not. Stay as long as you need to."

"Because if you do, I can leave. There are a hundred other places I could go."

"Stay," I said again. "I *want* you to stay." Even Mom would forgive that lie—I think.

Karen didn't look completely convinced, but she sank back against the pillow and plunged a chip into the salsa, and I figured she wouldn't be going anywhere soon.

I left her lying there, surrounded by junk food, and seriously annoyed that her binge wouldn't add one single pound to her delicate frame. Inside my room, I stripped off my clothes, tugged on my favorite ratty sweats and a wrinkled T-shirt, and crawled between the covers. After about five minutes, Max lost interest in the pity party and came to lie on the bed at my feet.

Good dog.

Even with Max's company, I had a hard time sleeping. Worry about Savannah got all mixed up with irritation over the way Karen and Bea had been acting, and that got me tossing and turning and punching the pillow which, for some reason, just didn't *feel* right. I kicked the covers off, thinking I was too warm. Ten minutes later, I decided I was freezing and pulled them back up to my neck, but I still couldn't sleep.

Savannah Horne was out there somewhere. It was just a matter of time until we found her.

I had to keep believing that.

I was up by sunrise on Sunday morning, gritty-eyed with exhaustion but too agitated to even pretend to sleep any longer. I downed two cups of coffee and a scrambled egg, then hurried downstairs to join the volunteers who were already starting to gather. Bea still wasn't happy with me, but she didn't let a little thing like irritation with me get in the way of her volunteer effort. I don't know, though, if it had any bearing on the assignment she gave me.

I spent two hours combing the brush along a stretch of riverbank, alternately praying that we'd find Savannah and hoping that we wouldn't. By ten o'clock, I stopped and went back to the store so I could open at noon. Sunday is one of our busiest days during tourist season, so the number of volunteers dwindled rapidly as shopkeepers returned to their own stores, but those who didn't have to be somewhere kept searching while the rest of us manned the cash registers.

Business was steady all morning long, but I still managed to steal a few minutes to place an online order with our paper goods supplier and a few more for a quick talk with Jawarski, who called to find out how the search was going. If Savannah stayed missing for another forty hours, we could officially turn the search over to the police. That made my stomach hurt.

Unless she was inside somewhere, safe and sound and laughing at all of us for scurrying around like ants, she was outside in the elements. I had serious doubts about anybody's ability to survive a January night in these mountains without the right gear.

Early in the afternoon, Dooley Jorgensen sent one of his part-timers down the hill to help out so I could rejoin the search. I gave the girl cursory instructions, told her to check with Bea if she had questions, and loaded Max into the Jetta a little after two o'clock.

Like it or not, I told myself as I drove away, it might be time to consider hiring someone else to help out around the store. Adding another staff member would cut my profit margin significantly, but I couldn't handle the business on my own, and unless Karen pulled her head out and I found a way to spend several mornings each week in the kitchen, we'd be in serious trouble soon.

Now that I was free to start looking again, I didn't know where to begin. Maybe I should have let Bea assign me a quadrant to search, but I had a feeling I'd be more effective listening to my own instincts.

Now, if only my instincts would start talking. I pulled to the side of the road and stared at the mountain peaks for a little while, as if I thought I'd find answers there. I didn't care what Delta said, I couldn't imagine Savannah simply disappearing without telling someone, and I wasn't convinced that she'd taken off to avoid Evie's accusations.

After a few minutes, I realized that the building I could see stretching across the hillside was the Summit Lodge—Savannah's hotel. Since that's the last place anyone saw her, that seemed as good a place as any to start looking.

The Summit Lodge is one of three new hotels built in recent years to accommodate Paradise's increased tourist traffic. Nestled against the mountains between ski runs and the new golf course, the lodge is a majestic collection of varnished wood and polished glass. From the look of things as I pulled into the parking lot, business was booming. I drove around at a slow crawl for a few minutes before I found a parking space between the Dumpster and the tarp-covered outdoor pool.

The walks had been cleared, but a thin layer of ice had formed over most of the parking lot, so it took a few minutes to reach the lodge's front doors. Inside, a fire blazed in the center of the lobby, and the honey-colored wood gleamed as if every inch of the building had recently been polished. I had to wait in line while a twenty-something clerk with a thin blonde ponytail checked in a handful of visitors, but at last she turned a practiced smile in my direction. "May I help you?"

"Yes, I'm looking for Savannah Horne, and I'm hoping you won't mind answering a few questions."

The clerk, whose nametag read Julie, smiled blandly and typed something on the computer in front of her. "Savannah Horne? I don't show her registered. Are you sure she's staying here?"

Her reaction confused me. Didn't the staff know Savannah was missing? I nodded slowly. "Yes, I'm sure. She's here with her husband, Miles."

She tapped something else on the keyboard and smiled with satisfaction. "Ah, yes. Here they are. Have you checked their room?"

"I don't know their room number, but that's not—"

The satisfaction on Julie's face turned into something closer to pity. "I'm so sorry. I can't give you that information." She brightened and said, "But I could put a call through to the room. You're welcome to use the courtesy phone at the end of the counter. Just dial zero."

I actually felt a flicker of hope as I followed her instructions. Maybe Savannah had come back last night. Maybe Miles would pick up the phone and tell me that everything was fine now.

My hope was short-lived. Six rings later, the call patched through to voice mail. I left a brief message, just in case, and replaced the receiver. "No luck," I told the clerk. "Have you seen Mr. or Mrs. Horne this morning?"

Julie shook her head. "I wouldn't know. We have one hundred thirty rooms, and they're all full. It's next to impossible to keep track of everyone who's staying here."

"Mrs. Horne is about my age. Tall. Long, dark hair. Very pretty."

Julie's pert smile drooped. "You've just described half our female guests."

"I understand that, but this is important. Mrs. Horne left the hotel to go jogging early yesterday morning. Her husband hasn't seen her since."

"One of our guests is missing?"

"You didn't know?"

She shook her head quickly. "No, but management

might. Information doesn't always filter down to the rest of us."

"She hasn't been missing long enough to get the police involved," I told her, "but her husband is getting worried, and so are her friends. If I could find someone on staff, or even another guest who's seen her, it would set everyone's minds at ease."

Julie shook her head slowly. "I'm sorry, but I can't help you."

"Were you working at five thirty yesterday morning?"

"No. I don't come on shift until seven."

"Then can you tell me who *was* here?"

Her frown deepened. "The only thing I can do is give you the name of our night manager. He might be able to help."

"I'll take it. Any chance I can get a phone number so I can talk to him this morning?"

Julie shook pale blonde bangs into her eyes and swept them away again. "That's against company policy, but he'll be on duty again at eleven. You could probably talk to him then." She wrote something on the back of a business card and pushed it across the counter.

I thanked her and jotted my cell phone number on the back of another card for her. "Thanks. I appreciate the help. If you see Mrs. Horne or run into someone who has, please give me a call."

Julie promised she would, and I skidded back across the parking lot to the Jetta.

Max was whining again by the time I got back to the Jetta, so I clipped on his leash and let him out into the frigid air. No matter how cold it is, Max seems to need time and space to take care of business, and I've learned not to rush him. I gave him his lead and followed him through the parking lot toward the mountain.

By the time we reached the service road that runs adjacent to the forest, Max began sniffing in earnest, but instead of settling on one of the perfectly good spruces or aspens surrounding us, he raced off in search of something better.

I fell into step behind him, a little nervous about running on the ice that still lined the unused road. I'm in better shape than I was before Max came to live with me, but I'm still not one of those people who hits the streets every day, come rain, shine, or snow, like Savannah.

Since I was occupied with other thoughts, I didn't notice the other set of footprints in the snow immediately. Even after I did, it took me a few minutes to figure out that Max was following them. I mean, it's not as if there were lots of choices about which path to take. The forest grows right to the edge of the road there, and the undergrowth is so thick someone could lie hidden in it for days.

That thought sent a cold chill up my spine, and for the first time, I wondered if Savannah had gone jogging on city streets, or if she'd chosen this more obscure path. As quickly as the thought formed, I dismissed it. Who in their right mind would run out here, alone, in the dark?

Whatever scent Max was chasing must have been a strong one. Eight inches of fresh powder lay in mounds between the trees, and piles of snow had been pushed against the shoulder of the road by the street crews. The cold air burned my lungs, and my fingers were already numb, but the dog showed no sign of letting up.

We rounded a curve in the road, and I sawed on the leash, trying to get Max to stop. "Come on, boy," I pleaded between gasps. "Let's go back. It's cold out here."

To prove which one of us was the boss, Max laid his ears back and started running faster. We'd probably gone half a mile from the hotel when I caught a glimpse of something red almost buried in the snow beneath the trees. I didn't even have time to register what I was looking at before Max lunged off the road toward it.

I was dimly aware of car doors opening and closing in

the parking lot behind us, but trees obscured the view. How odd. It seemed like we'd walked forever, but we'd circled around behind the hotel and only a few feet now separated us from civilization.

I fell twice as I struggled through the snow toward the red patch, and the burning cold turned my hands nearly as red as the mystery bundle I was heading for. After what seemed like an hour, I drew close enough to see that the bundle was some kind of fabric, and a panicky feeling fluttered in my stomach.

With a low growl, Max buried his nose in the snow and began to dig. Tugging him away was no easy feat, but I didn't want to just let him go. What if . . . Well, what *if*?

I secured the leash around a tree branch and, ignoring Max's unhappy whining, prodded the mound gently with the toe of my boot. When I realized that the red fabric was attached to something solid, I swear my stomach turned completely over.

Trying not to think, I dropped to my knees and scooped powder away with my already numb hands. But the snow was so light and dry it collapsed on itself. Each scoop I removed filled up again immediately.

Panting and exhausted, I sat back on my heels and tried to come up with another plan of attack. Maybe it was nothing, I told myself. Something tossed to the side of the road. A waste of my time.

But what if it wasn't? I shifted a few inches to my right and started digging again. In spite of the frigid air, sweat trickled down my temples and the back of my neck. I kept digging anyway.

After a few minutes, the snow fell away, revealing the slightly rounded curve of a shoulder, an arm, and one bare hand with skin an unnatural color of gray blue. The breath left my lungs in a rush, and I fell backward into the snow. I stared at the curled fingers in disbelief for far too long before the realization hit me that whoever it was might not be dead.

I went to work on the snow again with a vengeance, shoveling powder away by the armful and praying silently with every fear-filled breath. I don't know how long it took to uncover her head, but one look at her face and her eyes staring sightlessly at the ground convinced me of what I already knew: I was too late.

My stomach heaved, and bile shot into my throat. With my eyes blurred by tears, I crawled into the trees a few feet away and emptied my stomach. I could hear Max howling in the background, but I wasn't sure whether he was worried about me or eager to check out Savannah's lifeless body.

When I finally finished, I felt the strangest urge to lie down in the snow and let the cool white powder wipe the fever from my face, but I didn't have time to indulge myself. I had to let someone know what I'd found.

Naturally, my first thought was of Jawarski. I could use a friendly face right about now.

I'd been carrying my cell phone in my pocket all day, but I was in one of those sections of Paradise the satellite signal doesn't reach. Swearing softly under my breath, I shoved the phone back into my pocket and leaned my head against the tree where Max sat watching me. "What do I do, boy? I don't want to leave her . . ."

I know it doesn't sound logical. After all, she'd been there for more than a day already. What could a few more minutes hurt? But it was the principle of the thing. Nobody had known she was there before. I did know now, and I didn't want to just walk away and leave her lying there, cold and alone.

After a few minutes, the sound of voices cut through the haze in my head, and I realized that someone must be in the hotel parking lot. My throat hurt from being sick, but I forced myself to shout, "Help! Help me, please! I need someone to call the police."

The voices fell silent, but I shouted again, and a few seconds later, two women wearing hotel staff uniforms appeared through the trees. I stood and waved my arms over my head to get their attention. "Call the police," I shouted, struggling through the snow toward them. "Ask them to send Jawarski."

Chapter 9

"What made you decide to look for her out there?" Jawarski asked as he handed me a mug filled with cocoa a couple of hours later. I inched my shoulders under the blanket he'd brought me a few minutes earlier and took the cup with a grateful smile. It felt good to be inside where it was warm, surrounded by the familiar things in my apartment.

Karen was gone, but her clothes and bags were strewn all over my living room, so Jawarski and I had moved into the kitchen. Jawarski hadn't asked about the mess, and I hadn't offered an explanation, but the question floated in the space between us.

The cocoa had that pale, thin look you get from mixing that instant junk with water. I sipped it anyway and gave Jawarski an A for effort. "I wasn't really looking for her along that road," I said. "I was just taking Max for a walk."

"At the Summit Lodge?"

I shook my head and started over again. "I went to the lodge to look for Savannah, but the clerk I spoke to hadn't seen her. When I came outside again, Max made it clear that he needed to get out of the car. He's the one who found her."

Jawarski's glance settled on the dog, who lay curled at my feet as if finding a dead body was an everyday occurrence. Jawarski patted his side and straightened again. The man is tall and solid, with short-cropped hair, blue eyes, and a regulation police mustache that droops a little over his upper lip.

I can't deny that I'm attracted, but I'm determined to take things slow. My divorce is barely a year old, and my track record with men leaves a whole lot to be desired. I'd somehow managed to miss my ex-husband's affair until I tripped over it. Jawarski seems like a good guy, but so had Roger, and look how that turned out.

Those are my reasons for holding back. I don't know Jawarski's. He doesn't say a lot, and I don't ask. I figure he'll talk when he's ready. With any kind of luck, I'll still be around to listen when he does.

But none of that mattered. He was here for me now, his eyes gentle and filled with concern, his presence large and steady.

I shuddered, remembering how Savannah's hand had looked against the snow. "How did she die?"

"We're not sure. She's pretty battered, though. If I had to guess, I'd say it looks like a hit-and-run, but we'll know more after the autopsy is completed."

Images I didn't want filled my head. I forced them away and looked into Jawarski's eyes. "Has anyone told Miles that she's gone?"

Jawarski nodded. "Captain Palmer talked to him a few minutes ago."

"How did he take it?"

"He's pretty broken up. You can imagine."

Yeah. I could. That was the trouble. "Is somebody with him?"

Jawarski nodded again. "Svboda."

"Nate?" I gaped at Jawarski in disbelief. Nate Svboda might be a cop, but he's also a friend of my brother's—a middle-aged good old boy with the sensitivity of a Gila monster—and just about the last person I'd choose to console the bereaved.

I stood a little too quickly and felt my head swim. Jawarski caught my arm and kept me from moving. "Where do you think you're going?"

"To make sure Miles is all right. If I know Nate, he's showing Miles pictures from the most recent issue of *Playboy* to make him feel better."

"Sit down, Abby."

"I'll be fine. I just want to make sure—"

"I know you're fine," Jawarski snapped. "And so is Miles. Nate's a trained police officer. He knows what he's doing."

Jawarski's impatience irked me. "You don't know Nate like I do."

"I know he has everything under control. Now, sit down."

I could tell he meant business, and I didn't like it. Jawarski and I get along much better when he's off duty. I tossed the blanket over the chair. "Sorry, Jawarski. I know you're trying to help, but I've got too much to do to sit around feeling bad."

"What?"

"What do you mean, 'what'?"

"What do you have to do? The contest has been postponed, Bea's downstairs running the shop, and she'll be closing in less than half an hour. What's so pressing that you have to run off right now?"

"Closing the store is my responsibility," I told him, "not Bea's."

He moved his hand from my arm to my hand and rubbed a thumb gently across my knuckles. "Maybe so, but I think you need to take it easy tonight. You've been through an ordeal."

His touch did something to me. The urgency drained away, and my eyes burned, but I hate crying, so I pulled away slowly. I didn't want Jawarski to take it personally, though, so I smiled to ease the sting of rejection. "Not nearly as much as Savannah went through. I'll be all right. Just as soon as I can get the images out of my head."

Kindness warmed Jawarski's eyes. "That might take a little while."

"Or forever." I shuddered again at the memory and wished I hadn't been so quick to pull away. "I'm pretty sure that image won't ever go away."

"Seeing your first body is a shock," Jawarski agreed. "It gets easier, but I don't think the horror of that first one ever completely goes away."

"I'm going to have to trust you on that," I said. "I don't ever want to see another dead body." I sank back into my chair, reluctantly abandoning the idea of rushing to Miles's rescue. Maybe Jawarski was right. Maybe Nate wouldn't botch things too badly. He'd been on the force for at least a decade, and nobody had fired him yet. "What I want to know is, who did this to her?" I said. "Do you have any leads?"

Jawarski's expression grew solemn. "Not yet. There are more than a dozen sets of tire prints along the road, and no way yet of knowing which ones belong to the vehicle that hit her."

"But you'll be looking for it."

"Of course. But at the moment you're our only witness."

I pulled back sharply. "I didn't see the accident."

"No, but you were the first person on the scene. It's possible you saw something that might help us out." He nudged the cocoa toward me.

"I didn't see anything," I insisted. "I only wish I had."

I didn't want the cocoa, but I didn't have the heart to disappoint him. I sipped and forced a smile. *Yep. Thin. Watery. But warm.* "She was only about twenty feet from the employee parking lot, wasn't she? I wonder if one of the staff saw or heard something. Or maybe it was a staff member who hit her. Have you thought of that?"

Jawarski nodded. "Yeah. We've thought of that. But let's get one thing straight right off the bat, okay? I don't want you getting involved in this. Let us handle it. That's what we're trained to do."

I held up both hands. "Not a problem. I have no desire to get involved in your investigation."

"Even though you found the body?"

"Especially since I found the . . . her. I didn't *try* to find her, it was an accident."

"But you were searching for her."

"Well yeah, because you *told* us to."

"I told you?"

"When I called to ask you for help. You said that if Miles was that worried, he should look for her. So we did."

Jawarski rolled his eyes, but he couldn't argue with me, so he changed the subject. "Tell me about the altercation Savannah had with Evie Rice the other night."

"Why do you want to know about that?"

"I have a dead woman on my hands, Abby. I want to know about anything that might have put her here."

My heart slowed ominously. "Are you saying you think someone hit Savannah *deliberately*?"

Jawarski lifted one shoulder with exasperating nonchalance. "I'm just exploring every possibility, that's all. So what about the argument?"

I did my best to match his casual shrug. "There's not much to tell. Savannah took first place in last night's event, and Evie Rice accused her of cheating. End of story."

"Is it?"

"Of course it is." I remembered what Richie said about Evie's competitive nature and felt the sudden urge to start pacing. I made myself ignore it. Jawarski would suspect that he'd hit a nerve, and I didn't want him destroying the competition and sullying Divinity's reputation by accusing the contestants of killing each other.

He spotted a jar of Cappuccino Divinity on the counter and pulled it onto the table. He helped himself to three pieces and said, "I understand that several of you knew Savannah when she lived in Paradise before?"

It's hard to resist a man who so thoroughly appreciates what you do for a living. I tried anyway. "A lot of people knew her."

"And I understand that some people were upset with her for coming back to Paradise?"

"They might have been. But that still doesn't—"

"Including Karen."

A stupid statement like that made it easier to resist him. "You think *Karen* had something to do with Savannah's accident?"

"Do you?"

"Don't play cop with me, Jawarski. It's not going to work."

"I'm not playing, Abby. Mrs. Horne didn't just fall over in the snow. Someone knocked her down and made damn sure she wasn't going to get up again."

"Well, it wasn't Karen," I assured him, and for good measure added, "I can't imagine Evie doing something like that, either."

"What about Savannah's husband?"

I have to admit that Miles made more sense as a suspect than Karen did, but I had a hard time picturing the distraught man who'd been at Divinity all day as a cold-hearted killer. "I don't think he could have done it," I said. "He's been here for the past two days."

Jawarski licked candy from his fingers. "*All* day?"

"Most of them."

"You want to run through the timetable for me?"

The past forty-eight hours felt like a week. I had to think for a minute to remember everything. "Miles Horne called me early yesterday morning," I said. "I think it was around six thirty."

Jawarski pulled the notepad from his pocket and scribbled something. "You were already at work?"

"No. In fact, he woke me up."

Jawarski lanced me with one blue eye. "He had your home phone number?"

"I didn't give it to him, if that's what you're asking. But this is Paradise. I'm in the book."

He made another note and nodded for me to go on.

"When he called, Miles said he wanted to talk about the disagreement over the contest. He thought that Evie owed Savannah a public apology, and he wanted me to arrange it."

"And you agreed?"

"Not exactly. I was almost certain Evie would refuse to make any kind of apology. I agreed to meet with the Hornes because I was hoping I could get them to compromise."

Jawarski's head snapped up. "So you met with both of them?"

"No, Miles came alone. Savannah was out jogging, and he wanted to talk to me before she got there.

"Did he say why?"

"He was worried because Savannah and her sister don't get along. Savannah wouldn't tell him why, and he was hoping I would."

That earned me another sharp look. "Why you?"

"Because I'm in the same boat Savannah was—at least that's what Miles told me. I moved away, and I came back. He said I knew how hard it can be to insinuate yourself back into the community, and he thought I'd be sympathetic toward Savannah."

"And were you?"

I shrugged again. "Not really. Or maybe I was a little. I didn't exactly like her back in high school, but she seemed different when I talked with her that night."

"You talked with her? Was that before or after the argument with Evie Rice?"

"After. I ran into her while I was walking Max."

Jawarski stopped writing. "So you saw her alone? What time was that?"

"Ten thirty, maybe eleven. I didn't really notice the time, but all the excitement had died down and, like I said, I was taking Max for a walk, so it couldn't have been much earlier than that."

Jawarski bent and scratched Max's knobby head. "You get around, don't you boy?" Max responded with a noisy lick of the fingers, and Jawarski lifted his gaze to mine again. "So you spoke with her?"

"For a few minutes. Not long."

"How did she seem?"

"Fine. Maybe a little more quiet than usual." I worked up a sheepish smile and added, "More human, I guess. That's why I agreed to meet with her and Miles the next morning. I thought the Savannah I spoke with Friday night might have been open to a compromise with Evie."

"The old Savannah wouldn't have been?"

I shook my head. "I'll never be sure, but I doubt it. Savannah could be . . . unpleasant."

"In what way?"

I could have given him a nice long list, but what purpose would it serve? For all we knew, her death was an accident, so why stir up mud unnecessarily? "There's nothing specific," I said, trying to look honest and forthcoming. "She just had an abrasive personality. You know the type."

Jawarski nodded slowly. "I do. But her husband seems to think that a number of women here in Paradise hated her."

"She wasn't the most popular girl in our class at school," I admitted, "but *hate*?" I shook my head. "I think that's too strong to describe how people felt about her." Unless, of course, they came in second place in a contest or had too much to drink. I resisted the urge to glance at the mess Karen had left in my living room and kept my eyes locked on Jawarski's instead. "Why are you asking about that, anyway? You don't even know how Savannah died. All of this is pure speculation."

He stared at me for a long, uncomfortable moment. "Call it gut instinct. And you're right. I don't know how she died, but I will."

There was a faint warning in his words, but I ignored it. After all, *I* had nothing to worry about. "Are you through grilling me? Because it's been a long day, and I'm exhausted."

Jawarski's personality changed again right in front of my eyes. "Do you want me to stay here with you?"

It was a tempting offer, but I made myself shake my head. I've never been one of those women who gets nervous when she's alone, and I wasn't going to let myself start now. Besides, Karen would come back eventually, and I didn't want Jawarski around when she did. "I'll be fine, thanks."

"You're sure?"

"Absolutely. I have Max, don't I?"

Jawarski ran a skeptical glance across my face, but he didn't argue. I stood to face him, and for one brief moment, I thought he was going to put his arms around me. A tiny flutter of anticipation danced around low in my belly. After a long moment, Jawarski turned toward the door to the living room. I couldn't decide whether I felt relieved or disappointed.

He stepped across a mound of Karen's things and opened the front door. "You'll call if you need anything?"

"Sure," I agreed. And maybe this time, I actually would.

Exhausted, emotionally spent, and aching for a hot bath, I slumped down the hall to my bedroom. I wondered where Karen was but I told myself not to worry. She could be back with Sergio for all I knew, and when she got around to wanting her stuff back, she knew where to find me.

No sooner had I started picking up pieces of the paper towel roll Max had shredded sometime that morning, than someone knocked on my front door. With his stump of a tail wagging at the prospect of a visit, Max trotted toward the sound. I followed a little more slowly.

Maybe Jawarski had come back, but if all he wanted was the answers to more questions, I wasn't interested. Maybe it was Dooley checking up on me, but I wasn't in the mood for company. Finding Savannah had left me shaky and uncertain, and I needed time and space to figure out how I felt.

I yanked open the door, fully prepared to send whoever it was on their way, but it wasn't Jawarski or Dooley. My niece stood in the dim spill of light, her thin arms wrapped around herself, her small face clouded with misery.

"Dana?" I asked tentatively. I'm embarrassed to admit that I still have trouble telling sixteen-year-old Dana and her twin sister apart. Both have chin-length blonde hair, both have wide, expressive brown eyes. Their noses, chins, and mouths are virtually identical, and now that changing diapers isn't an option, I'm not likely to see which one has the small jelly bean–shaped birthmark on her hip.

Usually, I have to take my cues from Wyatt and Elizabeth or from the girls' brothers to identify the twins, but I didn't have that luxury tonight. This was the first time either of the girls had come to me on her own, and I wanted desperately to do and say all the right things.

My niece nodded. "Can I come in?"

Giving myself a mental pat on the back, I shoved the door open the rest of the way. "Of course. Is something wrong?"

"Kind of." She came inside, shivered elaborately, stared at Karen's mess, and dropped like a stone onto the floor in front of the ugly plaid couch.

More than anything, I want to be for Wyatt's kids what Aunt Grace always was for me: a soft place to fall, a shoulder to cry on, someone to talk to when I couldn't talk to Mom and Dad. I have a lot of time to make up for. Even knowing all of that, the nervousness that gripped me caught me by surprise.

"Let me take your coat," I suggested. "Then you can tell me what's wrong."

Dana shrugged out of her parka and pushed it toward me. "I need you to help me with thom-thing," she said without looking at me.

Her voice sounded funny—almost as if she was talking around a mouthful of peanut butter. I draped her coat over a pile of Karen's clothes and sat where I could get a good look at her. "Are you all right?"

Dana nodded and pulled her knees up against her chest. "I'm fine."

"Are you sure? You sound . . . different."

She slid a glance at me. "Do I really? Ith it bad?"

"Not *bad*, exactly. Just different." I leaned forward so I could see into her eyes. Wyatt and Elizabeth had recently separated, and the kids weren't taking it well. They needed more care and understanding than ever, and I wanted to dish up just the right amount of both. "Why don't you tell me what's up?"

Dana dropped her forehead to her knees and sat that

way for a minute or two before she finally lifted her head again and opened her mouth. It took me a second or two to recognize the green ball on her tongue for what it really was. When I did, my heart plummeted to the floor. "You pierced your *tongue*?"

Nodding miserably, Dana shut her mouth again. "Mom's furiouth."

I thought about Elizabeth, keeper of traditional family values and director of the choir for her church, and nodded slowly. For all of that, Elizabeth is the free-thinking one in the family. Compared to my brother, she's practically a raving liberal. "I'll bet she is. What does your dad say?"

Dana scowled up at me. "He doethn't know yet. That'th why I'm here. Mom thays I have to tell him mythelf."

An internal warning bell went off, but I ignored it. "When are you going to do it?"

Dana turned a set of dark brown puppy dog eyes on me full force. It was an unfair advantage, and I'm pretty sure she knew it. "Would you help me, Aunt Abby?"

"Help you?"

"Come with me to tell my dad," she said, her voice still thick and unnatural sounding. "Please? I don't know what to say to him."

And she thought *I* did? Every rational instinct I had screamed at me to stay out of this. But what kind of aunt would I be to say no?

"When are you going to tell him?"

"Mom says I have to tell him tonight."

"Tonight?"

"She says I have to before I come home," Dana mumbled unhappily, "or I can't go to the dance on Friday."

Once she told Wyatt, the dance would be out of the question, but I decided not to say so and dash all hope. "So what do you want me to do?"

Dana scratched Max behind one ear, and he sank onto the floor beside her. "Come with me to see my dad. Help me explain."

Explain? *This?* To my brother? Apparently shoving a metal rod through your tongue also scrambles the brain. Who knew?

No. Not a chance. Never in a million years. Absolutely not. The words were all right there, but I couldn't get a single one of them past my own tongue. Apparently, guilt does a bit of scrambling, too, because I actually felt my head bobbing up and down as if I agreed to help her. Dana launched herself from the floor and threw her arms around my neck, and for a few minutes I actually believed that things were looking up.

Chapter 10

Sid Lancaster has been serving greasy burgers and toxic coffee to the good old boys of Paradise for as long as I can remember. In all that time I don't remember the diner changing—not one little bit. From the chrome-and-Naugahyde stools, to the stained booths, to the curtains at the windows, everything's so old it's almost retro chic.

At any time of the day or night, you can step inside the glass doors at Sid's and be guaranteed to find three things: the scent of coffee left too long on the burner, Sid standing behind the stove wearing a greasy apron and a white paper cap, and at least one pair of Wrangler jeans planted firmly on a stool in front of the counter.

I found a parking spot near the front door and tried to convince Dana to wait while I made sure Wyatt was inside. I had about as much success with that as Elizabeth had trying to convince Wyatt to give up red meat.

Together, Dana and I trudged through the snow through the glass-enclosed foyer and into the overly heated diner. When I saw Wyatt's Wranglers hitched onto a stool next to Toby Yager's, I let out a silent sigh of relief.

I'd heard rumors that he'd been sighted having dinner with a couple of single female coworkers over the past few months. No doubt, Elizabeth had heard the same rumors, which is probably why she was keeping Wyatt at arm's length. I was afraid that she'd end up creating what she feared most if something didn't change soon. The longer Elizabeth kept him cooling his heels about coming home, the more determined he seemed to be to screw up his entire life.

Now that we were inside and surrounded by chipped yellow Formica and peeling red Naugahyde, Dana's bravado faded. She walked two steps behind me all the way to the far end of the counter where Wyatt sat with his back to us. We were almost upon them before Toby recognized me, and Wyatt spun around on his stool to see who Toby was looking at.

My brother is five years older than I am, and half the time he looks like someone who just stepped off the cover of a *Tombstone* video. Since leaving home, his dark hair has grown shaggy, and the mustache he's been cultivating since the summer he turned eighteen droops well past his chin.

He gave me a once-over that lacked warmth, but when he noticed Dana cowering behind me, his entire demeanor changed. "Hey, kiddo," he said, holding his arms wide and inviting his daughter close for a hug. "What are you doing here?"

I willed Dana not to speak, and for once someone listened to me. She turned those helpless eyes in my direction. I smiled encouragement, then took a deep breath and nodded toward an empty booth. "Mind if we talk to you for a minute?"

Wyatt grew immediately suspicious. "Why? What's up?"

"We just need to talk to you," I said, and to Toby, "this shouldn't take long."

Toby's probably in his mid-thirties, heavyset with a solid layer of muscle under the flab. He keeps his head shaved, but a fine layer of whiskers covers his cheeks and chin at all times. Guess you never know when you may have a facial hair shortage. "Take your time," he said, waving us away. "Me and Wyatt was just chewing the fat anyhow."

Dana flashed me a look filled with gratitude and, feeling auntlike and protective, I slid into the booth beside her before Wyatt could.

"So what's all this?" he asked as he sat across from us.

I gave him a don't-worry smile. "Dana just needs to talk to you for a minute."

In retrospect, maybe the don't-worry was a mistake. Wyatt's thick black brows knit together, and his mustache drooped a little lower. "And she needs help to do it?" He speared his poor daughter with a stare that made him look like Grandpa Hanks. "What's going on, Dana? What's this all about?"

Dana clamped her lips together and looked at me as if she expected me to make everything all right. Sucker that I am, I actually tried. I smiled at my brother and hoped I didn't look as nervous as I felt. "The thing is, Wyatt—"

He sent me another Grandpa Hanks glare. Don't get me wrong. Grandpa was just about the nicest guy who ever lived . . . until somebody crossed him. Then he was a force to be reckoned with. I'm not a chicken. I just didn't want to reckon with Wyatt tonight.

"Do you mind, Abby? I'd like Dana to tell me whatever it is that's bothering her."

Color flooded Dana's cheeks, but the girl ignored the question and embarked on an extensive study of her fingertips.

"I'm sure you'd like Dana to tell you," I said, trying

my best to sound empathetic, "but Dana asked me to come with her, and she's obviously uncomfortable."

"Uncomfortable? With *me*?"

Yeah. Go figure. "Maybe uncomfortable is the wrong word," I said quickly. "But she is a little worried that you'll be upset with her."

Grandpa Hanks disappeared. The ogre glaring at me now was pure Wyatt Shaw. "What for?"

I waved away the question and tried to keep my tone light.

"Promise you won't fly off the handle?"

"I'm not promising a damned thing. I don't care which one of you does it, but one of you had better start talking. *Now!*"

There didn't seem to be much point in avoiding the issue, so I nudged Dana gently with my elbow. "Show him."

Her surprised gaze shot away from her fingertips and up to my face.

"Show him," I said again. "He's going to find out sooner or later, and the longer you wait, the worse it's going to be."

Defiance followed quickly by resignation flashed through Dana's big brown eyes. I suppose she wanted to refuse, but even if she pulled that post out of her tongue, her dad would still find out what she'd done. Her mother and at least one or two friends knew, and secrets just don't last long in Paradise.

With a grudging scowl that made her look way too much like her father, she opened her mouth and stuck her tongue partway out. Wyatt's expression changed slowly as he realized what he was looking at; then he shot to his feet—or at least he tried.

The booth caught him in the midsection, and he fell back onto the bench bellowing like a bull elk. "What the hell is that?"

A dozen heads shot up, and I could feel every eye in the place turning to watch us. I kept my voice calm and hoped Wyatt would follow my lead. "That," I said, "is your daughter's new tongue . . . ring."

Looking all of about five years old, Dana finally made eye contact with her father. "It-th a barbell."

Blood rushed into Wyatt's face. "What in the hell is it doing in your mouth?"

"I put it there."

"I can see that," he shouted. "I'm not blind. What I want to know is why?"

"Becauth it-th cool, and becauth I like it."

I half expected steam to erupt from my brother's nose and ears. "Who did this to you?" he demanded. "Tell me right now so I can kill him."

Now, there was a strong incentive to rat out your friend. Dana scowled up at her father. "It was a friend, and I'm not telling you his name."

"Oh no? You think I can't find out on my own?"

The color in Dana's cheeks drained away. "Please, Daddy . . ."

"Does your mother know about this? Did she tell you it was all right? Because if she did—"

Dana shook her head miserably. "No. She's mad at me, too. She said I had to tell you before I could come home."

Wyatt slid to the edge of the booth and stood glowering down at his daughter. "Go into the bathroom and take it out."

As if she'd suddenly grown a backbone, Dana set her jaw and stared back up at him. "No."

"Do it, Dana. Now."

"I don't want to."

"I don't care what you want," Wyatt growled. "You're not old enough to make that decision."

"It's *my* tongue."

"Not until you're eighteen." Wyatt reached for her arm,

but she jerked away. Frustration darkened his eyes and formed deep lines around his mouth. "Dana Marie Shaw, take that damn thing out of your mouth this instant."

"No."

I might not agree with Wyatt's method of dealing with this, but Dana wasn't exactly winning medals for her brilliance either. I hesitated to get between them, but one of these days they'd both regret arguing in public, so I quietly offered a suggestion to my grim-faced brother. "Why don't you sit back down and talk this over with her?"

I should have known better.

"This has nothing to do with you," Wyatt snarled at me.

"Well, maybe not technically—"

Eyes glazed over with fury, Wyatt tossed a handful of change onto the table. "You can't just come back to town and start sticking your nose into everything, Abby. It doesn't work that way." He pulled Dana to her feet and clapped one hand to her shoulder to keep her there. "This is between me and my kid, so just stay out of it."

His words stung, but I was more angry than hurt. I shot to my feet and jabbed him in the chest with my finger as I talked. "Dana asked me to come with her." *Jab, jab, jab.* "That makes this my business whether you," *jab,* "like it or not. And if you," *jab, jab,* "were home with your family where you belong, she wouldn't have to ask me to get involved." I was living dangerously, but I didn't care. I'd had a rough day, and he wasn't helping.

Wyatt stiff-armed past me. "My family is fine. You don't know what you're talking about."

"Your own daughter's afraid to talk to you," I shouted after him. "That doesn't sound fine to me."

Wyatt whipped around again, his face terrible in his anger. For an old fart, he moved pretty fast. "What would *you* know about it, Abby? You're not a parent. Don't use my kids to give yourself some kind of maternal rush."

I felt myself recoil, and I could swear the blood drained from my face. I don't think Wyatt had any idea that he'd scored a direct hit with that one. After all, I'd never really talked to him about how much I'd wanted children during my marriage, how much Roger's lack of interest in a family had hurt, or how devastated I'd been to learn that my husband was having a child with another woman. If Wyatt had tried for a year, he couldn't have found a more hurtful thing to say, and I hated him fiercely in that moment.

"You're a bastard," I said through my teeth. I was dimly aware of Dana hovering behind a nearby table, of her frightened gaze darting back and forth between the two of us.

Tears burned the backs of my eyes, and the impulse to cry was almost as strong as the urge to shove my brother in front of a moving train. But Wyatt's so thick-headed, I'd probably get sued for damaging the train.

Steaming, I snatched my keys from the table where I'd left them and turned toward the door. "Come on, Dana. Let's get out of here."

My little niece hesitated for only a heartbeat before she fell into step behind me, but Wyatt caught her arm and stopped her. "Oh no you don't. The only place you're going is home with me. I want to see what your mother has to say about this."

"Leave her alone, Wyatt. I'll take her home."

"No thanks, Abby. You've already done enough damage."

A whole truckload of arguments rose to my lips, but what could I do? She *was* his daughter, poor thing. Besides, he might be angry, but I knew he wouldn't hurt her, and I was still reeling from the last blow he'd delivered. Wyatt didn't look anywhere close to backing down, and I wasn't sure I could survive another round.

"Your dad wants to take you home," I said to Dana. "Are you okay with that?"

She nodded uncertainly. I guess she knew as well as I did that we were beaten.

"Okay," I conceded, "but you know where to find me if you need me."

She nodded again, and her gaze dropped, but not before I registered the disappointment I saw there. Maybe it was a good thing I'd never had kids. I wasn't even a good aunt.

Chapter 11

Desperate to get away from Sid's before Wyatt and Dana could come outside, I shoved out into the cold night air and jammed the key into the Jetta's ignition. Instead of turning over the way it should have, the Jetta gave a couple of uninspired and useless clicks, then groaned and died.

Unbelievable. What now?

Wyatt and Dana burst out of the diner, but there was no way I was going to ask *him* for help, so I slid down in my seat and hid there until I was sure they were gone. Wanting to keep Max from lunging up at the wrong moment and giving me away, I clutched his collar until the roar of Wyatt's engine finally died away; then I tried the ignition again. No luck. I stared at the pointy snout and big brown eyes of my best friend and felt tears of frustration brimming.

I hate crying. It's messy and weak and embarrassing. I try not to do it more than absolutely necessary. It wasn't necessary now.

Swiping at my eyes with my sleeve, I tried to conjure

up a few bars of service on my cell phone. No luck. Surprise, surprise.

"Don't worry," I said to Max. "There's a solution. I know there is. It just might take a few minutes to find it." But I didn't want to bother Jawarski, and I couldn't call Karen. I didn't want to walk back into Sid's and face the crowd inside, but I couldn't sit in my car all night.

I don't know how long I sat there contemplating my fate before I noticed headlights shining on the snow that lined the highway. Hoping it would be someone I knew, I lunged out of the Jetta and raced across the parking lot, waving my arms frantically over my head. An Explorer rounded a curve in the road, and the headlights caught me, blinding me momentarily. The driver veered off into the parking lot, fishtailing to a stop on the ice only a few feet from where I stood.

I heard the whine of a motorized window followed by a woman's voice. "Abby? What on earth are you doing?"

I squinted into the headlights and made out a familiar silhouette framed by mousy brown hair freshly shaped and blown dry by the ladies at the Curl Up and Dye. "Faith! Am I glad to see you. My car is broken down. Can I catch a ride back into town with you?"

"Of course." She leaned across the car and opened the door for me. "What are you doing at Sid's?"

"Long story. Do you mind if I bring Max along?"

"You certainly can't leave him here. It's far too cold. Praise God, I came along when I did."

I gathered keys, purse, and dog from the Jetta, made sure it was locked, and scurried back to Faith's Explorer. When I had Max settled in the backseat and myself securely strapped in the front, Faith pulled back onto the highway. "I just heard the news about Savannah. Is it really true?"

I was too tired to think about Savannah's death, but I forced a nod. "I'm afraid so."

She mumbled something under her breath—another prayer, no doubt. "How did it happen?"

"The police don't know yet, but they're thinking it might have been a hit-and-run."

"A hit-and—" Faith broke off with an exaggerated shudder and shot a glance across the seat at me. "But that's horrible! Who would do something like that?"

"That's the million dollar question. I have no idea, but the police will find out."

In the dim reflection of moon, stars, and dashboard lights, I could see Faith's complexion grow pale. She chewed the side of her thumbnail and steered around a sharp curve in the road. "Do you think Delta did it?"

I stifled a yawn and tried to ignore the ache of exhaustion in my limbs. "I have no idea," I said again, "but I wouldn't rule out any possibilities." I studied her profile for a moment, and it occurred to me that she might know something I didn't. "Why do you ask about Delta? Do *you* think she did it?"

Faith shook her head uncertainly. "I don't know. It's just that—well, everybody's talking about how upset Delta has been since Savannah came back to Paradise. And everybody knows she didn't want to give Savannah any part of their mother's estate. It would have been the right thing to do—the Christian thing to do—but Delta won't hear of it."

"And you think Delta killed her so she wouldn't have to?"

Faith's eyes left the road for a split second. "I'm not accusing her of murder. I'm just trying to figure out what happened. Murder's a little disconcerting, don't you think?"

Well, yeah. To put it mildly.

"I suppose it's worse for us because we all knew Savannah," Faith went on.

"We knew her," I agreed, "but it's not as if any of us were all that friendly with her."

"Not lately." Faith's lips curved slightly. "Oh, maybe you're right. Nobody really liked her, did they?"

I sank down on my tailbone and tried to get comfortable. "Not much."

"I think it's so sad that she and Delta couldn't even get along. Just between you and me, Noah says Delta's been down at the church several nights this week talking to Pastor Ramsey."

That got me sitting up a little straighter. "About Savannah?"

"He didn't say. I'm not sure he knows. But what else could it be? I mean, here comes Savannah demanding half of their mother's estate—and after she did absolutely nothing to help when Victoria was so sick. On the other hand, Delta stayed here and nursed that poor old woman right to the end. If anybody deserves that house and what little money Victoria had, Delta does."

"Family is family," I said, as if that actually meant something.

Faith quirked a little smile at me. "That's kind of a naïve statement, isn't it? People in families hurt one another all the time. And I'm not accusing Delta of murder, anyway. It's just that Noah said she was awfully upset when he saw her, and now this. It's kind of an odd coincidence, don't you think?"

"I'm too tired to think," I said honestly. "It's been a long day. Like I said, I'm sure the police will figure it all out."

Faith fell blessedly silent for a few minutes, but it didn't last long. She'd seemed so quiet and reserved at the Curl, but this Chatty Cathy doll was more like the Faith I'd grown up with. "I heard that you're the one who found her," she said as we skimmed past the Pit Stop. "Is that true?"

I gave my head a weary nod. "Yes, it's true."

"And she was already dead?"

I nodded again. "Yes, she was."

"So she didn't say anything to you?"

What a strange question. "No, she didn't."

Did I just imagine the flicker of relief that darted through Faith's eyes? It was gone before I could be sure. "It must have been just awful for you. I don't even like to think about it. And her poor husband! He must be beside himself."

"I'm sure he's devastated."

"Especially being here in a strange city," Faith said, "without his usual support system. Someone really should see if there's anything he needs."

"Someone should," I agreed. Emphasis on someone *else*.

I didn't need to worry. Faith slowed as we hit the downtown traffic and waited at an intersection while crowds on either side of the street changed places. "Maybe I'll stop by the hotel on my way home and see how he's doing. You don't think that would be too presumptuous, do you? I mean, I haven't even *seen* Savannah since high school, so maybe I'm not the best person to do this."

Who better? "I'm sure he'll appreciate the concern," I assured her. The man's wife was dead, and if the good people of Paradise were suddenly going to show how compassionate and concerned they were, I wasn't going to argue. Still, it might have been nice if they'd been a little more friendly when it could have done Savannah some good.

I leaned my head against the seat and asked, "Is there *anybody* in town who stayed in contact with Savannah after she left here?"

Faith thought for a moment. "Have you talked to Marshall Ames?"

"I didn't realize he and Savannah were friends."

"Oh, sure." She flicked a glance across the seat. "Maybe not friends, exactly, but Marshall had quite a thing for Savannah back in school. I thought everybody knew that."

Not everybody. Maybe that explained why he'd jumped to her defense the night of the contest. "Did they date?"

Faith laughed and shook her head. "Are you kidding? Savannah wouldn't even give Marshall the time of day. He wasn't her type."

"Then why would you think they'd stayed in contact after she left Paradise?"

"Because I heard Marshall asking her about some letter he sent her."

"You did? When?"

"Friday afternoon."

Considering everything that had happened, it took me a few seconds to cycle back in time that far. "You mean before the contest started?"

Nodding, Faith cranked the wheel and turned onto Prospector Street. "A couple of hours before. They were just down the street from the post office, and I'd just come from mailing a few things. I overheard them talking." She stopped in front of Divinity and waited for me to get out. I had the feeling I should be asking her something, but I was too tired to wrap my head around the conversation we'd just had. I gathered my things and stood on the curb hanging on to Max's leash while she drove away. But one question ran relentlessly through my head as I stood there. What had Marshall told me about Savannah that night?

Hadn't he said that he hardly knew her? Yes, I was sure of it. But if Faith was telling me the truth, then Marshall had lied to me. And I wanted to know why.

* * *

Karen was asleep on my sofa bed when I climbed the steps and let myself inside, so I decided not to wake her. Maybe she wasn't willing to talk to me yet, but she was still willing to sleep on my couch, and that meant she didn't hate me.

I'd have to take what I could get.

Unfortunately, she was gone by the time I woke up the next morning. This time the sofa bed was neatly made and her suitcase was gone. I hoped that meant that she'd worked things out with Sergio. I wanted to believe that she and I would work through our differences, too, but I decided to give her a little more time to cool off first. Her marriage had to be first priority.

I dressed quickly and led Max outside into one of those ultracold days we sometimes get in January in the Rockies. The air was crisp and clear, but so dry and cold it almost sucked my breath away. It was too cold for the snow to melt, and the ice squeaked underfoot when I walked. Even bundled into my warmest coat, hat, gloves, and boots, the cold permeated everything, and the weather forecast called for temperatures to remain well below freezing all day.

I thought about Savannah, running along that service road by herself, and wondered if she'd seen the car coming before it hit her. Had she recognized her assailant? Had she known what was happening? Had she died immediately, or had she suffered? I hated the thought of her lying in the snow, thinking about the person who'd hit her and unable to let anyone know she was hurt. Nobody deserves to die that way.

I thought about Dana and wondered how the conversation with her parents had gone last night. I just hoped I hadn't let her down too far. I was disappointed enough for both of us.

For once, even Max seemed aware of the cold and took care of business in record time. On my way back to Divinity, I spotted Dooley Jorgensen through the window at Picture Perfect. He hadn't been over to see me for a few days, so I detoured and knocked on the door.

Dooley's a large man in his early sixties, round-faced and barrel-chested, with a shock of hair that used to be blond. He moved to Paradise a few years ago and immediately took Aunt Grace under his wing. After her death, he transferred his attention to me, and he was quickly becoming a trusted friend.

He hurried to let me inside, roughed Max up a bit, and gave me a quick once-over. "I've been wondering how you're doing with all the excitement that's been going on. I was going to stop over and see you this morning, but I didn't think you were there. Where's your car?"

"Out at Sid's. Dead battery." I made a face and stuffed my hat and gloves into my coat pockets. "I don't think I'd call what's happening around here 'excitement.' Whatever it is, I could do without it."

"Need help towing your car to the garage?"

I shook my head. "I'll call Orly at Paradise Auto Body later. He did a good job with it after my accident. I'll just have him fix it again."

Dooley put one beefy hand on my shoulder. "You doin' okay, sweet pea?"

I nodded without conviction. "More confused than anything else. I wanted so badly to make this year's contest as wonderful as it was when Aunt Grace was alive. Now I'll be lucky if I can even save it."

"It's not that bad, is it?"

"Just about." I trailed him through aisles filled with cameras, camera equipment, frames, and photographs of smiling people, to the long workbench at the back of the store. Even this early in the morning, the chemical scent of developer made me want to sneeze. "I've let Aunt Grace down, one of our contestants has been killed, I've upset Karen so she's not speaking to me, and Bea's not far behind her. Wyatt's mad at me, too, and I've discovered that I'm a lousy aunt." I grinned ruefully and leaned against the counter. "I'm doing just fine, Dooley. Thanks for asking."

He laughed softly and dragged a chair close so I could sit. "I doubt things are as bad as all that. "Do the police have any idea who ran that lady down?"

"Not that I'm aware of. Last I heard, they didn't have any leads."

"Well, they'll find 'em." Dooley slipped a stack of photographs into a protective sleeve and tucked it under the counter. "That friend of yours seems sharp enough to get the job done."

A silly grin tugged at my lips, but I fought it. My friendship with Jawarski was the one thing going right in my life. Getting all syrupy over him wouldn't help. "He does all right," I said. "I just hope they hurry and figure out what happened to her. I hate thinking that there's a murderer on the loose."

Dooley glanced at me over the rims of his reading glasses. "Could have been an accident. Woman jogging along in the dark on that road . . . would have been hard to see her."

I slipped Max a lemon drop from my pocket, and he settled at my feet to work on it. "That's true," I said, "but then why didn't the driver report it?"

"Probably doesn't want to get in trouble."

"Yeah, but—" I cut myself off with a shake of my head. "I don't know, Dooley. Something just feels wrong. I don't think it was an accident. I think somebody ran her down deliberately."

Dooley eyed me cautiously. "You got any reason for thinking that?"

"Besides the fact that half the people in town hated her? Not really."

"You know anybody with a real motive?"

I started to shake my head, then stopped myself. I didn't want to admit it, but Karen had a motive—or at least thought she did. And what about Evie? Was winning Divinity's contest enough to drive her to murder? Or what about Delta?

"It's not my problem," I said firmly. "The police will figure it out."

"Sure they will." Dooley glanced out the window toward Divinity. From this vantage point, he could see the kitchen window, the back door, and the park bench where Aunt Grace used to sit to work through her problems. "I don't suppose you know why they're so interested in Karen?"

A hollow pit opened in my stomach. "Who's interested in Karen?"

"The police."

"The police have been asking about Karen? When?"

"Couple of officers stopped by yesterday. Started off asking if I'd seen or heard anything the night of the contest, but they got around to asking about Karen pretty quickly. Seems she made quite a fuss down at O'Schuck's that night."

The hole in my abdomen widened. "What else did they want to know?"

"They asked about Karen's relationship with Sergio. Did they get along? Have I ever heard them argue? That kind of thing."

I couldn't sit still any longer, so I started to pace. "Well, of course they argue. Every couple argues."

"That's just what I told 'em."

"And?"

"They wanted to know if I'd ever seen Karen arguing with the dead woman."

"You said no." It wasn't a question.

I guess it should have been. Dooley's eyes filled with

misery, and he had trouble meeting my gaze. "I couldn't do that, pumpkin. I wanted to, believe me. I just couldn't."

"Does that mean you *did* hear an argument between them?"

"Didn't hear it so much as saw it," Dooley said, frowning. "I was working right here. Looked up and saw that lady—the one who died—standing outside your back door."

"What time was this?"

"I didn't notice, but it wasn't very late. Seven thirty, maybe eight."

"Was she alone?"

"At first—at least until some guy showed up."

"Do you know who it was?"

Dooley shook his head. "It was too dark, and they moved off into the shadows."

"Was he tall? Short? Fat or thin?"

"I didn't pay much attention," Dooley admitted. "The only thing I can tell you is that they had an argument of some kind."

"You didn't hear it?"

Dooley gave his head another shake. "I was working. I didn't think that much about it until Karen showed up. Even from here I could tell that she was upset, and by that time I was gettin' a little curious, so I decided to get a little fresh air."

The hole in my stomach turned into a yawning chasm. "What did you hear, Dooley?"

His gaze flickered away, as if he couldn't bear to look at me when he answered. "Well, now, I only heard a word or two. Keep that in mind."

I stared him right in the eye. "What words?"

"And I don't think you can put much stock in 'em, considering that I heard it all out of context."

"What did you hear, Dooley?"

He sighed and tugged the reading glasses from his

face. Regret filled his eyes, and I think I knew what he was going to say almost before he said it. "I hate to tell you this, sweet pea, but I heard Karen threaten to kill her."

My fingers grew cold, and my arms felt numb. That ever-present knot in my stomach grew cold and hard. "Are you sure that's what she said?"

"I'm sure. You don't know how bad I wish I wasn't."

That made two of us. "What happened then?"

"The lady laughed. Guess she thought it was joke."

"Maybe it was." I knew better, but we were talking about my cousin—a girl I'd grown up with, gone to the swimming hole with, partnered with in countless of Aunt Grace's taffy pulls, and taught to roller-skate.

"Yeah," Dooley agreed halfheartedly. "Maybe."

It looked bad. Even I had to admit that. But for the past year, I'd worked side by side with Karen at Divinity almost every day. She wasn't a killer—no matter *what* she said.

Chapter 12

"Where is it?" Evie Rice demanded a couple of hours later. She reached the bottom step, tossed her purse onto one of the wrought-iron tables, and came close to the glass display case separating us. "What have you done with it?"

I pulled a basket from the supply cupboard, lined it with metallic shred, and began filling it with a dozen varieties of licorice. Thanks to ski season, we had a healthy walk-in business, and more than a dozen customers were milling around among the various displays.

"Done with what?"

"My prize. The box of chocolates. It's crap, but I figured I might as well come and get it. Megan might want it."

I ignored the insult since she wasn't thinking clearly. "It's upstairs right where you left it."

Evie pulled her red ribbon from a pocket and waved it in front of me. "No it's not. This was all there was."

"But that's impossible. It was there Friday night when

I came downstairs, and I was the last person here. Nobody's been up there since."

"Well somebody must have been, because the candy's gone." Evie perched on the edge of a chair and crossed her legs. "I'll bet it was Savannah."

"I don't think that's likely."

"No, really. I'll bet she snuck up there and took it, and I'll bet she planned to bring at least some of it back as her entry the second night of the contest."

I might have laughed if Evie hadn't looked so serious. "Even Savannah wouldn't have dared to try that," I said. "She'd have been crazy to try."

Evie arched an eyebrow as if I'd just made her point for her.

I slid a package of licorice ropes into the basket, jammed my finger on a piece of wire, and swore softly. Turning away in exasperation, I ran cold water over my hand to wash away the blood. "First you were convinced that Savannah had downloaded her recipe from a website. Then you're convinced she was passing off candy made by someone else as her own. Why would she have done that?"

Evie rolled her eyes as if she was the one who should be exasperated. "I don't have all the answers, but I'm *convinced* that she was doing something wrong. It's a good thing she's not here anymore. The contest could have lost all credibility."

Yeah, but I happened to think a human life was worth slightly more than the reputation of a contest—even this one. "You don't have any proof," I told her, and added what I seemed to be saying to everyone these days. "You can't accuse her of doing something wrong just because you didn't like her."

Evie's gaze grew hard as peanut brittle. "No, I didn't have proof, but it probably wouldn't have been hard to get. That's why I wanted you to find out what kitchen she was using. She wouldn't have been able to tell you, you know. And that would have been your proof, right there."

I turned off the water and toweled my hand dry. "That wouldn't have proved anything. None of the contestants have ever had to reveal the location of their kitchen. I couldn't have singled Savannah out without a very good reason."

"You had a good reason," Evie insisted stubbornly. "She was accused of cheating—"

"By someone who has hated her for years. And this is a moot point anyway. She's dead. It's not an issue."

"She should never have been given first place that first night."

"And you want me to strip the blue ribbon from her posthumously?" Was she insane? Luckily, a couple of women in ski gear came toward the counter, and I had to pause to ring up their sales. "Look, Evie," I said when the door shut behind them, "I'm sorry, but the truth is that when it comes to Savannah, you're not the most reliable source of information, and I have no intention of taking away her blue ribbon."

Her eyes turned almost the same purple as a grape Fun Dip wrapper. "So you're not even going to listen to me?"

"Not if you want me to take a silly first place ribbon away from a dead woman."

"Well, you have to do *something*," Evie insisted. "She practically ruined the contest, and now, with that blue ribbon tied up this way, the rest of the contest can't possibly be decided correctly."

For the past two days I'd been struggling to hang on to my patience. For the past nine months, I'd been trying to keep a smile on my face and show everyone that I was as pleasant as Aunt Grace had ever been. But at that moment I didn't *feel* pleasant. In fact, my frustration level was off the charts.

"If the contest is ruined," I snapped, "Savannah won't be the only one to blame."

Evie pulled back sharply, and her cool violet eyes narrowed into angry slits. "Ex*cuse* me?"

A little voice in the back of my head told me to be careful, but I was too angry to care. "I know you're used to winning this contest, Evie. I know you expect to win again this year. But the fact is, you didn't take first place the first night. Not because Savannah cheated, but because the judges felt her entry was superior to yours. If you want different results when the contest gets under way again, I suggest you stop complaining and spend some time in the kitchen."

She drew herself up to her full five four and glared at me. "*What* did you just say?"

Again, that voice whispered caution. Again, I ignored it. Evie *was* one of Divinity's best customers, and she had a lot of friends. If I made her angry, she could do some serious damage to my business. But I was too angry to act logically. "The judges aren't going to change their decision," I snarled. "I'm not going to take Savannah's blue ribbon away. So get a grip. Move on. Let it go."

Evie drew herself up sharply, and for one terrible moment, she looked angry enough to kill somebody. She snatched her purse from the table and strode toward the door. "I can see I'm wasting my breath here. I should have known you wouldn't take care of this. I can't rely on anyone, can I?"

The look on her face made my stomach knot. She slammed out of the shop so hard, she knocked over two pint jars filled with jelly beans. And as I watched the colorful candies spill onto the black-and-white-checked floor, I wondered what it would take to make the world feel normal again.

* * *

The store stayed busy until I flipped off the lights and locked up again. Karen never bothered to put in an appearance, and since the search for Savannah was over, Bea had stayed away, too. That meant I'd had to do everything myself.

I hadn't even had time for lunch, so by seven o'clock I was hungry enough to eat my way across three states. Unfortunately, dinner would have to wait. I'd called an ad for a part-time salesclerk in to the *Paradise Post* earlier that afternoon, so I hoped the staffing crisis at Divinity would be short-lived. But even hiring someone new to help out wouldn't completely solve the problem. Karen had the past twenty years of Divinity's history in her head, while mine was blank on the subject. Like it or not, I needed her.

Carrying a healthy deposit to the bank made me feel marginally better. At least Savannah's death, the upset over the contest, and turning Divinity into Search Central hadn't ruined business completely. I'd even managed to pick up a catering job from a woman named Ruth Cohen, the wife of a movie mogul whose original party caterer had backed out on her at the last minute.

Catering isn't something we do often at Divinity, and the short time frame involved had almost convinced me to say no. But the generous paycheck Mrs. Cohen offered was hard to resist. When she also mentioned that she was staying at the Summit Lodge, my resistance had disappeared.

Listen, I know I'm not a private investigator, and solving Savannah's murder isn't my responsibility. I understand that completely. But *someone* out there had hit Savannah and killed her, either by accident or by design. After talking with Dooley, I figured it was only a matter of time until Jawarski got around to naming Karen as a suspect and maybe even arresting her. Having an excuse for spending time around the Summit Lodge staff seemed like a good idea. If Jawarski tried to cart Karen off to jail, maybe I could stop him.

After I locked the front doors, I brought Max down to my office, brewed a cup of herbal tea, and dug out Aunt Grace's recipe files so I could start making plans. Mrs. Cohen wanted to meet the next afternoon so she could look at the proposed menu and I could talk with the hotel staff about accommodations. Getting ready for that meeting would keep me busy, but there are worse things than having plenty to do.

I'd decided to serve pecan cream candy, Lady Slippers (actually butterscotch patties named after Grace's favorite wildflower), chocolate fondant dipped in white chocolate, toffee-coated popcorn, strawberry bonbons, Rocky Road Drops, and raspberry meringues, when I heard a knock on the kitchen door. I found Jawarski on the other side, but I didn't know whether I should be happy to see him or worried until I caught a whiff of the spicy scent of his aftershave and the faint mint of toothpaste as he squeezed past me into the kitchen. Both things told me he'd spruced up a little, and that convinced me that this was a social call instead of a professional one.

"You're working late," he said.

I nodded and led him into the office. "Trying to stay busy so I don't have to think too much. What's up?"

"I was just heading out to dinner. I know it's presumptuous, but I thought I'd see if you want to grab a bite."

I frowned with genuine regret. "I'd love to, but I really need to work. I've just signed on for a big job this weekend, and I'll never make it if I don't focus now."

"What about pizza? I can order in. Just please tell me you have a beer in your refrigerator."

I grinned. Couldn't help it. "I'll bet I could find a couple if I tried hard enough." I considered inviting him upstairs but decided against it. What if Karen came back? I wanted a chance to talk with her before Jawarski did.

We spent a few minutes arguing amicably over pizza toppings, compromised on the Gut Buster special, and made ourselves comfortable on opposite sides of the desk to wait for the Black Jack Pizza guy to arrive. That's when Jawarski brought up the subject he'd obviously been dying to discuss.

I'd kicked off my shoes and put my stocking feet up on the desk, and I was just dragging the afghan my mother had crocheted for me last Christmas around my shoulders when Jawarski said, "We found the car."

I froze in place. "The car that hit Savannah?"

"Yep."

Even Mom's afghan couldn't keep the chill away. I was almost afraid to ask, "Whose is it?"

Jawarski shrugged. "It's a rental. Picked up in Denver. Registered to a couple of musicians staying at Old Miner's Inn. They reported it stolen."

"And you have no reason to believe they're lying?"

Jawarski shook his head. "As far as we can tell, they have no connection with Mrs. Horne. We found fingerprints belonging to both of them in the car, but no others. Not surprising. Whoever stole it was smart enough to wear gloves."

I offered a halfhearted smile. "Don't be so sure about how smart that makes our guy. In this weather, even an idiot would wear gloves."

Jawarski laughed softly, and something I didn't want to feel curled through me. "Great. And here I thought I had the suspect list narrowed down just a little. Leave it to you to set me straight."

Yeah. Leave it to me. I snuggled a little deeper into the afghan as the seriousness of the conversation wiped the smile from my face. "So I guess that settles it? That's how she was killed?"

"I still don't know," Jawarski admitted. "It seems obvious that she was struck by the car, but whether or not the collision actually killed her is still up in the air. We won't know until the coroner tells us, and it could take a few more days to get the lab results back."

This was only my second experience with an autopsy, and I wondered if professionals ever got used to what seemed like an interminable delay. "So what happens now? Is Miles going to stay in town until you find out what happened?"

Jawarski shrugged again. "I don't know. He hasn't said anything about leaving, but I'd be surprised if he doesn't at least wait for the coroner to release the. . ." He shot a glance at me to gauge my reaction and finished with a quiet, "the body."

I'd seen the body, and though I couldn't get the image out of my mind, I had an equally hard time thinking of that cold, grayish thing as Savannah. I tried to wipe the image from my mind. "So you still don't have any idea who was driving?"

Jawarski propped his feet against my desk. "Not yet. We've been questioning staff and guests at the lodge, but nobody admits to seeing anything that might help us. One of the desk clerks noticed Savannah heading toward the back doors early that morning. A member of the housekeeping crew saw her crossing the parking lot, but that's where the trail ends."

"Nobody saw the car that hit her?"

"Nobody admits to seeing it." Jawarski ran both hands across his face and groaned aloud. He sounded as exhausted as I felt—maybe even more so.

If we'd been dating, I might have suggested skipping the pizza, climbing the stairs, and crawling straight into bed—*to sleep*. But we weren't anywhere near ready for that. I forced my eyes open a little wider. "What about Miles? What did he see?"

"He says he didn't see anything."

"He was awake when she left, wasn't he?"

Jawarski shook his head. "He knew she'd gone jogging because she runs at the same time every morning, and her exercise clothes were gone when he woke up, but he didn't actually get up himself until a few minutes before he called you."

"Six thirty?"

"That's what he says."

Something in Jawarski's tone caught my attention. "You don't believe him?"

His lips curved slightly. "I don't believe him, but I don't disbelieve him. We always look at the spouse when someone dies under suspicious circumstances. You can find some very interesting stuff that way."

Made perfect sense to me. I'm not generally bothered by murderous tendencies, but even I'd had a split-second urge to do away with Roger when I walked in on him rolling around on my bedroom floor with WhatsHer-Name.

Okay . . . and another when he told me about the baby they'd created.

But Jawarski and I hadn't progressed to the point of discussing our past romances, so I nodded, slipped a piece of toffee from the dish at my side, and passed the dish to him. "And have you found anything interesting about Miles and Savannah?"

Jawarski helped himself to two and grinned. "Wouldn't you like to know?"

"As a matter of fact, I would. I was dragged into this mess against my will, and I'll admit that I'm curious."

Jawarski's expression grew serious. "Yeah, you were dragged into it, weren't you?" His voice was soft and gentle. Enough to start that tingling again. "You got a little more than you bargained for out there yesterday, didn't you?"

The past few days had left me tired and overly emotional. A little sympathy was going a long way. "I'm fine,"

I said, but it took effort to keep the pathetic whine tumbling around inside me from coming out in my voice. "I just can't imagine who would want to kill Savannah."

Jawarski tapped his foot against the side of my desk. "Judging from the information I'm getting, I don't think the question is who wanted to kill her, but who didn't?"

So Karen wasn't his only suspect? Good!

"What about Evie Rice?" he asked. "She hated Savannah, didn't she?"

"I guess so, but I can't picture Evie stealing a car and running down another human being with it."

"People do strange things when they're pushed to the limit. Who else?"

I felt a little guilty witholding information from Jawarski about my cousin's own run-in with Savannah. "There's always her sister."

"Mrs. Walters?"

I nodded. "She and Savannah didn't really get along. I talked to Delta the other day, and she didn't have anything good to say about her sister."

Jawarski eyed me cautiously. "Anyone else?"

I wasn't going to mention Karen, and I hadn't had a chance to follow up on Marshall Ames and his mysterious letter, so I shook my head. "Not unless you count everyone Savannah screwed in high school—literally and figuratively. That probably amounts to half our graduating class, and I'm not counting the classes that graduated before and after we did."

"Popular woman, huh?"

Outside, a car door slammed, and heavy footsteps pounded up the stairs to my apartment. I started to slide out from under the afghan, but Jawarski motioned for me to stay put. "I told you I'd order the pizza. That makes it my treat."

"You're a charmer, Jawarski. I feel like a princess."

He grinned over his shoulder. "Good. That was my

plan." He hurried through the kitchen, paid the bill, and carried the pizza back to my office. Leaving the pizza in my care—a risky decision—Jawarski headed into the kitchen for the beer.

It had been a long time since anyone had pampered me—even to the extent of beer and pizza delivered to my office—and I had the uneasy feeling that this kind of treatment could go straight to my head if I let it. He came back carrying two bottles of Coors, paper plates, and napkins, and we spent the next fifteen minutes attacking the pizza like a couple of starving puppies. Finally, only one piece remained in the box, and I was far too ladylike to eat it, so I curled under the afghan again and watched Jawarski polish off the last of his beer.

"So what now?" I asked.

He quirked an eyebrow at me and settled back in his chair again, one foot tapping against the desk. "You asking about the murder investigation or something else?"

There was no clear answer to that, so I took the safe road. "The murder. What will you do now?"

"Keep looking. Keep checking. Talk to everyone who knew Savannah and do what we can to retrace her steps that morning." He sat back in his chair and linked his hands across his stomach. "And I want to talk to Karen. Find out what she knows. When do you expect her back?"

I felt the pleasure rush from my body. "Is that why you came by? So you could interrogate my cousin?"

Jawarski's foot stopped moving. "I'm going to have to talk to her, Abby. We have a witness who heard her threaten Savannah the night before the murder and a handful more who will testify that she went ballistic at O'Schuck's."

"She's a suspect?"

"She's a person of interest. Good thing she has an alibi, huh?"

The pizza and beer started churning like taffy on a puller inside my stomach. "Alibi?"

"She was here, right? She told Svboda that she got here about two thirty that morning."

I nodded quickly. "That's right."

"So she's off the hook."

"Yeah." I forced a smile and hoped Jawarski couldn't see how phony it was. "That's great."

The conversation wandered onto another topic, and I made no effort to drag it back. I tried to follow what Jawarski was saying, but I couldn't stop thinking about the empty sofa bed when I got up the morning Savannah disappeared, and the way Karen looked when she came back. I didn't like knowing that she'd lied to the police about where she was. I liked even less knowing that she'd used me to do it.

Chapter 13

Tired, cranky, and determined to get some answers, I pulled into Karen's driveway a few minutes before seven the next morning. Only a few wispy clouds dotted the horizon, and the sun, a pale lemon yellow, gave off enough heat to thaw some of the frozen landscape. It wouldn't last. By nightfall, all the running water would turn to ice again, but the warmth was a welcome respite.

Karen's split-level house was still dark when I arrived, but I didn't let that discourage me. It was a school day. She couldn't sleep forever.

I parked, blocking her side of the garage, then trudged up the walk to the front door. Little pebbles of snowmelt glowed pale blue in the snow and crunched underfoot—an odd touch of normalcy in a world that no longer made sense.

Karen finally stumbled down the stairs after the third ring and wrenched the door open. With her fiery hair tousled by sleep, a pair of Sergio's sweats bagging on her bony butt and chicken legs, and a wrinkled nightshirt hanging unevenly from her thin shoulders, she looked only marginally better than when she showed up at my door drunk.

A sort of general irritation at being woken up turned to a very personal irritation with me when she realized who I was. Glaring hotly, she folded her arms tightly across her chest and blocked the doorway. "What are you doing here?"

Good to see you, too. "We need to talk."

"Go home. I'm sleeping."

"After we talk."

"Later," she snarled. "I'll call you." Moving faster than I would have expected considering the state she was in, she tried to slam the door in my face.

I caught it with one hand and held it open. "I'm not leaving, Karen. Get used to it."

She raked her fingers through her matted hair. "Why? What do you *want*?"

I decided to start with the easy questions. "I need to know if you're planning on coming to work this morning."

"I haven't decided yet. Frankly, I'm not sure I want to keep working with you."

The feeling was growing more mutual by the second. "Don't you think you owe me an explanation?" I said. "Why are you so mad at me?"

Karen gripped the door with both hands and tried again to shut me out. "If you were paying the slightest bit of attention," she growled as she struggled against me, "you'd already know the answer to that."

I fought her using my shoulders and hips. "I *am* paying attention. I just can't figure out what's going on. Are you really angry with me, or are you just making up an excuse to take some time off?"

Karen stopped pushing abruptly. "What in the hell is that supposed to mean?"

I staggered inside, almost losing my balance in the

process. "You don't have to make yourself angry with me. If you want time off, just say so."

Her eyes sparked. "What makes you think I have to *make* myself angry with you?"

"Well, it's just that—" I sensed movement at the top of the stairs and glimpsed Karen's daughter, Paige, watching us with wide doe eyes. I smiled and tried to look reassuring. Judging by the look on her face, I don't think I succeeded. I wasn't going to tell her what Jawarski said in front of Paige, so I skirted around it. "Look, Karen, I know you're upset with me, but I need you down at the store. Can't we work out whatever this is?"

An acid laugh dripped out of Karen's mouth. "You *need* me."

"Yes, I do—and don't try to say I don't tell you that. I tell you all the time. I don't know what's going on with you, but I've got to tell you, I'm worried."

"Well don't be. I'm fine."

"You could have fooled me." I took a step closer and lowered my voice. "Whatever is bothering you, let's talk it over. Get the kids off to school, and then let's sit down together, just the two of us."

"No. There's nothing to talk about."

"I think there is."

"And I think you're wrong." Resigned to having me in the house, Karen shuffled up the stairs toward the kitchen. Paige darted out of sight, and I wondered if Karen was making the kids as nervous as she made me.

"This is Bea's doing, isn't it?" Karen shot back over her shoulder. "I heard she helped out at the store yesterday."

"She was there," I admitted, "but—" I stopped short when I saw the kitchen. Dirty dishes lined the counters and filled the sink. An empty fast-food bag lay crumpled on the floor, and old soda seeped through the bottom of a paper cup. Karen had never kept an immaculate home, but she'd never let things go like this before—at least not that I'd seen.

Karen didn't seem to notice. "Well that's just great. What business is it of hers what I do? That's what I want to know."

"She's concerned about you." I took another look at the kitchen. "So am I."

Growling under her breath, Karen set to work making coffee. "Bea doesn't know what she's talking about, but she sure likes to stick her nose in everyone else's business."

I watched her for a few minutes, taking in her jerky, nervous movements, the irritation that seemed to ooze out of her pores. "What's going on, Karen? Why are you acting like this?"

She looked at me from behind a veil of tangled hair. "Like what?"

"Like *this*." I waved a hand to encompass the house, the yard, the neighborhood . . . *her*. "The kids have to be to school soon, don't they? You're barely even awake."

"So?"

"So?" I stared at her with my mouth hanging open. "Are you sick or something?"

She raked her fingers through her hair again and shook her head. "I'm fine. Don't worry about it."

But I was worried about it, and anybody with two eyes and a brain would have been, too. "Where's Sergio?"

"Gone to work already. Why?"

Why? I checked over my shoulder to see if Paige was still there, but I couldn't see her. "Would it have killed him to clean some of this before he left? Or did he leave this mess as 'punishment' for you being gone?"

Karen glared at me as if I'd just called her baby ugly. "You're as bad as Bea. Maybe worse. You haven't even been around for the past twenty years, and now you're suddenly an expert on me and my life?"

Her anger floored me. I didn't know whether I was more angry or hurt, but I did know that I was tired of people flinging my past in my face. "This may come as a shock to you and everyone around here," I snapped, "but it's not a crime to live somewhere else for a while. And there's no law on the books that says people can't come back."

"Well you ought to know about the law." She spat out the last word as if it tasted foul.

"Is *that* what's bothering you? The fact that I moved away and went to law school?"

"No. What's bothering me is that you moved away, went to law school, and forgot the rest of us even existed until you needed something. You didn't have time for us when you were married to Roger, but the minute your marriage fell apart, guess who came scurrying back?"

I opened my mouth to argue, but in a strange and twisted way, she had a point. I finally found a few words and hurled them at her. "That was then. This is now."

"And what happens tomorrow, Abby? Huh? How long are you going to stick around? Forever? Or just until something better comes along?"

"How should I know the answer to that? Life isn't something you plan, Karen. Things happen. You meet people. Surprises come along. I didn't plan to be here now, I didn't plan to find my husband having sex with his mistress on my bedroom floor, I didn't plan to divorce him and move back to Paradise—but here I am."

She snorted and turned away.

"All I can tell you," I shouted, "is that I don't *plan* on going anywhere. I *plan* to stick around and run the shop and learn the business and live my life." I paced in the tiny space that housed her dining table, dodging books and backpacks and countless other things that had been left on the floor. "If you felt this way, I sure wish you'd said something about it before now. This isn't exactly the best time to have a meltdown, you know."

Wrong thing to say. I knew it the second the words left my mouth. The spark in Karen's eyes turned into a raging fire. "Oh? So you can't plan anything, but I have to plan my 'meltdowns' around you? You know what? Go to hell, that's what. I quit."

I was too angry to care. "Fine!"

"Fine! Now get out of my house and leave me alone."

"Gladly." Seething, I thundered down the stairs and slammed out of the house. The rattle of the glass in the window made me feel marginally better, but only for as long as it took to get back to my car. Within thirty seconds, I started thinking that I shouldn't have let Karen walk out on me, but I was still too consumed by self-righteous anger to turn around and go back.

If Savannah encountered this kind of attitude when she came back to Paradise, I thought as I ground the Jetta into reverse, she probably *threw* herself in front of that car. At that moment, I didn't blame her.

I was still fuming when I pulled up in front of Sergio's office building twenty minutes later. I didn't have time for this, but I had to know what was wrong with Karen, and I needed Sergio to talk sense into her. I just hoped he'd agree.

The parking lot was nearly empty, which I took as a good sign. The more private our conversation, the better. Inside the lobby, I scanned the directory, found the suite number for Vance and Stroud, Attorneys at Law, then hot-footed it up the stairs. I found the right suite with no trouble, but the glass door leading into it was locked tight.

I knocked, softly at first, then louder and longer until an annoyed-looking Sergio came to see what all the fuss was about. When he recognized me standing in the dimly lit corridor, his step faltered. In the next heartbeat, he pasted a broad smile onto his equally broad face and unlocked the door.

When we were younger, Sergio had the sturdy build of a football player. Now all that muscle has turned to something else, and the broad chest Karen used to rave about has sunk to a spot just above his belt. His thick hair is thinning, his hairline receding, and the pepper is liberally streaked with salt. Don't get me wrong—he's a great guy. I like him a lot. But he's not exactly what you'd consider a stud, and I had a hard time picturing Savannah being interested enough to jeopardize her marriage over him.

He swung the door open, and his thick brows beetled over his broad nose. "Abby? What are you doing here?"

I pushed inside without waiting for an invitation. "We need to talk."

"Now?" He shot a glance over his shoulder and frowned back at me. "This really isn't a good time."

I ignored him. "I just came from the house. I want to know what's wrong with Karen."

"You came from *my* house?"

I nodded. "She's a wreck. I woke her up. The kids aren't ready for school, and she's slumping around in your old sweats and a stained T-shirt. What's going on?"

Sergio glanced behind him again, then reluctantly jerked his head as a signal for me to follow him. He led me into his office, a large sunny room dominated by a U-shaped desk, and shut the door behind us.

I sat in one of the burgundy leather chairs facing the desk, Sergio settled behind it and linked his hands on the blotter. "What did Karen say to you?" he asked, his accent slightly more pronounced than usual.

"Nothing that made any sense. She's mad at me, that much I know. I'm just not sure why." Or maybe I didn't want to know. I crossed my legs. Uncrossed them. Hitched myself to the edge of the chair and sat back again. "She resents me for inheriting the shop, doesn't she?"

Sergio wagged his head slowly. "Don't read too much into this, Abby. It's not what it seems. She's just . . . in a mood."

"Well it's quite a mood." I almost let it go at that, but I couldn't. I'd spent two solid years skirting the truth in my marriage, and look how well that had worked. I didn't want to make the same kind of mistake now. "I need you to tell me the truth, Sergio. Karen wanted the store, didn't she? She thought Aunt Grace was going to leave it to her."

He shrugged one broad shoulder and sat back in his chair, but he didn't look any more at ease than I felt. "She's fine with the way things turned out, Abby. Just relax, okay? You're upset by everything that's been happening the past few days, and that's understandable. Karen's upset, too. There's a lot to be upset about."

I would have given almost anything to believe the answer was that simple. "I won't argue with you," I said, dredging up a half smile from somewhere, "but it's more than that. She seemed fine the day of the contest, but since then every time I see her it's like I'm talking to somebody I don't even know."

Sergio's gaze faltered. Landed on his pencil holder and stayed there. "She's under a lot of stress lately."

"What kind of stress?"

"Stress." He stood and turned his back on me, staring out the window at the cars pulling into the parking lot, but I had a feeling he wasn't really seeing anything. "It's just the normal, everyday stuff," he said after a lengthy pause. "Nothing to get all worked up over."

He was lying to me. I could see it in his eyes, I just didn't know what to do about it. I switched gears to see if I could jar something loose. "What happened between you and Savannah the other night? How much stress did that put Karen under?"

Sergio's eyes flew to my face, and color flooded his cheeks. "Nothing happened between me and Savannah."

"Are you sure about that? A little thing like a cheating spouse can put a whole lot of stress on a woman."

His expression turned to stone. "I have never cheated on Karen."

"Well . . . except that one time," I reminded him. It was harsh, but I didn't care. Playing softball wasn't working with anyone.

"We weren't even married then."

"No, but you were dating, weren't you?"

He let out a heavy breath and mopped his face with an open palm. "Leave it alone, Abby. We were kids. We've moved way past that."

"Maybe you have, but I guarantee that the minute Savannah Vance set foot on Paradise soil, time shifted backwards. Everything Karen felt then, she feels now."

He slid down in his seat and loosened his tie. "Nothing happened that night."

"So why were you with her?"

"I wasn't *with* her," he insisted. "I ran into her. I was looking for Karen."

"And stopped looking when Savannah walked in."

"It wasn't like that." Looking utterly miserable, he drummed the fingers of both hands on his desktop for a minute. "I was looking for Karen. She called and told me that she was taking Evie Rice out for a drink, and I got worried."

"Why?"

"Because Karen's not supposed to drink. It's against doctor's orders."

"Karen's been seeing a doctor? Why?"

"I told you, she's been under stress. The point is, I was trying to find her. She told me about the argument between Savannah and Evie, and she said you asked her to take Evie out and calm her down."

"Only because I didn't know that might cause a problem."

He waved away my protest with one beefy hand. "I know, Abby. It's all right. I didn't do anything at first. About eleven o'clock I called Karen, only she didn't answer her cell phone. I didn't know if she couldn't hear it or if something was wrong, so I decided to go looking for her."

"And you ran into Savannah."

He nodded unhappily. "I saw her before she saw me. I thought about leaving—which is exactly what I should have done—but what if Karen was inside? Savannah was sitting at the bar talking to somebody, and I convinced myself I could sneak into the club without her seeing me."

"It didn't work?"

"Not even close. I wanted to avoid her, but she seemed . . . I don't know . . . different. She'd had a drink or two already, so maybe that was it."

"Maybe," I said uncertainly, "but I saw her about an hour before that. I don't think she'd been drinking when I saw her, but she seemed different to me, too. So what happened then?"

I think Sergio's cheeks actually grew flushed. "I didn't want to seem childish, so I asked about her husband and the big job in New York. She said she didn't want to talk about it."

"About her husband or about the job?"

"About either, I guess. I got the feeling they were having some kind of trouble."

I nodded slowly, trying to remember exactly what I'd overheard when I passed them in Candlewyck's doorway. "I think they had an argument just before I saw them," I said. "I didn't hear much, and Miles walked away a minute later, but Savannah told me that everything was okay."

"Maybe she lied."

"Maybe. Or maybe Karen's right, and Savannah was making a play for you. Some men have trouble resisting a damsel in distress, you know."

No question this time. He glanced down at his too-soft middle, and color flooded his cheeks. "Twenty years ago, yeah. We all know what happened then. But look at me. I'm not exactly Antonio Banderas."

"But she had drinks with you."

"A drink. One."

"And whose idea was that?"

"Hers. She said she was waiting for someone, and she didn't want to be alone."

"Waiting for someone? Do you know who?"

Sergio shook his head. "We ordered. The drinks were delivered. I leaned too hard on the table and spilled drinks everywhere. We were laughing about what a klutz I am when Karen and Evie came in."

I wanted to believe him, but I wasn't going to jump to conclusions. I've heard more convincing stories that turned out to be lies. "What did Karen do?"

"What do you think? She freaked out in front of everybody."

I could almost see it happening in front of me: the bar filled with noisy patrons, music blasting over the speakers, a Nuggets game playing on the overhead television sets. How many people would have heard the commotion? Probably not many except those at nearby tables. "Where were you and Savannah sitting?"

"One of those little round tables on the floor by the bar."

"Who else was there?"

"The bartender. The waitress. Some of the other ladies from the contest. Why?"

"The police consider Karen a 'person of interest' in Savannah's death. But what if somebody overheard her at O'Schuck's—somebody with a grudge against Savannah? What if that person decided that Karen's hysterics were the perfect opportunity to get away with murder?"

Sergio stared at me, uncomprehending. "What are you talking about?"

"Somebody killed Savannah, right? And I think we both agree it wasn't Karen."

"Of course it wasn't, but are you saying that you think somebody set her up?"

"It's better than thinking she stole a car and killed Savannah in cold blood, isn't it?"

"Well, yes, but who would have done a thing like that?"

"I don't know. Who else could have overheard her? Which ladies from the contest were there?"

He shook his head slowly, trying to remember. "Meena Driggs. Nicolette Wilkes, I think. Yes, I'm pretty sure she was there. Rachel Summers." Voices in the hallway filtered in through the closed door, and he scowled with irritation. "Talk to them. See if they can remember who else was there. I have a partners' meeting in ten minutes, and I'm not ready for it."

I might have argued, but I'd been an attorney myself, and I knew the kind of pressure he was under. I stood and crossed to the door. "You'll call me if you think of anything else?"

"Of course."

I started to open the door, but stopped when I realized there was one question I still didn't have an answer for. "What is Karen seeing a doctor for, Sergio? Be honest with me, please. I can't fix what's wrong between us if I don't know."

He stood slowly and spent an annoyingly long time pulling files from the credenza behind his desk. "She doesn't want everyone to know," he said after what felt like a year. "She's clinically depressed, and she's on medication for it."

"That's nothing to be ashamed of."

"You know that, and I know that, but Karen has a real problem with it. You know how her parents are."

My aunt and uncle were old-fashioned, but not unreasonable. "They have a problem with it?"

"They don't know, and if Karen has her way, they never will. She does okay most of the time, but occasionally she needs her meds adjusted, and sometimes when things have been going well for a while, she stops taking them. That's when the real trouble starts. You saw the house today. That's only part of it. It's like . . . like all the cylinders aren't firing. She makes rash decisions. She does stuff without thinking. She takes off and leaves me with the kids for a day or two, doesn't bother to tell us where she is, and then is shocked and hurt to discover that we were worried."

"So what do you do?"

"Get her to the doctor. Adjust her medication. Make sure she's taking it. Once everything gets adjusted, she'll be fine."

"How long does that take?"

"She starts getting better within a few days once she sees the doctor. It's getting her there that's the problem. She doesn't always want to go when she needs to."

Well, now, *that* sounded like Karen. It was the first thing I'd heard all day that did. But I wondered as I was driving away just how far off-kilter her "cylinders" became when her depression got bad. I just hoped it wasn't bad enough to hurt someone.

Chapter 14

I didn't get a chance to think about Karen and Sergio again until nearly noon when, blessedly, Bea showed up to handle the store while I focused my attention in the kitchen. I needed to make samples of candy for my meeting with Ruth Cohen, and I'd convinced Bea—with some effort—that I couldn't be two places at once.

Trouble was, she felt compelled to keep an eye on me as I worked. Even though I knew that Karen's anger with me was being fueled, at least in part, by her medical condition, my argument with her had either made me paranoid or more attuned to the disapproval I could feel radiating from my older cousin.

Between customers she hovered, watched my every move, checked the recipe over my shoulder, scowled a great deal, and made an occasional tsking noise with her tongue.

It wasn't easy, but I tried not to let her bother me. Aunt Grace had always found comfort in the kitchen, and if ever I'd needed comfort and a little peace of mind, I needed them today. Ignoring Bea, I focused on the steps that were becoming familiar again: stirring together sugar and corn syrup, bringing it to a boil, brushing down the sides of the pan when crystals began to form. In the past few months I'd been training myself to work slowly and carefully, to find joy in the process, not just in the results.

We danced around each other for most of the morning—Bea disapproving, me pretending not to notice—until the front door opened a little before noon and Rachel Summers breezed inside as if it were an ordinary day.

Rachel might run Candlewyck, but she's determined to make a life for herself as a plus-sized model, and never a day goes by that she isn't ready to be discovered. She wore a bright red satin blouse untucked over satin pants, stiletto boots that would have resulted in a broken neck if they'd been on my feet, and more silver jewelry than I've ever seen on one person.

"Hey Karen," she called out even before she was all the way inside. "Fix me a Coke, would ya? Extra large. And give me a couple of those chocolate-covered mints—the milk chocolate, not the dark." She plucked a maple cream from the free sample dish, popped it into her mouth, then stopped in her tracks when she saw Bea behind the counter. "Karen's not back yet?"

Bea transferred two mints to a paper plate and passed it across the counter. "She's still not feeling well," she said, running an assessing look along Rachel's ample figure. "*Diet* Coke?"

"No, make it a regular. I can't stand the taste." Rachel leaned across the counter to wave to me, then sat at one of the wrought iron tables and put her feet up on an empty chair. "It's been unbelievably busy on our end of the street today. How's it been up here?"

"It's been a good day," Bea said. "Are you sure you wouldn't rather have a medium? It's much easier to carry."

Apparently oblivious to Bea's thinly veiled insults,

Rachel shook her head. "I'm *dying* of thirst. I'm going to need the big one to get through the afternoon." She leaned up from her chair and studied the glass display case. "What's your featured candy today?"

Bea turned away, her opinion of Rachel's order written all over her face. "Rocky Mountain Cherry Bars."

"Ooh." Rachel ran her tongue along her glossy red lips. "Those are so good. You'd better give me a couple of those, too."

Bea's face froze. "You want those *and* the mints?"

Rachel must have felt the sting that time, but she merely shrugged. "I'll get on the treadmill later. I haven't had a Cherry Bar in months."

Bea's expression clearly said, *not long enough*, but she wisely kept the thought to herself. "Aunt Grace's bars are the best around," she said with a prim smile. "They've always been popular."

I'm sure it was only my argument with Karen that made those words resonate. Even *I* thought of all the candy at Divinity as Grace's. But Aunt Grace hadn't made a batch of Rocky Mountain Cherry Bars in more than nine months, and I suddenly wanted all the cousins who thought Aunt Grace had been wrong to leave me the store to know it. I just didn't know how to say so without appearing childish.

Rachel munched happily, oblivious to the undercurrents raging around her. "So what's going on with the murder investigation, Abby? Have they arrested Delta yet?"

The abrupt change of subject caught me by surprise, and it took a minute to make the mental shift. "Delta?"

"She's the one who did it, isn't she?"

"I have no idea. Is that what you think?" Silly question. Of course it was. I guess if I had to pick a prime suspect, Delta would have been it—but I was still scrambling to shift gears.

Rachel stopped chewing and turned so she could see me better. "Well, sure. Who had the strongest motive for killing Savannah? I know Evie's upset about the contest, but we're just talking about a few hundred dollars in prize money. Hardly worth committing murder for. If you ask me, Delta's the one. She's trying to hang onto an entire estate."

Bea blew out a sharp breath. "An *estate*? That's a bit of an overstatement, isn't it? Mrs. Vance wasn't worth much when she died."

I didn't have time to stop working, so I spoke over my shoulder as I pulled molds from the supply cupboard. "She wasn't?"

Bea shook her head firmly. "There's the house, but it's not worth much. Someone told me she had only about ten thousand in the bank, and they had to cash in her life insurance a couple of years ago to help pay her medical expenses."

Rachel licked chocolate from her fingers. "Ten thousand might be a lot of money to Delta."

I agreed. "People have committed murder for a lot less."

Bea sniffed and slipped out from behind the counter. "It would be a lot less after you take out funeral expenses, attorney fees, and then divide it in half. I don't know why we're talking about this anyway. The police will figure it all out."

Rachel and I both spoke at once. "Oh. Yeah. Of course." . . . "Naturally. Nobody's suggesting—" . . . "We're just tossing out ideas, really."

Bea picked up something from the counter and tossed it into the trash can. "Abby, you of all people should know not to get involved in something like this. Look what almost happened to you last time."

"Don't worry," I assured her. "I don't want to get involved in the murder investigation, but it's normal to speculate, isn't it? Especially under the circumstances. You know . . . me finding her and all."

Bea rolled her eyes in disbelief. Rachel polished off the last of her mint, eyed the bag holding her Cherry Bars for a moment, then crumpled the paper plate in her fist. "So who does Jawarski suspect?"

"He's not saying much."

"But he was here last night . . . wasn't he?"

A silly grin tugged at my lips before I could stop it. "He wanted to make sure I was okay after finding Savannah."

"Well, isn't that nice?" Rachel turned a Cheshire cat grin on Bea.

Bea actually smiled back. "Knowing that the police care that much about the citizens of Paradise certainly makes *me* feel safer."

I glanced away from the mold I was filling just long enough to scowl. "You two are hilarious."

Rachel snorted a laugh and wiped chocolate from the corner of her mouth. "Oh come on now," she said, her tone mocking. "I'm sure Jawarski would be just as concerned if either one of us had found Savannah. I'll bet he'd stay and have pizza, too."

I sprinkled a little sugar into my smile. "I'm sure he would. Now, can we please talk about something else?"

Rachel shrugged, and I took that to mean that she agreed.

Bea scowled and asked, "Like what?"

Nothing that would make Bea think about Rachel and her eating habits or Jawarski and me. I seized on an idea that had occurred to me earlier that morning. "Well, like, what we should do when the contest gets under way again. We can't just go on as if nothing has happened. We need to acknowledge Savannah's death somehow."

Tiny pinch marks formed over Bea's ski-jump nose. "What do you want to do?"

"I don't know exactly. I just think we should do *something*. Maybe somebody could say a few words. . ."

"You want them to be *nice* words?" Rachel asked. "Because if you do, you're going to have to hire somebody who never knew her."

"That's pretty harsh," Bea said, pulling a roll of gold-edged labels from the supply cupboard and slapping them onto half-pound bags of taffy I'd filled earlier. "I hope you don't let her husband hear you talking like that."

"Of course I won't," Rachel said, "I'm not stupid. Besides, I feel sorry for the poor guy. Not only did he have to put up with Savannah twenty-four hours a day for however many years they were together, but now he has to go through this. God only knows what else Savannah put him through."

"The good thing is, people are concerned," I said. "I talked to Faith Bond the other night. She was planning to check on Miles and make sure he has everything he needs."

"Well, that's good." Bea's scowl relaxed slightly. "I didn't realize Faith knew Savannah."

"She would have known her in school," I said. "At least a little. Our graduating class wasn't that big."

"Well, I hope theirs isn't the only church that makes an appearance at the lodge. If you want my opinion, the entire town should rally around that poor man."

"I'm sure people will, once word gets out," I assured her.

"Not if Delta has anything to say about it," Rachel said somberly. "She'd like to see him leave town and never come back."

I nodded, still bothered by the lack of familial closeness. "And she'll get her wish, I'm sure. He'll have to start that new job in New York soon, won't he?"

"Is he going to New York?" Bea stopped working and frowned at the price stickers I'd made earlier. "I thought he was going somewhere else. The half-pound bags are three *forty*-nine, Abby. Don't you have Grace's price list?"

"I do. I decided to raise the price last week. When did you see Miles, and what gave you the idea he was going someplace besides New York?"

Bea found a pen and started writing new price stickers. "I really don't think that's wise, Abby. People are used to the way Aunt Grace did things when she was alive. That's why they come to Divinity. If you start changing everything now, you could lose business."

Tension knotted in my neck. "I'm not changing everything," I said, struggling to keep my voice sounding normal. "I changed one thing. One tiny little thing. I raised the price of a half-pound bag of taffy by a dime. I hardly think ten pennies are going to cause a revolution."

Bea stared at me, unflinching. "You're missing my point, Abby."

I stared back. "Actually, Bea, I don't think I am. You want to tell me how to run the store. The point *you* seem to be missing is that Aunt Grace left Divinity to me. That means she trusted me to make decisions, to raise prices, to add products or even discontinue them if I think that's what's best for business. Nowhere in her will did it specify that I had to take a family vote every time I want to blow my nose."

Bea's shoulders stiffened, and her chin lifted. "Don't be ridiculous. Nobody ever said anything about taking a family vote, and all I'm doing is trying to help. Obviously, you don't appreciate it."

"I do appreciate it," I assured her, still thinking I might be able to sound calm and rational. "I just need you to support me instead of second-guessing me."

"I see. So you want me to just keep my mouth shut when I see you making a mistake?"

Yes! "No. I want you to let me make decisions and then

see what happens. Some of them might be mistakes, but making mistakes is part of learning, isn't it?"

"Under other circumstances I'd say yes, but your mistakes could destroy something near and dear to all of us."

First Karen, now Bea. How many other cousins were out there filled with resentment over Aunt Grace's will, waiting to see me fail? I hoped not many. I wasn't sure I could stand up to the whole family.

You have to understand one thing about the Shaw cousins. They don't respect a quitter, and they don't respect anyone who won't fight back. We might have some knock-down-drag-outs from time to time. The finger-pointing and name-calling might get a bit severe. But you're a whole lot more likely to keep their respect if you go nose-to-nose, give as good as you get.

"You're so certain I'm going to destroy Divinity," I shouted, "you're standing here with your arms out, waiting for the chance to catch what falls. Well, I just might surprise you, Bea. I might not destroy the store after all."

"You will if you mess with Grace's formula for success."

"Grace didn't *have* a formula," I snapped. "She rolled with the punches, and she changed with the times. That was the best thing about her. If she'd taken your attitude, we'd still be charging forty-nine cents for that half pound of taffy. And I don't think Aunt Grace would be all that happy listening to you insult the customers."

Cheeks aflame, Bea tugged off her apron and tossed it onto the counter. "It's obvious that I'm not appreciated around here, so I'll leave. You can mail my check."

In case you haven't caught on by now, my family is a passionate lot. Some might even say we tend toward the melodramatic. "You *can't* quit. There's no way I can handle the party this weekend and run the store. And what about my appointment with Ruth Cohen?"

Bea stopped with her hand on the door and glowered

back at me. "I have absolutely no idea what you're going to do, Abby, but I'm sure you'll figure it out. After all, this is *your* store. So go ahead. Do what you want with it. Just don't ask *me* for help next time you run into a brick wall."

She slammed the door behind her, and I turned, wild-eyed, to Rachel. "What just happened?"

"I think she quit."

Thank you, Captain Obvious. "Was I *wrong*?"

Clearly, there was only one right answer to that question, but Rachel didn't seem to realize it. She gave a laugh and gathered her things. "Oh no you don't. I'm not getting in the middle of a Shaw family argument."

"But—"

"I have to get back anyway. My break is over."

And just like that, she was gone, leaving me alone with a store to run and half a dozen samples to make before tomorrow's meeting. I was just naïve enough to think things couldn't get any worse.

The rest of the day went by in a blur of customers, telephone calls, and planning everything I could on paper, since I couldn't spend time in the kitchen. I told myself that writing everything down would save me time once I closed the shop and started cooking.

I had just finished a sale for a woman wearing far too much makeup when the phone rang. Grabbing the cordless with one hand and several boxes of peanut brittle I needed to reshelve, I scooted out from behind the counter. "Divinity Confectioners, making every day a little sweeter."

"Abby? Brenda Hayden here." My confused silence must have warned her that I didn't place her name because she added, "from the classifieds at the *Post*? You talked to me the other day about a want ad in this week's paper?"

"Oh. Sure. Yes. What can I do for you?"

"I'm afraid we have a problem. I didn't get a chance to

run the credit card you gave me until this morning, and the bank won't honor the charge. It says here that your account is over its limit—?"

I dropped one box of brittle but managed, barely, to hang on to the rest. "Impossible. That's a business account. I don't use it for anything else."

"Well, I'm sure you can clear that up with your bank. Our problem is that without payment, we can't run your ad."

"I'll stick a check in the mail. You should have it by tomorrow."

"I'm afraid that won't be good enough," Brenda said. At least she managed to sound regretful. "The deadline is five o'clock today. If I don't have your payment, I have to offer the ad space to someone else."

"But you can't do that! I need that ad to run."

"It's only four o'clock," she said, trying, I'm sure, to be helpful. "There's plenty of time to get your payment here before five."

"Except that I can't leave the store because I'm alone here. By the strangest coincidence, that's why I need that ad to run." The past few days had taken their toll. I didn't mean to get testy with Brenda. I just couldn't seem to help myself.

"Listen," she said, showing remarkable patience, "I understand completely. I just need you to understand that my hands are tied. Sloan has issued a moratorium against extending credit to *anybody*. If I let you slide, even until tomorrow, he'll fire me."

Sloan Williamson is the editor/owner of the *Post*, and though I seriously doubted that he'd fire anybody, I wasn't certain enough to put her job at risk. Having one of us on the line was enough.

"Just see what you can do to get the payment over here, okay?" she said. "I'll hold your spot as long as I can, but

I'm only here until five thirty, and I can't even guarantee it that long."

I assured her that I understood, slid the rest of the peanut brittle onto the shelf, and started running down my A-list for the third time in as many days. When my sister-in-law, Elizabeth, answered on the first ring, I hoped my luck was changing. But when she worried that she couldn't make the drive to town in time herself and suggested that I call Dana, who just happened to be in town with Wyatt, hope dwindled again.

Unfortunately, time was running out, and I didn't see many other possibilities dancing out there on the horizon. Lucky for me, Dana answered her cell phone and promised to come right over—which I took to mean that her dad wasn't sitting right there monitoring her every word. And that, I figured, had to be a good sign.

Dana arrived ten minutes later, red-cheeked from the cold and still sporting a rod through her tongue. I was encouraged to discover that not only had Wyatt caved in at some point, but there was a fairly good chance that my customers might actually understand Dana when she spoke to them.

Vowing to catch up on all the details later, I grabbed my checkbook and dashed outside just as a group of teenage boys piled out of an SUV laden with snowboards and headed toward the shop. Looked like Dana was in for a good time.

Long afternoon shadows stretched across the street, and I stood for a minute, watching my breath form clouds around me, while I debated whether to take the long way around or climb the three sets of stairs that led up the mountain to Escalante Street. Under normal circumstances, it would have been a no-brainer, I'd have hopped in the Jetta and driven myself there. But the roads were already clogged with tourists, and my watch said four thirty. I didn't want to take any chances.

I was seriously contemplating my last will and testament when I finally reached the end of my climb. The temperature couldn't have been more than twenty degrees, but I'd worked up a healthy sweat as I climbed. I did my best to ignore the trickles of perspiration snaking down the sides of my face and inching down my back, and kept walking.

With just ten minutes to spare, I pushed into the *Post*'s brick-front building and asked for Brenda Hayden. She kept me waiting so long, I was starting to get antsy again, but finally a short, round, redhead with no eyebrows and a smile that lit up her face cruised toward me with one hand outstretched. "Abby? Brenda. I'm so glad you were able to get here on time."

"You're not the only one." I shook her hand and pulled the check from my pocket. "So we're okay? The ad will run as scheduled?"

"We should be fine. Sloan wants me to phone the bank to make sure this will clear." She leaned in closer and dropped her voice. "You know, because of the other thing. That's not a problem for you, is it?"

"Not at all. There shouldn't have been any problem with the credit card, either." I was ninety-nine percent certain that my balance was at least eight hundred dollars below my limit, and I *knew* I hadn't ordered that many supplies.

Brenda smiled. "I'm sure it's just some kind of bookkeeping snafu." She started walking back the direction she'd come, nodding to indicate that I should walk with her.

I figured she probably wanted me to wait until she cleared my check, and I was happy to do it. I'd rather not make another mad dash up the steps if I didn't have to. I followed her down a long corridor lined with offices, some of which were empty, while others buzzed with activity as the staff tried to put this issue of the *Post* to bed.

"You're lucky we had space enough for a few want ads this week," Brenda said as she ushered me into a cramped office at the end of the hall. "Sloan cut out everything he deemed unnecessary to make room for the Savannah Horne murder. What a tragedy."

I agreed that it was and made myself relatively comfortable in a hard wooden chair in front of her desk.

Brenda patted the mounds of paper covering her desk, apparently looking for something. After a minute, her face brightened, and she pulled the local phone book from beneath a stack of colored file folders. "That poor, poor man," she said as she flipped through the Yellow Pages. "My heart just aches for him."

I assumed she was talking about Miles, so I agreed again. "It would be hard enough to lose your spouse, but to have it happen in a strange place would make it all that much harder. Have you heard whether his family will be coming?"

Brenda found the number she wanted and dialed. "What family?"

"I thought he had family," I said, trying to remember why I thought that.

"Not according to what he told Sloan this afternoon." Apparently on hold, she cradled the phone between neck and chin and leaned onto her desk eagerly. "He told Sloan that he's alone in the world now. Did he tell you something different?"

I thought back, trying to separate actual conversations from impressions and assumptions, and finally shook my head. "I'm not sure why I thought that. I've heard so many things over the past few days, I probably misunderstood."

The expectant smile faded from Brenda's face, and she punched a couple of numbers on her phone. "You and me both. I swear, if I didn't write everything down—" She broke off, spent a few minutes speaking with someone at the bank to verify that I actually had money, and finally disconnected with a smile. "Looks like you're in business. The ad will be in tomorrow's paper. You should start getting calls soon."

Terrific. Positive steps. That had to be better than waiting around for Karen to come to her senses and realize what a mistake she'd made. If I waited for *that* to happen, I might never leave the shop again.

Chapter 15

The sun had disappeared behind the mountains when I stepped outside again, so I decided to take the long way back to Divinity. Dana would be all right for a few more minutes, and my legs were still shaky from the climb. I didn't trust myself to go down three flights of steep, narrow stairs in the dark.

Maybe I should have gone straight back to the shop, but when I reached the corner of Prospector and Forest and spotted Paisley's yellow bug sitting in front of the Curl Up and Dye, I decided to take a brief detour.

I was still bothered by that offhand comment about Miles having no family. Still trying to remember why I thought he had. If anybody knew the answer, Delta would. Yes, I still thought she might be the one who ran Savannah down, but I didn't intend to let her know that I suspected her. And maybe I would have to dance around Paisley's efforts to give me a makeover, but it was just one quick question. I would be in and out. Surely, I could hold Paisley off for that long.

Paisley was in the middle of giving a haircut when I

came through the door, but she beamed with delight when she saw me, abandoned her customer, and bounced up to the counter. She's a short woman with freckles that she tries to hide under a thick layer of foundation and powder.

It doesn't work.

Unlike her clientele, Paisley's hair changes style and color at least once a week. I think she considers herself a walking billboard for the salon. I think she might be more effective if she wasn't perennially popping a wad of gum.

This week's hair was pale blonde and layered, shades of Farrah Fawcett in her *Charlie's Angels* days. In honor of her look, Paisley wore a pair of pink leggings, an oversized shirt belted at the waist, '80s style, and a pink tunic—paisley patterned, of course.

She held out both arms as she came toward me, as if we were the dearest of friends. "Abby! It is *so* great to see you here." *Chomp! Pop! Chomp!* Sit down and make yourself comfortable. I'm almost finished with Natalie, and I don't have another appointment between now and closing."

I backed up a step, but I also tried to look regretful. It seemed like the polite thing to do. "Thanks, Paisley, but I'm not here for a cut. I'm looking for Delta. Is she working tonight?"

Paisley's face fell. "No." *Pop! Snap!* "She asked for a couple of days off. I'm sure I don't have to tell you why."

I wasn't surprised. Disappointed maybe. I didn't want to drive out to Delta's house just to get the answer to one little question. "Do you know if she's at home?"

"Well, now, I'm not sure." Paisley tapped the comb she held against her hand and popped and chomped some more. "She asked for the time off, but I didn't ask what she was planning to do with it. I can call and ask if you want me to. No sense driving all the way over there for nothing."

"Thanks," I said, "but I'm not even sure if I'll attempt it tonight. I have a million things to do." And I didn't want to warn Delta that I was coming. I think you get a more honest answer when you catch someone off guard.

Since I wasn't about to become a paying customer, Paisley popped a bit more while she ran a glance from head to toe—one of those assessing looks that inevitably makes you squirm, I don't care who you are. "You're not going to upset her are you?"

"I don't plan on it."

"Because she's upset enough."

"I'm sure she is. I promise I'll be careful."

Apparently that wasn't good enough. Paisley narrowed her eyes and locked on me with a frown. "What do you want to talk to her about?"

"Nothing bad, I promise." I turned toward the door, ready to put an end to the conversation.

"Because the thing is," Paisley went on, undaunted, "I heard that you were getting kind of friendly with Savannah's husband."

That stopped me in my tracks. "Excuse me?"

"I don't mean *that* way," she assured me quickly. "But everybody's talking about how he was at your shop the day Savannah died. And now, with what that attorney told Delta, I'm not sure either of you are on her list of favorite people."

I took a couple of steps away from the door. "What attorney, and what did he tell her?"

Paisley flapped a dismissive hand. "Whatever attorney she's been using to settle her mother's estate." *Chomp!* "Apparently, he told her this morning that Miles is going to inherit Savannah's half, after all. Can you believe that?" *Pop! Pop!* "Poor Delta. Things just keep going from bad to worse for her."

"She didn't expect Miles to inherit?"

"Well, no! I mean, why would she?"

"I don't know. Maybe because Savannah and Miles were married?"

Paisley tsked and slipped the comb into the pocket of her smock. "Savannah told her that she and Miles had separated their assets. She *promised* Delta that Miles wouldn't get his hands on anything that was their mother's."

"Are you sure about that?" I wondered why Savannah would have done that. Maybe more importantly, why Delta wanted it done.

"I'm absolutely sure. Delta *hates* Miles. Always has. That's why she and Savannah didn't speak to each other for so long."

That surprised me. "They didn't speak because of Savannah's marriage to Miles? I thought it was because Savannah left Delta here to take care of their mother."

Paisley popped twice and waved away my silly notion. "No. Delta wasn't upset about that. Not really. She knew what Savannah was like, and she knew Savannah would have been miserable here. What really frosted her was the way Miles acted."

"What way was that?"

"Oh, you know . . . like he was so much better than everybody else. This job in New York was really a corker, you know? Before this, he was just the world's most annoying man, always talking about Harvard and making sure Delta and Charlie knew how smart he was. But this really put him over the top. He's been shoving everything he does under Delta's nose since the day he met Savannah. Like he just *has* to remind her that Savannah married him while Delta was stuck here in Paradise with old Charlie."

"Old Charlie" had been unemployed so many times over the years, I don't think anybody seriously expected him to hold down a job anymore. It wasn't that he was lazy or even a bad worker. He'd just been seriously unfortunate in that department.

I was having a real struggle to readjust my thinking and figure out how this fit with the hit-and-run that killed Savannah. "So Miles is annoying. Is that why Delta hates him?"

"She doesn't trust him, either. And that's all I know. You'd have to ask her the rest."

"Thanks, I think I'll do that." I turned toward the door again, then remembered one last question. "Has Delta ever mentioned whether Miles has family?"

Paisley gave that some thought and shook her head. "I don't remember. Sorry. But listen, anytime you want to come in here and let me fix you up, you just let me know, okay? You let us get to work on your hair, those eyebrows, and that little shadow on your upper lip, and you'll feel like a new woman."

Gee, thanks! I left there feeling almost as attractive as the night Grandma Hanks told me my shoulders were too broad for the lace dress I wanted for my graduation from junior high school. I guess some things never leave you.

I stayed up half the night finishing the samples I wanted for my meeting with Ruth Cohen, but by the time I crawled into bed I was satisfied with my efforts. Early the next morning, my sister-in-law showed up to work the store so I could meet with Mrs. Cohen and, hopefully, move Divinity up another rung on the ladder of success.

By nine o'clock I had my hair as under control as it ever gets and started packing the Jetta with samples. I heard the phone ring, but since I'd stuffed myself into one of the suits left over from corporate law days and jammed my feet into heels, I wasn't moving all that quickly. By the time I hobbled inside, the ringing had stopped.

I checked voice mail and found a message from Jawarski. I was just telling myself what a pleasant way that was to start the day when he ruined everything.

"Got the autopsy results back. Thought you might be interested to know that the ME found poison in her system. Amitriptyline. I'm not planning on making that public right away. Want to see if I can shake things up a bit. But I wanted you to know."

My hand was shaking as I disconnected. I tried calling him back, but he was already busy with something else, so I left a message and stared at the wall in front of me.

Poison!

It was almost too terrible to think about.

I paced around the kitchen for a few minutes, but I couldn't bear to do nothing. I wasn't scheduled to be at the lodge until ten thirty, but in desperation I decided to follow up on that question I wanted to ask Delta Walters.

Delta and Charlie live in a sleepy neighborhood on the outskirts of Paradise, in the sagging two-story frame house that used to belong to Delta's mother. Last I heard, Charlie was between jobs—but like I said, Charlie is usually between jobs.

Delta's green Ford was sitting in the driveway, so I parked on the street and followed the narrow trail someone had scooped out of the snow and ice to the front door.

I rang the bell twice and was just turning away when the door creaked open on rusty hinges, and Delta peered out at me. She was still in pajamas covered with a ratty chenille robe. Her hair stuck out on one side and lay flat on the other. Dark ridges of old mascara formed rings beneath red, puffy eyes. She looked horrible. But was she grieving her sister's death? It seemed unlikely if she'd been behind the wheel of that rental car, and even less likely if she'd been cold-blooded enough to poison her own sister. At least with a hit-and-run I could delude myself into thinking it had been a crime of passion.

Maybe Delta was grieving the news that Miles was entitled to half of everything she owned. She blinked a couple of times, as if she was having trouble focusing on me. "Abby? My goodness. You're all dressed up today. What are you doing here?"

"Paisley told me that you'd taken a few days off."

Delta nodded and squinted into the morning sunlight. "Yes, but—"

"I'm sorry about Savannah," I said quickly. "Are you holding up okay?"

She looked me over with eyes narrowed in suspicion. "I'm holding up, but that's about all I can say. But I'm sure you didn't come over here to ask me that. What is it you want?"

So much for the polite small talk portion of our visit. Since I wasn't sure if she was a killer or a mourner, I decided to ease into what I really wanted to know. "I guess you probably know that we postponed the finish of the contest at Divinity. I've been thinking that it might be nice to have a short memorial for Savannah before we get started again."

"A memorial? In a candy store?" Delta laughed softly and fiddled with the worn collar of her robe. "Well, I guess that's more appropriate than a church." From inside the house, an electronic buzzer sounded, and Delta seemed to realize for the first time that I was still outside. She stepped aside and motioned me through the door. "My coffee cake is ready to come out of the oven. Would you like some?"

I couldn't tell whether she wanted me to say yes or no. I wasn't sure I could eat even a crumb and still sit down in the skirt I was wearing. And I wasn't all that eager to eat something baked by someone who might have spare poison hanging around the house. But I'd just gotten started, and refusing would look suspicious, so I nodded and moved into the overheated, overcrowded house. Large pieces of heavy furniture lined every inch of wall space and jutted into the center of the living room. Gold brocade drapes, out of style for at least the past thirty years, blocked out most of the daylight, and the scent of cinnamon warred with the musty smell of a house that hadn't experienced fresh air in far too long.

When I realized that Delta was watching me, I worked up a smile and said, "You have a lovely home."

She gave a little shrug and headed toward the kitchen. "You're not a very good liar, Abby. The house is a mess, and you know it. There's too much furniture and not enough light, but it's what I'm used to." She waved me toward a round table in the center of the attached dining alcove and snatched up a couple of pot holders from the counter. "So you want to have a memorial for Savannah? Do you mind telling me why?"

"She was a contestant," I said again. "It doesn't seem right to just go on as if nothing has happened."

Delta pulled the cake from the oven and set it on a wire rack to cool. "Well, fine. What does any of this have to do with me?"

I made a solemn vow not to eat a single bite unless she ate some first. "You're her sister. I thought you might like to know, in case you wanted to be there. And, of course, if you want to say a few words—"

Delta's head shot up and a tight laugh escaped her lips. "It's a lovely sentiment, I suppose, but I guarantee you don't want me saying anything."

"But she's your sister."

"Was." Delta pulled a couple of plates from an overhead cupboard. "The fact is, Savannah hadn't been a sister to me in years. She left right after high school and couldn't be bothered with any of us she left behind."

That kind of comment always made me uncomfortable. Hit too close to home, I guess. "You didn't stay in contact?"

Delta gathered forks from a drawer. "Oh, sure. I'd say, 'Hey, I need help with mother,' and she'd say, 'Leave me the hell alone.' It was an ideal relationship . . . on her side."

Her bitterness didn't surprise me, but I wasn't comfortable with it. "Okay," I agreed cautiously, "I won't ask you to speak, but you're welcome to come if you'd like. I'm sure there are a lot of people who'd like to offer their condolences, and I'll bet there are people willing to help in whatever way they can."

Delta's sharp laugh sliced through the stuffy air. "One of your friends helped me already, didn't they?" She slapped two pieces of cake onto the plates and carried everything to the table. "Whoever it was should have left well enough alone."

"You think someone connected with the contest killed Savannah?"

Delta slid a piece of cake in front of me and plunked herself down in a chair. "It was either somebody who waited twenty years to get their revenge, or somebody who had something to lose right now. Which do you think?"

I wasn't about to point out that she had a strong motive herself. Not while I was sitting across the table from her and she had sharp objects at her disposal.

She didn't seem to notice my silence. "If you want my opinion, I think Evie Rice did it." Not for the first time, she sounded disconnected, as if we were discussing the death of a stranger. It bothered me as much this time as it had the last.

"I don't know," I said cautiously. "This seems too cold-blooded for Evie."

Delta forked up a mouthful of cinnamon cake and stared at it for a long moment. "You could be right, I guess. There's no shortage of people who hated my sister. I guess it could have been just about anybody."

"I know she wasn't the most popular person in the world," I said, "but I don't think Paradise is overrun with people who wanted to kill her."

"Maybe not *now*." Delta's mouth curved into a knowing smile. "But half those people probably wanted to kill her at one time or another. I'm afraid you won't find many people around here who'll appreciate what you're trying to do with this memorial service of yours." She finally put the cake into her mouth, and I felt myself relax.

"Maybe not, but I still think it's something I should do. Do you have any suggestions about who I might ask to speak?"

She eyed me skeptically. "How would I know?"

"You knew Savannah better than anyone when she lived here," I pointed out. "There must be someone who was a friend back then and who's still around here." *Someone who isn't on the suspect list.* "Marshall Ames was in our class at school," I said, watching her reaction from the corner of my eye. "Maybe I could ask him."

"Marshall Ames? Is that supposed to be a joke?"

I choked down a mouthful of dry coffee cake. "No. Is there some reason it should be?"

"I take it you don't know about Savannah and Marshall?"

Faith had mentioned something hadn't she? But I really didn't know anything. Since I couldn't speak, I shook my head. If there was poison in the cake, it sure wasn't in liquid form.

"Well, suffice it to say that Marshall has hated Savannah for years."

Sorry. Not sufficient. I needed to know *way* more than that. "I talked to Marshall the other day. I didn't get that impression at all."

"That's because Marshall is very good at hiding what he feels."

I forced down another bite of cake and asked, "Do you know why he hated her?"

"Oh, it was typical Savannah, really. Marshall had quite a thing for her from the time they were about fourteen."

"Marshall did? I would never have guessed."

"Then you must not have seen the two of them together. This was all back when Mother was still young and vital. She knew Marshall's mother somehow. I forget exactly how, but we spent quite a bit of time together in those days. Anybody in the same room could have seen how Marshall felt about Savannah, but she wouldn't give him the time of day."

That did sound like vintage Savannah, and it matched what Faith had told me. But Marshall had seemed so . . . so what? Innocent?

"It didn't matter so much when they were young," Delta went on, "but when they got into high school and Savannah started dating—" She broke off with a scowl and corrected herself, "By the time Mother *knew* she was dating, it became pretty clear to everyone that she wasn't . . . How should I say this? She wasn't exactly discriminating."

That was a very nice way of putting it. "So what happened?"

"Well, even then, even when she was going with almost any boy who'd look at her twice, she acted as if she didn't even know Marshall was alive."

"Are you sure about that?"

"She and I lived in the same house, didn't we? I saw it all. Marshall asked her out I don't know how many times. She always said no, and always in the meanest way possible. Marshall wasn't stupid, either. You'd have thought that eventually he'd get it, but he was like that Energizer Bunny. He just kept going and going and going . . ."

"So she was mean to him, but he didn't seem to notice. That's hardly a motive for murder twenty years later."

Delta held up a hand to stop me. "Things might have kept going like that forever, but during her senior year, Savannah finally said yes."

That surprised me. "I don't remember the two of them going out."

"That's because they didn't. Savannah told that poor boy she'd go to the Senior Ball with him, but she accepted a date with another boy for the same night. Poor Marshall showed up here dressed in a rented tux, carrying a corsage of roses, and driving his daddy's Cadillac, only to find out that Savannah was already gone with someone else."

"That's sad," I agreed, "but people get stood up every day." It had even happened to me a couple of times. I ate the last of my cake and pushed the plate to one side so Delta wouldn't get any bright ideas about offering me seconds. "That's not a reason to hate someone for twenty years."

"Oh, it was more than just that. Savannah wasn't content with just standing him up. She taunted him with it afterward. For months after the ball, she'd laugh about it, treat it as if it was the biggest joke—not the fact that she'd stood him up, but that he'd been stupid enough to take her seriously in the first place." Delta carried both plates to the sink. "I know it doesn't sound like much, but you didn't know Savannah that well, did you? You don't know how cruel she could be."

"No," I said. "Maybe I didn't. I was talking to someone the other day who said she overheard Marshall and Savannah talking about a letter. Do you know what that could be about?"

Delta shook her head. "Probably some love missive Marshall wrote to her."

"Then or now?"

"Then. Definitely. I think he eventually got over her, or maybe he just wised up."

She sounded so harsh, I winced inwardly. "Savannah seemed different to me when I talked to her the night before she died. She even sounded like she might be thinking about staying here."

Delta turned back toward me, wearing a touch of pity in her expression. "Savannah here? For good? That would never have happened. Savannah loves—" She cut herself off, and an expression I couldn't read darted through her eyes. "She loved things. She loved money. She loved the kind of life she couldn't get here in Paradise."

"That might have been true twenty years ago," I said, "but it's not so true today. Paradise has changed a lot."

Delta glanced out the window toward the hillside where a coven of new condos scrambled toward the summit. "Yes, it has," she agreed softly, "but Savannah would never have chosen to stay here when that husband of hers was offering Manhattan. Never." Another shadow passed across her expression, and she turned back to me quickly. "I wish you luck putting together your memorial service, Abby. But don't expect me to take part in it. That chapter of my life was over a long time ago. Now, if you'll excuse me, I have an appointment in town in an hour, and I'm not ready."

I nodded mutely and headed for the door. A dozen unanswered questions were racing around each other inside my head. Had Marshall harbored a hatred for Savannah all these years? Or was Delta merely trying to throw me off her trail? "Thanks for the cake," I said and tried to sound as if I meant it. "And if you change your mind about the service, you'll be more than welcome. I'll let you know the details when they're decided."

Delta's lips curved, but the smile didn't make it to her eyes. "I know what you're thinking, Abby. It's written all over your face. But what you don't understand is that I don't need to attend some memorial service for Savannah. I don't know the woman who died here in Paradise the other day. The truth is, I mourned my sister a long time ago."

Chapter 16

I was still mulling over my conversation with Delta as I drove out of her neighborhood a few minutes later. I couldn't decide how I felt about her reaction to Savannah's death. Did I believe her or not? It seemed immeasurably sad that the one person who should have loved Savannah hadn't.

I gave myself a mental shake. Maybe her sister had been cold and distant, but it wasn't as if no one had loved her. One person had loved her deeply, but for some reason I'd been avoiding him since I found Savannah's body along the roadside. I wasn't even sure why, except that it's hard to know what to say to a grieving person, especially one you don't know well.

I couldn't help wondering how he was holding up, though, and I felt responsible for the poor man in some odd way. Since I was going to the Summit Lodge anyway, maybe I'd stop in to see him while I was there.

During my meeting with Mrs. Cohen, I managed not to embarrass myself too badly and even managed to impress her with a couple of my creations. I left with a contract in hand to cater a soiree on Saturday night for a hundred guests. I don't mind admitting that I was stoked.

I took the samples back to the car, then hurried back into the lodge to check on Miles. This time when I asked the desk clerk to put me through to his room, Miles answered. He seemed pleased to hear from me, and five minutes later, I was knocking on the door to room 845.

Miles had sounded almost normal over the phone, but up close and personal was another matter entirely. His eyes were bloodshot and red-rimmed. His hair looked as if it hadn't been brushed in days. A fine stubble covered his cheeks and chin, and his hands were trembling—but I thought genuine relief flashed through his eyes when he saw me standing there.

After ushering me into the two-room suite and closing the door behind me, he indicated Continental breakfast for two on the round table near the window. "I'm trying to make myself eat something," he said, his voice gravelly and low. "I hope you'll join me. I couldn't bear the thought of ordering just for one, so there's plenty."

My thighs and hips begged me to refuse, my waist screamed for relief from the band of my skirt, but I didn't have the heart to say no. I settled myself in a chair overlooking the front parking lot, but Miles seemed preoccupied and flighty. He moved around the room quickly, touching this, moving that, all without any apparent purpose. When he finally perched on the edge of a chair across from me, I asked, "How are you holding up?"

Very slowly, he dragged his gaze from the white porcelain coffeepot to meet mine. "I don't know. It's still so unbelievable, I'm not sure how I feel. She's gone. I know that, yet every once in a while I'll have this moment when life seems normal. As if the door will open and Savannah will come breezing in, laughing about this or complaining about that . . ." He let his voice trail away and followed up with a deep sigh. "But then I remember, and it hurts so much it's like I've just lost her all over again."

I touched the back of his hand briefly. I wanted to offer some kind of comfort but didn't want to cross that invisible line between comfort and familiarity. "Have the police turned up any more leads? Do they have any idea who did this?"

He shook his head, and some of the sadness in his expression made way for anger. "They're still saying they have no leads, but what the hell do they need? A signed confession? Anybody with half a brain could figure out who did it."

I don't know why his vehemence surprised me. I'm sure I would have felt the same way if Roger had been killed back when I still loved him. "Who do you think it was?"

"You mean *you* don't know either?" He laughed without humor and slid a cheese Danish from the serving tray onto his plate. "So maybe it's not as obvious as I think. Here I thought Delta was the obvious suspect."

I selected an apricot Danish and a blueberry mini muffin, then speared two pieces of cantaloupe so I could tell myself I'd had a balanced meal. "I'm sure the police are considering her," I assured him, "but I just came from talking to her, and I have to admit I'm not convinced she's guilty."

"Then who else *could* it be?"

I shook my head to say "I don't know" and helped myself to coffee. "Did Savannah ever talk to you about a man named Marshall Ames?"

"Not that I recall. Who is he? Someone you suspect?"

I shook my head again. "I don't know. He's one of the judges in our contest, and Delta was just telling me about some trouble that happened between him and Savannah when they were kids. I wondered if Savannah had ever mentioned him."

Miles looked interested at that. "You're talking about the blond guy with the glasses? What kind of trouble did they have?"

"According to Delta, Marshall had quite a crush on Savannah when they were teenagers." I tossed off a weak smile. "She didn't reciprocate."

"And Delta thinks he's the one who killed my wife?"

I shrugged. He hadn't said anything about the poison, so I could only assume that Jawarski hadn't told him yet. I was tempted to say something, myself. He deserved to know. But Jawarski would skin me if I did, so I kept my mouth shut. At least about that.

"She suggested the possibility," I said, "but I don't know . . . all of that happened so long ago, why would he suddenly freak out about it? Even if he was upset enough to kill her twenty years ago, that kind of anger just doesn't last. I talked to Marshall on Friday night, and he didn't seem upset with Savannah at all."

"Not everything is what it seems," Miles reminded me. "Not everyone is who they appear. Some people make very convincing liars."

I grimaced. "Yeah, and I've known a few. But I just can't believe it of Marshall. Of course, that doesn't mean anything. I've been wrong once or twice in the past."

Miles almost smiled. "Not often though, huh?"

I managed a grin of sorts in return. "Not often."

Sobering again, Miles spent a few seconds picking at his Danish. "Much as I'd like some definitive answers, I have to agree with you about Ames. I saw him talking to Savannah the night before she died, and he certainly didn't seem upset with her."

"You did? When was that? Before the contest or after?"

"Actually, I saw them talking twice. Once outside the

kitchen door at Divinity. I went looking for Savannah for some reason—I don't remember why anymore. She said she'd gone outside for air. Marshall said he'd been having a smoke. I believed them at the time, but now I wonder."

"And the second time?"

"We went to dinner at a restaurant just down the street. He was there. Savannah left our table to go to the ladies' room, and this Ames guy stopped her on her way back."

"Could you hear what they said?"

"No, but I'd swear on my life they weren't arguing. If anything, this Ames guy was a little *too* friendly, if you know what I mean."

"He was flirting with her? In front of you?"

Miles peeled a section of Danish away, but he didn't actually eat. "I wouldn't say flirting, exactly, but he was standing quite close to her. Leaning in, I guess you could say. I noticed it. Even asked her about it when she got back to our table."

Interesting. "And what did she say?"

"Oh, she laughed. Said it was nothing for me to worry about. And, of course, I didn't give it another thought—until you mentioned his name." Miles ran a hand across the stubble on his chin. "Have you told the police about this?"

I shook my head. "No, I haven't had time. I came straight here for a meeting after Delta told me about it."

"You will though, right? I mean, there's no telling what might be important."

He was right, of course. Maybe I couldn't imagine Marshall as a ruthless killer, but that didn't give me the right to withhold information from the police. I'd done that once to protect Wyatt, but it wasn't a habit I wanted to get into. "Of course I'll tell the police," I said. And I had every intention of doing it. Really.

Everything I'd learned about Marshall Ames had me floundering. I still wanted to hold the memorial service, but I wasn't sure Marshall was a good choice, or even an acceptable choice to offer a few words. On the other hand, if I didn't ask him, who could I ask?

I decided to let Miles decide that.

"This brings up another question," I told him. "I'm planning a brief memorial for Savannah when the contest gets started again, and I was thinking of asking Marshall to say a few words. Do you have any objections to that, or would you prefer that I find someone else?"

Miles blinked a couple of times as if he was fighting back tears, pulled a handkerchief from his back pocket, and blew his nose loudly.

He seemed so overcome, I looked away and gave him as much privacy as I could to pull himself together. After a few minutes he cleared his throat and stood. "Sorry about that. I just wasn't expecting anyone here in Paradise to care." He mopped at his eyes and tried to smile. "A memorial service is a wonderful idea. Savannah would be so pleased."

I guess maybe she would have been. "So is it all right if I ask Marshall to speak?"

Miles shook his head slowly. "I guess so. I wish there was someone closer to her who could do it. A real friend. But I guess this is what happens when you stay away from a place for twenty years, huh?"

I polished off the last of my breakfast and reached for a napkin. "I'd be happy to ask someone else, but no one I've talked to has seen or heard from Savannah since high school graduation. If you know of anyone else—"

Miles lifted a miserable gaze to meet mine. "Nobody. To the best of my knowledge, she never even spoke with anyone here except for that one woman."

That set off a buzzer inside my head. "Which woman was that?"

"I don't know her name. Savannah just pointed her out to me the other day. She said that everybody else in town had been glad she was gone, except . . . whoever she was, but that *she* only stayed in touch because she needed something."

I could have sworn my heart stopped beating. "Do you know what she needed?"

Miles shook his head. "Savannah didn't say, but she gave me the impression that whatever it was could cause a lot of trouble for the other woman if it ever came out."

My heart started beating again—a little too rapidly. If I could find someone with a *real* motive, maybe the police would stop being interested in Karen, and maybe my life could get back to normal. "Where were you when Savannah told you about this?"

Miles looked surprised. "Why, we were at your shop. Whoever she was, she was there for the contest."

"Was she a contestant?"

"I don't think so. In fact, I'm almost positive she wasn't competing. Just one of the people there to watch, I guess." His expression grew hopeful. "She was there when everyone was searching for Savannah, too, but I didn't ever catch her name."

"Can you describe her?"

"A lady. Savannah's age. I'll confess, I didn't pay that much attention." He sighed heavily and looked away. "I've been racking my brain, trying to remember anything that might help the police figure out who did this. I'm afraid I'm not coming up with much."

The weariness on his face made me realize how much of his time I'd taken up, but there was still one unanswered question I had to ask. I stood and touched his shoulder briefly. "You're doing fine. Probably better than most of us would do in the same circumstances. This wouldn't be easy, even if you were in your own house, surrounded by family and friends. I'm sure

Delta's not being very supportive. Do you have anyone else? Maybe someone could come and stay with you until this is over?"

Miles shook his head again and looked away. "I know it probably sounds odd, but I prefer to be alone. My family never really approved of my marriage to Savannah. They thought she was too opportunistic." His gaze shifted back to mine. "They didn't know her like I did."

So there *was* family out there. Family who apparently felt about Savannah the way Savannah's family felt about him. Maybe theirs had been one of those marriages where the partners bring out the worst in each other. But why had he told Sloan Williamson that he had no family? It didn't make any sense to me.

"I was under the impression that you didn't have anyone. I don't know why. Did I read that in the paper or something?"

"That's what the paper said, but they obviously got it wrong. I hope the guy who wrote it isn't a friend of yours, but I have to say he's not exactly a world-class reporter."

Sloan isn't a friend, but the tone Miles used put me off a little. Maybe he had been offered a job with a Fortune 500 company, but that didn't make him superior. Of course, I reminded myself, he *was* grieving, and I couldn't expect him to be at his best. "So where is your family?"

"In Gunnison, most of 'em."

"And you're sure you don't want me to call one of them? It might help to have someone who loves you around."

"No. Thanks. I'll be okay once the police catch the killer."

There seemed to be nothing left to say, so I turned to leave.

Miles trailed after me. "Thanks for stopping by, Abby.

It helps to know that I have at least one friend here in Paradise. And thanks for the chocolates you sent over. I don't have much of a sweet tooth, I'm afraid, but Savannah was delighted."

I stopped walking. "Chocolates?"

He nodded and wagged a hand toward one of Divinity's gold-edged two-pound boxes nearly hidden behind a stack of books, file folders, and a digital camera. "It was really very thoughtful of you."

"I'd love to take credit for that," I said, "but I didn't send any chocolates."

The smile slid from his face. "Oh, but I—" He looked from me to the box an back again in confusion. "I just assumed."

"Was there a card?"

"No. Just a message on our phone when we came in that night after the contest. Someone left the candy with the front desk, and I just assumed it was you. I mean, who else would have done it?"

I shrugged as a disturbing thought crossed my mind. It was a long shot, but I had to know. "Do you mind if I take a look?"

"At the candy? Sure. Why not?"

As I reached for the box, I brushed the stack beside it, and a file folder and a stack of documents and letters spilled onto the floor. They looked important, so I bent to pick them up, but Miles beat me to it. "So the candy," he said with a jerk of his head toward the box. "Are you looking for something special?"

I couldn't voice my suspicions aloud, so I shook my head. "Not really—unless there's something special about the selection that might help me remember who ordered it."

I worked off the lid and checked inside, but when I saw that my worst suspicions were confirmed, my heart fell. We'd made up only one box in the combination I found myself looking at. One row of assorted fruit-filled chocolates, one row of almond bark. The middle rows alternated between chocolate caramel, peppermint crunch, and English butter toffee. Somehow, Evie Rice's missing box of chocolates had ended up in Savannah Horne's hotel room. Three of the fruit-filleds were gone, along with several pieces of toffee. The question was, had Evie sent them and pretended they were stolen to divert suspicion away from herself? Or was someone else trying to make Evie look guilty? Whoever sent the candy had taken the box from Divinity somehow—but how? And when?

Besides myself, only two people had access to that room before the candy went missing: Bea and Karen. Karen hadn't set foot in the shop. She'd just been in my apartment. But she could have let herself in to the second-floor meeting room through the back door and down my brand-new back steps.

My heart dropped, and a chill ran up my spine. I would have bet everything I owned that the poison was inside the candy I held.

"So? Do you remember?"

The question snapped my head up and reminded me that Miles was there, waiting for me to say something. My throat was so tight and dry I had trouble getting words out. "I—I'm not sure." I tried to look casual and even slightly bored. "Do you mind if I take this with me? Maybe I can figure out who sent it."

"Sure. Take it. I'm not a big fan of chocolate, so it won't matter to me."

Head reeling, I managed a smile, mumbled something I hoped sounded reasonably intelligent, and let myself out into the hall. I kept my head up and my eyes straight forward while I walked to the elevator, and I clutched the box so tightly I thought my fingers were going to put holes through it, but I couldn't seem to make myself let go.

The answer to Savannah's murder was inside that box. I knew it. I could *feel* it. I didn't say a word to anybody until I was locked safely inside the Jetta, then I pulled out the cell phone and punched Jawarski's number.

Chapter 17

"How long will it take?" I paced nervously along the floor in an unused interrogation room at the police station where I'd been waiting for an hour already. I don't mind admitting that I was getting antsy over the delay and more than eager to see the lab results.

My suit jacket lay abandoned, slung over the back of a chair near the door. I'd kicked off my shoes long before that. And I wished I'd thought to bring along a pair of jeans. The waistband of my skirt was probably creating permanent indentations in my skin.

Jawarski watched me from a chair in front of the two-way mirror. His lips curved at my nervousness, and his gaze strayed occasionally from my face to my legs. I just couldn't tell whether he appreciated the view or merely wondered why I'd exposed them to the world.

"Shouldn't be much longer," he said. "O'Keefe told me he'd put a rush on it."

"Do you think I'm right?"

He patted the seat beside him, waited for me to sit, and

lifted a shoulder. "I don't know. It's possible. Guess we'll find out when the lab results come back."

I'd been pacing, nervous, shaking and sick with dread at the possibilities since I arrived at the police station. Someone had used Divinity to commit murder. Someone had roamed around inside the store without me knowing it. I felt exposed and violated. But Jawarski's little joke actually made me smile. "Yeah, I guess we will."

He looked me over again carefully. Long enough to make me stop shaking with fear and start trembling for another reason entirely. Long enough to make my stomach do a little flip-flop and turn my blood into something resembling melted caramel. Who was he? I suddenly *needed* to know. I don't mean that I was mildly curious, or that I wanted to know more about him. I mean that I needed to know with a desperation that frightened me.

He watched whatever was happening on my face, leaned a little closer, and nudged me with his shoulder. "You okay, kid?"

I nodded without taking my eyes from his. They were deep and blue today, and I wondered what the world looked like from his end of it. "Yeah, I think I am."

"Want to talk about it?"

About what? About his past? About where he came from? Whether or not he'd been married before? What brought him to Paradise? Yes, to all of that and more. But I knew he didn't mean any of that, and what more was there to say about Savannah's death until we knew the truth?

I was terrified that the lab technician would find the poison in the chocolates, and even more afraid that Karen would turn out to be the person responsible. But how could I admit that aloud? Especially to Jawarski?

All I really wanted was to lean into those solid arms of his and lay my head on his shoulder—just for a minute or two.

Or maybe longer.

I shook my head, but it took just about everything I had to make it move in that direction. "What will you do if the poison is inside the chocolates?"

"I guess we'll start interviewing people to find out who had access to the second-floor of your building. We'll probably start with you."

That's what I was afraid of.

He nudged me again, and in spite of the topic we were discussing, the caramel in my veins took another sluggish turn. "Want to tell me about it now?"

I put a little distance between us—not because I wanted to, but because it seemed smart. "What is this, Jawarski? Some new investigative technique?"

I regretted the question the instant it left my mouth. He straightened sharply, and the softness in his eyes cooled and hardened. "No, Abby. It's not. If you'd like to see one, I can oblige. Just in case we find something in the chocolates, why don't you tell me who had access to the second-floor meeting room this week, starting with the day of the contest and moving on."

"Look, I'm sorry. I didn't mean—"

"Don't worry about it," he said, waving away my apology. But the moment was lost, and I regretted opening my big mouth. He stood, stretched, and moved to the other side of the table. "So what do you know about the chocolates?"

Stupid tears welled up in my eyes, but I refused to cry over a man—even Jawarski. "Nothing. They were there when I locked up on Friday night. I didn't go upstairs again until Evie told me the box was missing."

"Who did go up there?"

"I don't know. Nobody could have gone up there between the contest and when Savannah went missing. There wasn't time, and the store was locked."

"Somebody must have."

"Yeah. I know."

"Did anybody stick around late or show up early the next day?"

I sat back in my chair and tried to think back that far. It had only been a few days, but it felt like a year. "Karen and Evie left before a lot of people. Meena Driggs was one of the last contestants to leave. Marshall Ames stuck around and helped me wash up. As a matter of fact, you might want to talk to Marshall. I don't think he's involved in Savannah's death, and I'm sure he didn't go upstairs that night, but Delta says that he had a big old grudge against Savannah because of the way she treated him back in school, and Faith Bond mentioned a conversation between him and Savannah about some letter."

Now that I'd gotten started, pieces were beginning to snap into place. "Miles was telling me about some lady who was at the contest and also came in to search. According to him, Savannah knew something that would mean big trouble for this woman if it ever got out."

Jawarski seemed interested in that. "Any idea who she is, or what it was?"

"No, but he saw her twice and recognized her the second time, so maybe he'll see her again somewhere and point her out." I propped my feet on an empty chair. "It can't be Evie Rice. He'd know who she was. She's been at Divinity at least two times that we know of. Maybe she'll come again for the memorial service."

Jawarski's big head bobbed up and his eyes locked on mine. "What memorial service?"

"I thought maybe I should do something before the contest gets under way again. You know—a few minutes to remember Savannah and maybe get somebody to say a good word about her."

"I guess that sounds all right."

"What are you doing, Jawarski? Giving me permission?" Sometimes I just can't keep my mouth shut, even when I know I should.

His expression became even more brittle. "Have you got a problem with me, Ms. Shaw? If so, would you kindly get it off your chest?"

"How could I have a problem with you, Jawarski? I don't know the first thing about you." I told myself to stop. This wasn't going to accomplish anything. But I'm not good at taking advice—not even my own. "I don't know who you are, I don't know where you came from, and I don't know what you're doing here. I don't even know what *we* are. Friends? Acquaintances? More? Less? Are we dating, or am I just one of the guys you happen to share a pizza with now and then?" And there they were, emotions I hadn't even let myself acknowledge, much less process, dropped onto the table between us like a big, shapeless mound of taffy.

I hated that I felt that way. It seemed needy and weak, and I hated even more that I'd let it all slip out like that.

Jawarski's expression didn't change. He just stared at me for a long, uncomfortable moment. "What do you want to know?"

"Nothing. Everything." I shot to my feet and turned my back on him so I wouldn't have to look into his eyes. "I don't know. I'm tired. I'm confused. I'm stuck in the middle of another suspicious death, and now it looks like whoever did this may have used Divinity in some way. I've managed to make everybody around me angry, and I don't even know what I'm saying."

He stood, and I had one brief moment of hope that he'd leave, then another even stronger moment of fear that he would. He stepped up behind me, put his hands on my shoulders, and very gently turned me around to face him.

Was I still breathing? I couldn't be sure.

Was *he*? Yes, I could feel the gentle in and out of his

breath, smell a hint of garlic from his lunch, feel the warmth on my cheek.

I stood there, unmoving, unthinking, as he leaned in close and touched his lips to mine. It was over before my heart could beat twice, but it sucked my breath away.

He straightened. Grinned down at me. "Hope that answers at least one of your questions. Now sit down. Rest for a few minutes. I'll be back when I have the lab report." He stepped into the hallway and started to shut the door. "Want a Coke or something?"

I think I nodded. I can't be sure. He was gone before I could figure it out.

He came back twenty minutes later, two Cokes clutched in one hand (that answered *that* question) and a couple of official-looking documents in the other. "You were right," he said as he handed me one of the cans. "The candy was laced with amitriptyline." He held up the papers, a visual reference.

"So what's that?"

"A drug commonly known as Elavil. Antianxiety drug used to treat depressive neurosis, manic-depression, and anxiety associated with depression." He opened a folder and ran his finger along the page. "According to this, an overdose would cause tremors, seizures, changes in blood pressure, irregular heartbeat, heart attack, heart failure, stroke, and death, to name just a few. Reaction time, fifteen to forty minutes. Somebody meant business."

"And they put that into a box of Divinity candy? What if the wrong person had gotten into it? One of the housekeeping staff or a kid? What if Miles had offered a piece to someone who came to visit him?" I shuddered at the thought.

"Then we might have had an even bigger tragedy on our hands. We're lucky this stuff was contained." Jawarski drummed his fingers on the tabletop and read over the report again. "Whoever it was, they must have injected the poison"—he glanced at me and tossed off a lopsided grin—"unless *you* poured it into the whole batch."

The time I'd spent alone had helped me get a grip on myself, so I grinned back. "Sorry, Jawarski. I know that would make your job easier, but I can't help you. You're going to have to look for a crazed madman running around Paradise with a loaded syringe."

"That's what I was afraid of." He tossed the file folder onto the table and cracked open his Coke. "She was poisoned, but it was the impact of the car that killed her. The question now is, why poison her and then run her down?"

"Maybe we're not talking about just one person," I suggested.

One eyebrow arched high. "You think this is like *Murder On the Orient Express*? Everybody did it?"

I shook my head. "I don't know. It's a thought, that's all." I stood and stretched, trying to make this latest news make sense. "There are plenty of people with motive to kill her. Anybody could have walked into the hotel and left a package for a guest. What about the car? Do you have any leads on who stole it?"

Jawarski skimmed a disapproving glance over me, and I knew we were straying into questionable territory. I could talk about the poison because the candy came from Divinity, but asking about the car meant I was getting involved in the investigation. "Not yet," he said slowly, "but we're working on it. I'll be going out to the Old Miner's Inn in a few minutes to talk with some of the staff there. I'm still hoping we can find somebody somewhere who saw or heard something that morning."

"Do you have any idea when the car was taken? Could it have been taken the night before?"

Jawarski shook his head. "The guys who rented it were out late. They say they pulled in from Aspen at about two in the morning. Unless they're lying—and they have no reason to—the car was stolen between then and five thirty."

"So we're looking for someone who had motive and opportunity and who also has no alibi for the middle of the night." I shrugged and put my feet up again. "Piece of cake, Jawarski. I don't know why you're still sitting here. What are you going to do? Run through the phone book starting with A?"

"Pretty much."

"I could make it easier on you. I could put together that memorial service, and we could use that to see if we can draw the killer out."

The smile slipped from his face. "Hold on a second, Abby. Let's get one thing straight. There is no *we*. Not when we're talking about the investigation. I appreciate you bringing me the evidence. I appreciate the fact that you figured out the poison was in that box of chocolates, and I appreciate the fact that you're willing to help, but there's no way in hell I'm going to let you get any more involved than that."

"*Let* me?" This time, my eyebrow arched.

"This isn't a man-woman thing," he snarled. "This is a police-civilian thing."

I shrugged to show that he had me on that one, but I wasn't ready to cave in completely. "Let me put it this way, Jawarski. I'm *going* to hold a memorial service. When I do, I'm going to make sure Miles Horne is there." I dropped my feet to the floor and leaned closer. "When he is, he might just be able to identify the woman Savannah told him about. If he does, wouldn't you like to be there?"

"You think your mystery woman is the killer?"

"I have no idea, but it's a possibility, isn't it? Even if she's not, I'll bet the killer *will* be there. At the very least, the poisoner will almost certainly be there. Unless, of course, the poisoning was a random act of violence that just *happened* to occur on the same day as the hit-and-run accident that killed a universally disliked woman who just returned to her hometown after a protracted absence." I pretended to consider for a moment, then nodded. "Could happen."

"Yeah." Jawarski actually smiled. "In Abby-world." He sobered again and locked eyes with me. "Put together your memorial service, and I'll be there—unless I already have the murderer in custody. But you do *one thing* to put yourself in jeopardy or hinder this investigation, and I'll—" He broke off as if he'd just confused himself and stood so he could tower over me. I guess it made him feel better. "Just don't do anything to interfere with my investigation, Abby, that's all."

"I wouldn't dream of it. Believe it or not, I really don't have any desire to become involved. But finding that candy . . . well, that made it personal somehow. Somebody used *me*—my store, at least, to kill another human being. I hate that."

"It had nothing to do with you or with the store. The candy was handy—"

"You don't know that. In fact, the candy *wasn't* handy. Someone had to get up to the second floor where Evie left that box of chocolates—and who would have known it was even there? It's not something that somebody just stumbled across between one night and the next morning."

"Maybe somebody else noticed that Evie left it behind."

"That's possible, of course, but they couldn't have gotten into the store—unless my security is a whole lot worse than I think it is."

Jawarski put a hand over mine. "We'll figure it out, Abby. Try not to worry. Something will occur to you, or we'll find a clue that will lead us in the right direction."

I tried to look reassured, but no matter how hard I thought or what angle I looked at the problem from, I was pretty sure I already had the answer. Only one person could have gotten to that candy.

My cousin. The one on antidepressant medication.

Chapter 18

I called Elizabeth from my cell phone as I left the police station and asked if she'd mind watching the store for another hour. She agreed, so I drove down Twelve Peaks to Marshall's restaurant. He'd been at Divinity with me the night of the contest. Maybe he'd seen something or someone I hadn't.

Gigi is a chic place, streamlined, modern, all wood and metal and straight lines. I parked—not an easy task with the lunch crowd already gathering—and followed a laughing group of sunburned skiers toward the door. Already, the line of customers waiting to be seated filled the foyer and spilled out onto the sidewalk.

It was probably the worst time in the world to talk with Marshall, but I didn't turn away. This was too important, and if I was wrong and he *did* have something to do with Savannah's death, catching him now might make it harder for him to script his answers.

I jostled my way through the crowd, ignoring the grumbles of protest in my wake, and gave my name to the young woman at the front desk before leaning into a corner to wait.

Delta's dry coffee cake and the Danish had long since worn off, and the scents of beef and garlic, the sight of tray after tray laden with meals being delivered to nearby tables made my stomach cramp with hunger. I'd have given almost anything for time enough to enjoy a leisurely lunch, but I'd already been away from Divinity all morning. No matter how willing Elizabeth was to help, I didn't feel right leaving her there much longer.

Just when I was starting to think that I was wasting my time, Marshall swooped into the waiting area. He wore an obviously expensive black suit and white shirt, the top two buttons of which had been carelessly (or care*fully*) left open. His pale hair and glasses gave him a slightly boyish look, and I wondered again why I hadn't noticed him in high school. Maybe he was just a late bloomer.

"Sorry to have kept you waiting," he said. "We're shorthanded in the kitchen, so today's rush has been even more hectic than usual."

"I completely understand. Actually, I probably shouldn't even bother you. I'll just take two minutes if you can spare them."

With a grin, Marshall nodded toward the dining area. "I can give you five, but you'll have to walk with me."

"Deal."

"So what brings you out in the middle of the day?" he asked over his shoulder as we walked. "Is there some kind of trouble?"

"Not really. I came by to ask a favor."

He paused at a table and spent a few seconds chatting with the customers sitting there, then resumed his journey. "Favor huh? Such as . . .?"

Now that I was there, it suddenly seemed crass to talk about Savannah's death in front of all those people. But I'd chosen the time and place, and I was too worried about

Karen to wait for the crowd to leave. "I want to have a short memorial service before we start the contest again. It won't be anything fancy, but I do think we should acknowledge what's happened."

Without breaking stride, Marshall picked a drooping petal from the rose centerpiece on an empty table and dropped it into his pocket. "That's probably a good idea. What did you have in mind?"

"Nothing too complicated. Some quiet music and a few nice words about Savannah ought to do it."

Marshall stopped walking abruptly. "Don't tell me. That's why you're here? To ask me to do it?"

I nodded. "Delta refuses to, Miles is too upset, and there's no one else."

Marshall nodded slowly. "Sad, isn't it, to think that somebody could live their entire life in such a way that nobody would want to speak for them at the end?"

"Sad doesn't even come close to touching on it," I said. "Does that mean you won't do it?"

Marshall sidestepped a waiter and tugged me out of the way with him. "I don't think I'm the right person for the job, Abby. I mean, it's not as if Savannah and I were close. I hardly knew her."

"Really? But I understood you actually saw quite a bit of one another when you were younger."

He smiled, but it was a token gesture. "Who told you that?"

"Delta mentioned that your mothers were friends." I wondered how much more to say, but curiosity has always been a powerful motivator where I'm concerned—far more powerful than discretion. "She also said that you were pretty much head-over-heels for Savannah back then."

Marshall looked away and took a few seconds to compose himself. "Delta's exaggerating," he said when he looked back at me. There was a challenge in his expression—as if he dared me not to believe him. "I probably had a little crush on her for a while, but it wasn't anything serious."

"She told me about the senior prom."

The smile on his face grew cold. "I think maybe we ought to finish this conversation in my office. Do you mind?"

I followed him through the kitchen, down a brightly lit and freshly scrubbed corridor, and into a small, windowless office at the back of the restaurant. "I can just imagine what Delta told you," he said when we'd both settled into chairs, "but it wasn't nearly as bad as she makes it sound."

"She said that you asked Savannah to the prom, and that Savannah stood you up."

He nodded slowly. "That part's true enough, but I'm hardly the only kid in the world who's ever been left holding a corsage."

Or the only girl left waiting for one. "She also said that Savannah was pretty mean to you about it afterward."

He gave another slow, wary nod. "She was, but that was Savannah. You must know that."

Well, yeah. "So you didn't hate her?"

"Lord no!" He leaned back in his chair and linked his hands behind his head. "I'm not going to tell you we were best friends or anything, but she didn't destroy me—at least not for long."

Frankly, I was glad to hear it.

"When you think about it," he went on, "I shouldn't have been surprised that she stood me up. She was way out of my league, and I was dreaming to think she could ever reciprocate my feelings. I'm just too damn thick-skulled. At least, that's what my mother used to always tell me."

"She knew how you felt about Savannah?"

He nodded. "And discouraged me from feeling it. She always said that Savannah would be way more trouble to some poor man than she'd be worth. Maybe she was right. I don't know. It was a long time ago, and I didn't like listening to her."

"Were you upset when you found out she was back in town?"

He lowered his hands slowly. "Not a bit, but why all the questions? Don't tell me you think *I'm* the one who ran her down."

I laughed uncomfortably. "Of course not. I'm still just trying to find someone who'd be willing to say something positive about her at the memorial."

A slow smile spread across his face, and I had the distinct impression he was trying to decide whether to believe me or not. That was only fair. I wasn't sure I believed myself. "I guess I could help you out," he said at last. "If you don't think that having one of the judges memorialize a dead contestant would taint the contest or add fuel to Evie's fire."

"I'm sure Evie will try to make something of it," I admitted, "but I think we should all put our differences aside and just be adult about this."

Marshall laughed. "I think you're talking to the wrong crowd. But if that's what you want, I'll come up with something."

"Thanks. I appreciate it."

He made to stand, so I asked my next question quickly. "The night of the contest, when you stayed late to help me clean up, did you notice anyone else around? Anyone coming downstairs after I did, maybe?"

He sank back into his seat and shook his head. "No, why? Something wrong?"

"Maybe. I just came from the police department. The autopsy report on Savannah is back, and it appears she was poisoned before she was hit by the car. The poison was in a box of chocolates from Divinity."

Marshall's eyes flew wide behind his horn-rims. "No kidding? So she was poisoned?"

"Yeah, but it was the car that killed her."

"Can you trace the box of chocolates?"

"Unfortunately, yes. I've made up only one box like that. It's the box Evie Rice won for second place that night."

"Well, then, there you go!"

"I wish it were that simple. Evie left the candy behind. It was still upstairs when I shut off the lights and came to the kitchen. That's when I ran into you. You didn't see anyone else in the building? No one who ran down the front stairs a minute before I came down?"

"No. But couldn't somebody have gotten it later?"

"Not much later. She had to have ingested the poison between the time I saw the box upstairs, and when she went jogging at five thirty the next morning, and she probably ate some of the candy about half an hour before she died."

Marshall looked surprised. "She was eating chocolate at five o'clock in the morning?"

"Some people do that, you know."

He laughed and tugged off his glasses to clean them. His face seemed weak without them, and I suddenly remembered the nerd he used to be. "Yeah, I guess they do. I really wish I could help you, Abby. I just can't. I didn't see anything."

I was surprised to discover that I liked Marshall, and I didn't want to find that he was hiding anything. But, of course, he must be. Otherwise, I wouldn't have to ask my next question. "What about the letter?"

His eyes grew wide, but he hid them behind his glasses and spent a few seconds stuffing his handkerchief into his pocket before he looked at me. "What letter?"

"The one you were talking to Savannah about on Friday afternoon."

"I don't know what you're talking about."

But he did. I could see it in his eyes. That made me a trifle nervous. "Look, I'm sure it's no big deal. It's just that you told me on Friday night that you barely knew Savannah and you hadn't seen her in years. But somebody overheard the two of you talking about some letter on Friday afternoon—before the contest. So what was that all about?"

His entire demeanor changed. "If you think I killed her, you couldn't be more wrong."

I believed him. More than that, I realized right then and there that he still loved her. "Had you been writing to her?"

"No."

"How did you know where to find her?"

"I didn't. I never wrote to her."

"Then who did? Whose letter was it?"

Marshall sat back hard in his chair and let out a deep breath. "It wasn't mine, that's all I can tell you."

"Come on, Marshall. A woman is dead. A woman I think you cared a whole lot about. Are you really going to hide something that might bring her killer to justice?"

"The letter has nothing to do with the murder."

"How do you know?"

"Because Faith wouldn't—" he broke off suddenly and shot to his feet. "Forget I said that."

Not likely, bud. "Are you talking about Faith Bond?"

"Forget it, Abby. I'm not saying anything else." He took two jerky steps toward the door and yanked it open. "You have to leave. They need me out in the house."

I shrugged and stood. "Okay. Fine. I'll just go ask her, then."

"No! You can't do that. You just can't. It doesn't have

anything to do with Savannah's murder, I swear. Promise me you won't talk to her."

"Then tell me what you know."

He looked miserable—like a kid who's gone wild in a candy store for several hours. His face was flushed, his eyes a little unfocused. I really thought he might throw up. Head hanging, he shut the door and sat down again. "All right. It was my letter."

"To Savannah?"

He shook his head. "From her."

I gave him a look. "A love letter?"

"No. Nothing like that."

"Like what, then?"

He mopped his face with one hand and kept going right around to the back of his neck. "Savannah wrote to me a long time ago to tell me about something. It was something she did for another person."

"Something she did for Faith?"

He nodded.

"Are you going to tell me what it was?"

He stood again, apparently too agitated to sit still. "She let Faith stay with her for a few weeks once."

"When she lived here?" So, what was the big deal about that?

Marshall paced in the space behind his desk. "No. It was after she left here. A year after, maybe less."

"How did Faith know where to find her?"

"I told her. She came to me. Said she needed to reach Savannah, and she figured I'd know where she was."

"And you did."

Marshall actually looked sheepish. "What can I say? I was a kid obsessed. Anyway, I told Faith where she was."

"So? That's nothing to get all worked up over."

"It is if she lied. She told Noah she was going to stay with her aunt."

I didn't know Faith's husband well, but I couldn't understand why that would be a problem. Noah was a little stiff. Some might even call him self-righteous. Okay . . . *many* might call him self-righteous. And judgmental. But I still didn't get it. "So she took off for a couple of weeks. It's not as if they were married back then. What did she do, have an affair or something?"

"No! It wasn't anything like that."

"Then what was it?"

"She was pregnant, okay? Nobody's supposed to know, and the only reason I do is because Savannah told me."

I could only stare at him for a long time. "Faith Bond was unmarried and pregnant?"

"Yeah, but Abby, you can't tell anybody—especially not the police. You know how Noah is. It would kill Faith to have this come out after all this time."

"Yeah. Maybe. But I'm confused. She went to stay with Savannah for a couple of weeks. When? At the beginning? Before she delivered?" I did a quick mental calculation, but the numbers just didn't add up right. None of the Bond kids were old enough. "Did she give the baby up for adoption or something?"

He shook his head. "She lost it."

"So are you saying that Noah doesn't know about the baby?"

"Good God, no. Can you imagine how he'd treat Faith if he did?"

I didn't even want to try. "You realize this gives Faith a motive for killing Savannah."

"But she didn't do it. She couldn't have."

"How do you know? Can you give her an alibi?"

He started to say something but cut himself off and shook his head. "No, but you know Faith. There's no way she'd harm another human being."

"Maybe not under normal circumstances," I agreed, "but people will do strange things if they're pushed hard enough." I stood and crossed to the door. "One more thing," I said with my hand on the door. "Is Faith by any chance taking an antidepressant?"

The question seemed to catch Marshall off guard. "I have no idea," he said. "You'd have to ask her."

Thanks. I had every intention of doing just that.

Chapter 19

The latest word, straight from Faith Bond's neighbor (who I found outside knocking icicles from her eaves) was that Faith had gone over to the church for a meeting of the women's group or the food pantry . . . or something. The neighbor didn't seem to know, and it didn't really matter. Faith, bless her heart, spent more time at the church than she did at her own house. At least that's what her neighbor said.

The Shepherd of the Hills Church is one of the first things you see when you approach Paradise from the north. It started life many years ago a small wooden building with enough room for about six rows of pews. It's been added onto and expanded so many times it's become large and sprawling and, frankly, ugly.

I parked in the nearly empty parking lot (an oddity for Paradise in January) and let myself in through the front door where the blast of warm air knocked me back half a step. I stripped off my coat and listened for sounds of life. I could hear voices, but it took a few minutes to track them to the gymnasium that doubles as a cultural hall.

Two rows of metal chairs had been formed into a semicircle near the stage, and Faith stood in front of a group of concerned-looking citizens, her hands clutched together in front of her and a look of supreme benevolence on her face. "I handed the woman that box of food," she said, her voice almost whisper quiet, "and then I hugged her. I simply couldn't help it. When I did, I was overcome by the oneness of the human race. We were the same, she and I, in spite of the obvious outward differences." She took a deep breath, and when she went on her voice sounded stronger. "*This* is what I want to bring to Paradise. This recognition that *we are all one* as God intended us to be."

A woman at the far edge of the circle burst into spontaneous applause, and most of the group joined in. I had nothing against the sentiment, but I wondered what a handful of determined Christians could to do turn the rest of us into human beings who really loved one another instead of injecting each other's chocolates with poison.

Faith noticed me standing there and waved me forward eagerly. I didn't want to join in, but I felt a little foolish backing out. I picked up a folding chair from a stack at the back of the room, tiptoed across the polished wooden floor, and set myself up a little behind the rest of the group. No sense giving the impression that I was there to experience oneness or anything.

The meeting lasted about twenty minutes longer, a mishmash of stories about experiences helping others and rah-rah about how much better Paradise was going to be once this committee started passing out Bibles and bread to people. I could see it happening. Just not in this lifetime.

I had to stay through all the post-meeting chitchat, smiling pleasantly through introductions to people I planned never to see again. Only when everybody had scurried to escape the dreaded task of putting away the chairs did I get a chance to talk with Faith alone.

"It's lovely to see you here," she said as the door closed behind the last conscientious avoider. "I had no idea you were interested in helping the community."

"I'm not." I realized how that sounded and laughed. "I mean, I *am*, but that's not why I'm here."

She moved a couple of books from a table to the stage and grabbed the end of the table as if she wanted to move it, too. "That sounds mysterious. Why *are* you here?"

I shifted to the other end so I could help. "I'd like to talk to you, but this might not be the best place."

"Oh? Now *that* sounds ominous." She laughed, and we rotated the table onto its side so we could break down the legs. "What do you want to talk about?"

"Savannah Horne."

The smile left her face as if I'd flipped a switch. "What about her?"

Is there any smooth way to tell someone you know a secret they've kept hidden for two decades? I couldn't find one. "I know that you went to stay with her for a while after we graduated from high school. I want to know more about that."

She forced a laugh, but it rang hollow. "Who on earth told you I did that?"

"How many people know?"

"Nobody knows. It never happened."

Mmm-hmmm. Just take a look at your face, honey, the truth is written all over it. "You were pregnant," I said. "You turned to Savannah for help."

The table slipped from her fingers, and the crash reverberated around the gym. "You're wrong."

"You turned to Savannah for help," I said again. "You left town and went to stay with her. Why her? Were you friends?"

Faith tossed a frantic glance over her shoulder, no doubt making sure nobody was listening. "I was never friends with Savannah."

"So why did you go stay with her?"

"I didn't."

"Apparently, there's a letter in Savannah's handwriting that says you did."

The color drained from her face, and I even think her knees buckled. "Where?"

I didn't want to put Marshall's butt on the line. What if she *was* the killer? So I tried to be clever. "It's around."

"You've seen it?"

"I have." Okay, not true, but when you're talking to a frightened woman who may or may not be injecting chocolates with lethal substances, it seems smart to appear strong. From a strictly selfish standpoint, if she believed there were two of us who knew, there was a fifty-fifty chance she wouldn't come after me first. Not that I wanted to put Marshall in danger—

She looked so shaken, I didn't know if she was about to faint or lunge at me with a syringe full of Elavil. "Don't tell me *that* was the letter they were talking about."

I didn't.

"So then you know." She looked at me with eyes filled with such pain, my heart constricted.

The correct, clever response to this is to agree that yes, you know everything. I nodded, thinking that might give her that impression without actually making me lie inside a house of worship. "Why did you go to Savannah for help?"

She shook her head and glanced toward the doors again. "You're right. I can't talk about this here. We're going to have to go somewhere else."

I'm not the I-told-you-so type, so I kept my mouth shut and followed her outside. But that's where I took charge. There's no way I was going to climb into her car and let her drive me somewhere. I don't have nougat for brains.

Neither of us said anything until we were seat-belted in place and I had the heater running. Since I had control of the wheel, I asked, "Is there anyplace in particular you'd like to go?"

She shook her head, then leaned against the seat and stared out the window. "Anywhere, as long as it's away from here. If Noah ever hears about this, he'll leave me."

"Why?" The question popped out before I could think about it. A reason occurred to me half a breath later. "Was it his baby?"

Her head jerked up and shot around to glare at me. "Of course it was his baby. He's the only man I've ever been with."

"So what was the problem? You didn't think he'd support you?"

"In having an abortion?" A cold, hard laugh escaped her lips. "Is that a serious question?"

An abortion? That's what this was about? I tried to hide my surprise, but I must have failed miserably, because I watched the realization dawn in Faith's eyes. "You *didn't* know, did you?" She leaned back against the seat, and weariness dragged at her expression.

I decided to be honest. "No, I didn't know. Not everything." I pulled out of the parking lot and drove for a while, giving her time to collect her thoughts. Doing the same for myself. "So you realized you were pregnant, and you went to Savannah because you believed she could help you. Did she ever threaten to tell Noah?"

From the corner of my eye, I saw Faith nod. "She never came right out and said that she would tell, but it was always there. You know what Savannah was like. She could look so innocent, and all the time she was ramming the knife into your chest."

"When she came back to town you must have been terrified."

"I was. I didn't know what she'd do."

"What did she do?"

"Nothing. I waited and waited for her to call me, or to

do something, or say something, or hint that she was going to talk to Noah. She never did. Finally, I couldn't stand it anymore, so I decided to talk to her. That's why I came to Divinity the night of the contest."

"And did you talk to her?"

She nodded. "Yes, but not there. I waited until she slipped outside for something, and then I followed her. But she was in the middle of an argument with somebody, so I left."

That got my attention. "Do you know who she was arguing with?"

"A man. That's all I know. They were in the shadows, and I couldn't see him."

"Could you hear what they said?"

"I heard a little. Savannah was really upset, I can tell you that. Whoever it was had lied to her, and whatever he'd said, it must have been a doozy." Faith's thin lips curved at the edges. "I heard him ask her not to tell anyone. He said they could figure out a way around it. She told him that she was going to let everyone know what he'd done, and that he'd wish he was dead by the time Jason got through with him."

I took my eyes from the road for a second. "*Jason*? Who's Jason?"

"I don't know. I didn't stick around to find out."

"That's all you heard?"

"That's it. I was just relieved that she had something else besides me and my stupid mistake to think about. I thought maybe, if whatever this was kept her busy, she wouldn't have time to tell Noah what I'd done."

I parked on the side of the road and shifted in my seat so I could look at her. Since I had to ask, I asked straight out. "Did you kill her?"

"No."

"Do you know who did?"

"No, but I'd give anything if I did." She looked down

at her hands in her lap and twisted her fingers together nervously. "I would have, though. I really think I would have, and I hate knowing that about myself."

I felt this strange need to console her. "I don't know, Faith. If push had come to shove—"

She cut me off. "No, Abby, I would have. I mean, I killed my own child, so what's to stop me from killing someone else?"

I hated seeing her so consumed with guilt. I'm torn on the issue, myself, so I wasn't entirely convinced that she was doomed to burn in hell for what she'd done, and I wanted to believe that twenty years of marriage would count for something. "Noah would forgive you, you know. Maybe he wouldn't understand, but he'd forgive you."

"No. He wouldn't." Her eyes brimmed with unshed tears, and the misery on her face made my stomach knot. "You don't know Noah. He doesn't believe in abortion for *any* reason."

"But he loves you. You've been together since you were kids. You've got twenty years of shared history."

"Yeah, and all but two of them based on a lie. He'd leave me, Abby. I know he would, but I couldn't bear it. I don't think I could survive without him." She gave in to the tears and buried her face in her hands. Sobs racked her body, but I didn't try to stop her. Meaningless platitudes wouldn't help, and I had nothing else to offer.

Would she survive without Noah? Of course she would—but I was convinced she wouldn't want to.

I put the car in gear again and drove some more while Faith cried until she had no more tears left. She had twenty years of guilt, fear, and anger stored up inside, so it took a while. I thought a lot as I drove—about Savannah, about the past, about Delta and Karen and Evie and Marshall and Faith.

Faith certainly had a strong motive for doing away

with Savannah, but I simply didn't believe that this distraught woman with the red, puffy face had injected poison into a box of candy or run Savannah down with a car. Maybe I was wrong. I might live to regret my decision. But I chose to believe her.

So that left who? Karen? All the signs kept pointing to her, but I couldn't believe it. I wouldn't believe it.

How about Delta? She certainly didn't seem to be grieving over her sister's death, but had she killed her to save half of a small inheritance? It seemed unlikely.

Evie didn't have a strong motive, either. Unless she was completely off her rocker, why would she kill Savannah over a few hundred dollars in prize money and a plaque from a candy-making contest? Even taking in her fierce competitive streak, it didn't make sense.

Marshall? His motive seemed weakest of all—unless there was something else going on that I didn't know about. Could he have been the man arguing with Savannah the night of the contest? He'd been one of the judges, in plain view all night. I didn't think he'd had time to slip outside for an argument with anybody. He'd barely had time to escape to the men's room.

So then, who? And who was Jason?

Maybe finding the answer to that question was the key to everything else. Find out who Jason was, and I'd have a better idea who Savannah argued with outside Divinity. I might even know who killed her.

In a perfect world, I could have run down the mysterious Jason in an afternoon. Unfortunately, I live in Paradise, where I had a candy shop to run and a sister-in-law waiting impatiently for me to do just that.

Since I hadn't eaten more than a few bites all day, I pulled through the drive-through window at Arby's, loaded up on a roast beef sandwich with a side of stuffed jalapeños and sucked down a Coke on the way back to Divinity.

Elizabeth was waiting for me when I parked, her brown eyes snapping and her mouth pulled down in a frown. "You said you'd be gone another hour," she shouted at me across the parking strip. "You've been gone half the day."

"I know. I'm sorry." I gathered empty containers, the agreement I'd signed with Ruth Cohen a lifetime ago, and my lunch from the car and hurried toward her. "I was at the police station when I called you, and everything got just unbelievably complicated." I dumped everything onto the counter and turned back to face her. "I'm really sorry."

"You should be." She brushed a lock of reddish blonde hair from her forehead. "I was supposed to take Dana to the doctor at one. Did you forget that?"

I had, but I didn't want to admit it. I already had too many points on the "bad aunt" tally. "Did you cancel?"

"Oh yeah. Late. We're going to have to pay for the visit anyway, that's office policy."

"I'll pay for it," I offered quickly. "It's my fault."

"Okay. I'll let you." Elizabeth slipped the strap of her purse over her shoulder. "So I guess this means you're playing private detective again."

That hurt. The last time I "played" private detective, I'd saved her husband from a murder charge. Okay, the fact that he's also my brother played a minor role in my decision to clear him, but still . . .

"I'm not *playing* anything," I told her. "I was there in Miles's room. I saw a box of chocolates. He thanked me for them, but I knew I'd never sent them. His wife just happened to be murdered a few days ago, so what did you want me to do? Pretend I didn't notice anything out of the ordinary?"

Elizabeth leaned against the counter and crossed one foot over the other. "No, but you don't need to put yourself in dangerous situations, either. Believe it or not, we all love you, Abby. We finally have you back after all these years. None of us want to see you get hurt."

Her words were so unexpected, she caught me by complete surprise. I blinked. Felt the burn in my eyes and the lump swelling in my throat. I knew I wasn't going to be able to outrun this one, but I was sure going to try. I tried to clear my throat, but the lump refused to budge, and I had trouble getting words out around it. "I—I don't—"

My sister-in-law pushed away from the counter and closed the distance between us. Before I knew what she intended, she pulled me into a tight hug and spoke softly into my ear. "You're surprised we feel that way?"

I could only nod. Tears were splashing out of my eyes onto her shoulder, and I couldn't do anything to stop them. My nose stuffed up almost at once, but I couldn't change that, either. I stood there, sniffling and splashing and feeling quite pathetic until Elizabeth released me.

Okay, even after she released me, I felt pretty pathetic. But I also felt something I hadn't felt in a long time—not since Aunt Grace died, I guess. Maybe even since I was a kid. I just couldn't wrap my mind around it.

"You're Wyatt's kid sister," Elizabeth said as she pulled away and stepped back. "For all his bluff and bluster, he adores you. Surely you know that."

I half nodded, half shook my head. Frankly, I didn't know what I knew and what I didn't. Our last encounter hadn't left me feeling especially adored, but we were talking about Wyatt, not Mr. Rogers. "But the kids—"

"Are thrilled to have you living here now. Look who Dana ran to when she was mad at me. She knows you're her dad's soft spot."

That startled a few coherent words out of me. "I didn't even know Wyatt *had* a soft spot."

"Yeah? Well he does, kid, and you're it. So please, I know you're curious, and I know you can't help yourself, but please, for *us,* be careful what you do?"

How could I say no to that? I'm not *stupid*. "Of course I will."

And right that minute, I had every intention of honoring that promise.

Chapter 20

I don't mind telling you, the afternoon crawled by. Business was brisk, but I couldn't stop running over all the conversations I'd had over the past few days and wondering what I'd missed. Someone had gone to the second floor of Divinity when no one else was around and swiped that box of candy. Someone had injected that candy with Elavil. Someone had stolen a car. And someone had run Savannah down while she jogged along the side of the road.

And that someone was probably a person I'd talked to face-to-face in the past seventy-two hours or so. That made me a little nervous.

When I wasn't thinking about the murder, I was remembering the conversation with Elizabeth and trying to reconcile what she'd told me with the feelings I'd been carrying around for the past few years.

With all that going on, I had a tough time concentrating on business. I took a large order over the phone from a woman in Mississippi who'd driven through Paradise during the summer and had fallen in love with our strawberry bonbons. I answered a long-overdue e-mail to a web designer I'd been consulting with about taking Divinity online, ran a duster across the displays in the east room, refilled several baskets of candy that were dangerously depleted, and restocked the glass display case by the cash register.

I locked the front door at seven and pulled out the vacuum, but I *still* couldn't stop thinking about Savannah's murder.

I know I told Miles that some people eat chocolate at five o'clock in the morning, and I'm sure some do, but it did seem strange that Savannah would pop out of bed that early, down two or three rich chocolates, and then head out to jog. But that's precisely what she'd done. If she'd eaten the candy the night before, she would have died in the hotel room from the Elavil overdose. She *must* have eaten the candy within half an hour of leaving the hotel.

And then what?

She must have gone out through one of the hotel's back doors, across the parking lot, and along the service road. It seemed like an odd choice to me, especially at that time of day right after a heavy snowstorm, but I couldn't argue with the facts, and the fact is, that's where I found her. And the fact was that she'd been poisoned by someone and then struck by a car and killed.

I finished vacuuming the small east room and moved into the large room. Someone who knew she was going to be jogging at that time of day? Or someone who chanced along the road and hit her accidentally? That was my biggest sticking point.

If her death was the result of a random hit-and-run, we might never figure out who did it. But if it was someone who went gunning for her—so to speak—then how narrow did that make the playing field?

I couldn't imagine how Karen would know that Savannah went jogging at five thirty every morning unless she'd overheard either Savannah or Miles say so. Ditto for Evie—unless Savannah had shouted something about her jogging habits while they were scrapping over the contest. Marshall spoke with Savannah on Friday night, so he *could* have known, although it seemed unlikely that Savannah would have thought to discuss her exercise routine while her mind was on Faith Bond and emotional blackmail.

Finished vacuuming, I dragged out the mop and pail. So who did that leave? Delta, of course. She was Savannah's sister, and even though the two hadn't seen each other in years, she certainly could have known her sister's habits. And Miles. Of course he knew.

I ran over the timeline a dozen times while I worked. Miles said that Savannah left to go jogging, as she always did, at five thirty the morning she died. She never came back. Before she left, she ate a handful of Elavil-laced chocolates. Sometime between eleven o'clock at night and five in the morning, somebody got into the upstairs room at Divinity and then delivered the chocolates, anonymously, to the Summit Lodge. I tried to remember what time Miles said they arrived, but it couldn't have been earlier than ten thirty or eleven, because that's when I'd seen the box sitting upstairs—and I *knew* there was only one box like that.

Unless, of course, Karen made up another one without telling me.

Ugly thought. Not even worthy of a moment's time.

I shook it off and carried the dirty water to the utility sink.

Okay. Square one. Begin again. Just like following one of Aunt Grace's recipes. What had she told me? I remembered standing in the middle of the kitchen surrounded by what seemed to me a hundred ingredients, tools, molds, liquid colors, and flavorings. It had felt to me like uncontrolled chaos, but Grace had smiled at my confusion.

Follow the steps, Abby. There's order in the chaos if you know where to look.

Unfortunately, I doubted that even Aunt Grace could make order out of the chaos in my mind. I wondered what she would have done if she'd been in my shoes—but it was a foolish question. I knew what she would have done.

I put away the cleaning supplies and moved into the kitchen, where I pulled condensed milk, coconut, strawberry gelatin, almonds, almond extract, and confectioners' sugar from the supply cupboard. I found the red and green food coloring in the drawer, and heavy cream in the refrigerator. Working methodically, I measured the cream, coconut, gelatin, almonds, and almond extract into a bowl and spent a long, long time getting the mixture the exact shade of red I wanted.

Remembering the way Aunt Grace's gnarled hands had looked as she worked, I covered the bowl and put it into the refrigerator to chill. Strangely, I *did* feel a little more grounded.

I had an hour to wait, so I filled a glass with ice and carried it to the table with a Diet Pepsi.

Square one.

Miles said—

My thoughts broke off abruptly mid-swallow. *Miles said.*

Miles said Savannah went jogging that morning. Miles said Savannah went jogging every morning. Miles said the candy was delivered to the front desk of the lodge.

Miles *said* a whole lot of things, but how many of them were actually true?

I nearly choked as I tried to get down that swallow of Pepsi. My fingers tingled, and the hair on my neck stood up. Thoughts boiled around together in my head, crashing in on one another as I tried to work through the story without relying on what Miles said.

Maybe Savannah hadn't gone jogging that morning. Maybe she didn't always go jogging at five thirty. But that still didn't explain who stole the candy from the second-floor meeting room. It must have been taken between eleven o'clock on Friday and . . . sometime on Saturday morning.

Too wired to sit, I stood and began to pace. Who was here? Me. Max. Karen.

And Miles.

I stopped walking so abruptly I nearly tripped myself. Miles was here that morning. Miles, who sat at my table and worried about his wife and ate my chocolate French toast and lied through his teeth to me. I knew that now as surely as I knew my own name.

Miles was the last person to see Savannah alive. She could have left the hotel room at any time. With her husband. Without him. Alive. Drugged. He was also the only one of the suspects I hadn't watched fairly carefully the night of the contest. I hadn't thought twice about him, in fact. He could have slipped outside at any time for an argument with Savannah.

Maybe I hadn't thought of him then, but I sure did now. I thought about how he'd looked that morning. About his odd request that I tell him all about Savannah's squabbles with her sister. Details he claimed not to know about his wife's life. How he'd engaged me in conversation for a while and then suddenly changed his mind.

And why?

To establish an alibi. Nobody ever suspected him because he was with me, drinking coffee and playing the concerned husband. I wanted to throw up. My stomach pitched, and bile rose in my throat. My hands grew clammy and tears—of anger this time—burned my eyes.

Leaving the kitchen a mess, I grabbed my coat and

keys and hurried outside. Jawarski needed to hear about this, and I wanted to tell him in person. I figured I'd be a lot more convincing in person.

The first few flakes of a new snowstorm were falling as I stepped outside. Normally, I'd stand there in the silence and enjoy the moment, but with a killer on the loose and the possibility that I knew his identity, it just didn't seem like a good idea.

I was halfway inside the car when I realized that I hadn't fed Max or let him outside in hours. Swearing at the delay, I bounded up the steps, clipped on Max's leash, and did my best to ignore the toilet brush, bra, shredded roll of paper towels, sock, shoe, and VCR remote scattered around the living room floor.

Back inside ten minutes later, I filled his food and water dishes, thought about taking him with me, but decided to let him stay behind and eat. So he chewed another shoe or ten. So what?

I promised to come back soon, locked the door, and hurried downstairs again. It occurred to me, as I pressed the unlock button on my keychain remote, that I still had a couple of missing puzzle pieces. I had no idea why Miles might have wanted Savannah dead, and I still couldn't connect the mysterious Jason to any of the puzzle in front of me. Who was he? How did he fit into all of this, and why would Miles care if he was upset?

It still didn't make much sense to me.

"Abby?"

An unfamiliar male voice brought me around on the balls of my feet. When I saw Miles walking toward me, his hands inside the pockets of his overcoat, a bland smile on his face, my heart stopped.

"Miles," I said. And then my brain stopped working. Or my mouth did. Whichever it was, I couldn't seem to figure out what to say next. I tried a smile. It froze on my face for reasons that had nothing to do with the weather.

"Going somewhere? Did I catch you at a bad time?"

Oh, the responses that raced through my head! "Actually, yes," I said, struggling desperately to sound normal. "I was just on my way to—" *to where?* Not to the police station, that's for sure. "—meet a friend. For dinner."

"Ah." He tilted his head back and gave a jerky nod, all without taking his eyes from my face. I didn't take that as a good sign. "Having dinner out?"

"Yeah." Inwardly, I felt myself recoiling, but I tried not to let him see my reaction. I could hear Max whining on the other side of my apartment door and cursed myself for not bringing him with me.

"Someplace special?"

I shook my head and scrambled for an answer. "No, not really," I said. "I'm going to my cousin's house, in fact." I pretended to glance at my watch and sidled closer to the car. "Wish I had time to talk, but I'm running late as it is."

"The cousin who killed my wife?"

"She didn't kill Savannah," I said automatically.

"I think she did. It's no secret she hated Savannah."

"A lot of people did," I reminded him. *Including you, apparently.*

"Yeah, but not everybody caught their husband hanging all over her." He moved closer quickly—too quickly for me to react. Wearing a thin, frightening smile, he leaned against my car door and folded his arms. "It was a shame, that. Don't you think? All those years as a devoted husband, and then along comes Savannah, and the whole thing goes right out the window."

I toyed with the idea of mollifying him, but he'd already blocked my best escape route, and I didn't think I stood much of a chance, anyway. Since flight looked like a slim option, maybe my best option was fight—at least until I could call attention to my plight.

"The only trouble with that story is, I don't believe that's what happened."

"And yet it did."

"I know Sergio and Savannah had a drink together, but that's all."

Miles pretended to be surprised. "Oh come on, Abby. I gave you credit for being smarter than that. That was never all when it came to Savannah."

He was wrong. I knew it. He'd planned this somehow, coming to town and stirring up all the old controversies Savannah had been embroiled in to create a long list of suspects. Pretending he knew nothing about Savannah's past here had all been part of his plan. But I had no way of proving any of this, and I wasn't even sure I'd get the chance.

He was too cold. Too much in control. Every move, every word had been calculated, maybe months before. My only chance was to take the control out of his hands, but how should I do *that*? If I goaded him into losing control, I might very well meet the same fate Savannah had. Then again, that was probably going to happen if I let him move through the orderly steps in his head. "Did it bother you?" I asked. "The way Savannah played up to other men?"

"Bother me?" He barked a laugh. "Why would that bother *me*? I'm the one she came home to. I'm the one she chose to be with. I gave her everything: money, position, respect. I took her from being the town tramp to being one of the most respected women in Colorado. She would *never* have left me."

The slight emphasis on that word made me wonder if she'd been about to walk out on him. Maybe I was just reading too much into what he'd said. I could feel my heart pounding in my head, my pulse thrumming in every pore. "Did she know it was you, Miles?"

"Me?"

"Behind the wheel of the car."

He laughed again, and the sound rumbled like distant thunder in the space between us. "You think you're clever, don't you, Abby? You're going to trick me into confessing my sins." He pushed away from the car and moved in close. I could smell onion on his breath and grease. Burgers, I thought irrationally. He'd had fast food for dinner. "But I'm afraid I'm going to have to disappoint you. I have nothing to confess."

Focus, I told myself sharply. *Find a weakness. Figure out what makes him vulnerable.* He'd been so cool through this whole ordeal. He'd played his part perfectly. How was I going to find a chink in his armor?

His eyes bored into mine. I didn't want to look, but I couldn't turn away. "I think," he said, his voice soft and oddly compelling, "I think you're going to have to disappoint your cousin. Poor thing. First her husband. Now you. I hope it's not enough to send her completely round the bend."

He was looking for *my* weaknesses. I could see it in his eyes. I reached into the bag of tricks I'd used during my courtroom days and pulled out my game face. Completely impassive and unrattled. "Oh, I think she'd survive. But I don't have any intention of changing my plans. Now, if you'll excuse me."

I tried to slip past him, but he blocked my path and clutched my arm with a monster grip.

Instinctively, I tried to pull away, but he was too strong. That wasn't the way to fight him anyway. I'd had self-defense courses. I knew what to do, if I could only remember.

"Come on. We'll take my car."

No. I realized I hadn't spoken aloud, so I tried again. "No, Miles."

"I'm afraid you don't have a choice."

Think!

He started walking, dragging me along behind him. I tried going limp, hoping that dropping with my full weight might break his grip. It didn't seem to make any difference. I couldn't get close enough to jam my heel into his instep or attempt any of the clever thumb-to-eye—or was it thumb-to-throat—maneuvers that were chugging around in my head. The only chance I had was to outsmart him.

I was in serious, *serious* trouble.

"You were good," I told him, still making efforts to resist. "It took us a while to figure out what you'd done." We drew even with the kitchen door of Divinity, and I tried again to break free.

No luck.

He didn't seem to notice the "we" I'd purposely thrown at him, so I tried again. "We know you did it. We know you injected the poison into the candy, and we know you ran Savannah down while she was jogging. The only thing we can't figure out is why you did it. I mean," I said, trying in vain to latch onto a streetlamp with my free arm, "why both? The poison would have worked, wouldn't it?"

He didn't say a word. What was *wrong* with him? I thought all villains were supposed to leap at the chance to share their brilliance.

"So what went wrong? Didn't it take effect fast enough? Were you so determined to get rid of her that you couldn't wait?"

Something happened then, but I couldn't put my finger on what it was. A slight shifting of his shoulder? The faint hesitation over his next step? Whatever it was, I decided I'd touched a nerve. At least, I hoped I had. "You really needed to get rid of her, didn't you?"

We reached the street, and though I didn't think it was possible for his grip to get any tighter, somehow he managed it. Through clenched teeth bared by a cold smile, he said, "Just shut up. We're going to walk to my car, and we're going to look happy about it. A couple of friends going to dinner together."

"I'm not your friend."

He pretended to be hurt. "Oh, but you *were*."

Yeah. Just stamp Sucker on my forehead. But I was letting him retain control. I couldn't do that. "I felt sorry for you. That's completely different."

"It's good enough for me."

Okay. Another about-face. He'd be a harder nut to crack than Faith had been, but I was desperate. "I saw Savannah that night. Did she tell you?" And just in case he didn't catch my meaning, "You two were arguing just down the street there, by the candle shop."

That finally got his attention. I felt a definite shift in his stride. "You're bluffing."

"Am I? We talked afterward. You came up the street in this direction. She and I walked the other way. I guess I don't need to tell you what we talked about."

A muscle in his jaw jumped, but then he smiled again. "If that were true, why haven't the police been knocking on my door?"

Okay. Hold on. That was almost a confession. My stomach turned over, and the blood moved like sludge through my veins. My brain fell all over itself trying to find something to say. "You're not the only one who can wait for something," I said, and I prayed frantically that the raw fear in my throat didn't come out in my voice. "Things aren't always the way they appear, Miles. You know that better than anybody."

I didn't know exactly what I'd said, but he stopped walking abruptly and gripped both of my arms tightly. Pulling me close, he looked me hard in the eyes. "And I won't let anyone ruin what I've worked so hard to create. Now *shut up*."

He was rattled. I just didn't know if that was a good

thing or a bad one. "But she was going to ruin it, wasn't she? She told me all about it. She was going to tell Jason."

White-hot anger exploded behind his eyes. I wanted to duck and close my eyes, but I forced myself not to move. I wasn't even sure I wanted to breathe. "She would have destroyed it all. Everything. And why? Because she suddenly developed principles?"

He let go of one arm, but the circulation was nearly cut off in the other. He began to walk quickly now. His stride was longer than mine, and I instinctively tried to match my pace to keep up with him before I remembered that I couldn't let him take me anywhere if I wanted to stay alive.

Prospector Street was teeming with people window-shopping, laughing together, and talking. No one had noticed us yet, but obviously something had to change.

Miles had some momentum going, and I'd never be able to match his strength, but one thing I've always been good at is being a loudmouth. I pulled back hard and turned myself into dead weight, opening my mouth and letting out a bellow at the same time. "Help! Somebody help me!"

It took a couple of steps for him to react to my screaming, and sure enough, just like all those self-defense experts had promised, he let go of me as if my arm had burned his hand. I fell on the icy sidewalk, *hard*! My leg twisted under me, and pain tore through my knee and shot through my hip.

I ignored it and kept shouting.

Miles backed away, slowly at first, then faster. I saw him reach into his pockets, pull out his keys, and dart toward his BMW. "Don't let him get away," I shouted, but either the stunned people staring at me couldn't understand what I said, or nobody wanted to get involved.

I tried lurching to my feet so I could go after him, but

I couldn't get my leg to hold me up, and the excruciating pain made me almost sick to my stomach. I fell back to the sidewalk and lay there while people, finally beginning to realize that I was hurt, gathered around and asked if I was all right.

And while they worried about me, a cold-blooded killer drove off into the night.

Chapter 21

I don't know who finally helped me to my feet, but someone did. I remember handing over my keys to a woman, who unlocked Divinity's front door, and I remember someone else bringing me the phone so I could call Jawarski.

Naturally, he didn't pick up. I left a message on his voice mail and tried his number at the station. When I rang through to his voice mail there, I tried one more call to the main switchboard.

I tried very hard to make the good old boy who answered understand that he had an emergency on his hands, but good old boys will be good old boys, and I've never met one of them who will take a "little woman" seriously. By the time I realized I wasn't going to get anywhere with him, my head was throbbing, and my knee felt twice its normal size.

Someone brought me some ibuprofen and a swallow of water. I took both gratefully and tried to think what to do. I couldn't drive. My knee would never stand the clutch work. But I couldn't just sit here while Miles got away. I needed someone willing to drive me, which meant I needed someone adventurous enough to do something dangerous, but not stupid enough to get us killed.

I did the only thing a girl *can* do under such circumstances—I called my big brother.

Wyatt arrived within minutes, mainly because since his separation, he doesn't have anything else to do in the evenings. He left his big red Dodge truck idling at the curb and burst inside like Divinity was the OK Corral. The way his mustache swagged down across his lip told me he was ready to take care of business, which was exactly what I wanted.

He scooped me up like I was nothing more than a twenty-five-pound bag of sugar, waited impatiently while my rescuers filed out the front door, and locked up behind us, then settled me in the truck's cab and hoisted himself inside. "Any ideas which way he's gone?"

I could smell oil—the kind you use to clean guns—which didn't surprise me. Wyatt's been working at Harrison Rifle Works since he was a kid. He's not the type to head into trouble without a gun. While guns usually terrify me, tonight Wyatt's obsession gave me an odd sort of comfort.

In answer to his question, I shook my head. "I have no idea. He might have gone back to the hotel so he can clear out, but he might have done his clearing out before he came after me."

Wyatt slid the truck into gear and jerked his head toward me. "You got that cell phone of yours on you? Call 'em. See if he's still registered."

Brilliant. I should have thought of that myself. The irrational thought that I'd have to pay forty-nine cents for directory assistance shows just how jumbled my thoughts were right then.

Now that Wyatt was with me, the reality of what had happened finally started to hit. My fingers trembled as I pushed the numbers on my phone pad, but I only needed to push three of them. I went through all the rigamarole to get connected, asked for the front desk, and found myself talking to a soft-spoken man who identified himself as Shane.

I did my best to sound normal while Wyatt, the truck, and I careened around a corner and my head began to pound. "Could you tell me if Miles Horne is still registered there?"

Shane clicked around on the keyboard for a minute before he answered. "I'm sorry. It looks like Mr. Horne has checked out already. Is there something else I can help you with?"

I could feel Wyatt watching me, so I shook my head once to give him the answer. At the speed we were traveling, I wanted his eyes on the road. Turning my attention back to Shane, I said, "Do you have any idea how long ago he checked out?"

"Only a few minutes, and I believe he's gone back upstairs for his things."

I think I remembered to thank him before I disconnected. I'm not sure. "He's still there," I told Wyatt.

He planted his foot even harder on the accelerator. "You know what this guy drives?"

"A black BMW."

He rolled a look at me. "Great. I'll bet there's only one of *those* at the Summit Lodge. Hell, Abby, I'll bet that description fits half the cars up there."

"Yeah, but there will only be one with a murderer frantically tossing his suitcases into it."

Wyatt grinned as we shot through the intersection with Doc Holliday Road. "You have a point." He nodded toward the lodge, its honey-colored wood gleaming in the glow of a thousand clear lights against the backdrop of the mountains. "I don't know how you feel, but this might be a good time to talk strategy."

"I just want to keep him from getting away until the police can get here."

"And how do you plan to do that?"

"I don't know. I guess that's going to depend on what he does. If he tries to make a run for it in his car, we can head him off. If he takes off on foot," I said with a grin, "you can run after him."

"And if he pulls a gun?"

I hadn't thought of that. "We duck?"

Wyatt chuckled and rolled through the stop sign at the corner of Grandview and Lucky Strike. "Great plan, sis. I feel a whole lot better now."

Maybe he didn't, but I did. It had been years since the two of us had gone off on an adventure together. Of course, those adventures had been a far cry from trying to beard a killer in his den, but almost anything seemed safer with Wyatt at my side.

I called both of Jawarski's numbers again. Ran into his voice mail both times. In frustration, I suggested something I would never have considered under normal circumstances. "What about Nate? Is he on duty?"

Wyatt shook his head. "I don't think so. He's watching the Nuggets, I think. Want to call him?"

I'd sooner chew tree bark, but I didn't want Wyatt talking on the phone and driving like a maniac at the same time. Wyatt gave me the number, I dialed, and a few seconds later I had Nate Svboda on the phone.

"Nate? It's Abby Shaw. I'm with Wyatt and we have a—"

"Wyatt? What the hell's he doin'? Tell him I thought he was comin' over here to watch the game with me."

"Nate, listen, we have a prob—"

"Tell him it's his turn to bring the beer, too. Sumbitch left me holdin' the tab last time."

"Nate, *listen*! I know who killed Savannah Horne. Wyatt and I are—"

"You what? Listen, Abby, this habit you're gettin' into is a dangerous one. You're gonna—"

"Nate!" I shouted, "would you shut up for a minute and listen to me? Miles Horne killed his wife. He's already checked out of his hotel, and if you don't do something right now, he's going to get away."

"Miles Horne? What makes you think that?"

"He confessed!" Not entirely true, but you can't be subtle with Nate. "You've got to get up to the Summit Lodge right now. Wyatt and I are on our way—"

"He confessed? Are you sure? What exactly did he say?"

"Nate! Listen to me! He's going to get away if you don't do something."

"Well, now, just who did he confess to?"

"To me. To me while he was trying to kill me. Nate! Get off the couch, turn off the game, and *do* something!"

I hadn't even finished my sentence when Wyatt grabbed the phone from me. He snarled, "Do it, Nate," into the phone, and passed it back to me. Nate was already gone before I could get the phone to my ear.

While I was relieved to know that the police would be coming, it galled me for all the obvious reasons that Nate wouldn't move until Wyatt told him to. But none of that mattered now.

We reached the turnoff to Summit Lodge, and I clutched the dashboard with both hands while Wyatt cranked the wheel and sent us shooting onto the single paved lane. The drive wound through the trees and opened into the parking lot where row upon row of cars sat lifeless and ghostlike in the pale moonlight.

Wyatt looked to me for direction. I started to shrug, but a flash of inspiration stopped me. "The back parking lot," I said. "He's going to sneak out using the service road."

Wyatt gunned the engine, and we careened around the side of the lodge, fishtailing as we hit patches of black ice neither of us could see. Now that we were this close, my heart drummed in my ears, and I could feel myself shrinking in apprehension. The memory of Miles's cold, empty eyes left me feeling small and frightened.

I was torn between praying that we hadn't missed him and hoping that we had. Let the police find him. Let them take him into custody. They had all kinds of equipment I didn't have—like guns. That thought got me reaching under the seat for one of Wyatt's rifles.

He caught my movement and asked, "What are you looking for?"

"You've got a rifle under here, don't you? I thought I'd pull it out—just in case."

"What are you going to do with it?" he asked as we pulled into the back parking lot. "You haven't touched a rifle in twenty years."

"Yeah, but all things considered, I think I can remember what to do." I stared at the three long rows of cars stretching the length of the lodge, but I couldn't see any signs of life. Had we missed him? I couldn't find the rifle, so I scooted as far as my knee would let me and tried again to get my hand under the seat. "Where is it?"

Wyatt slid a glance at me. "Not here."

I sat bolt upright and gaped at him. "What do you mean, not here?"

"I mean, it's not here. I took it out when Dana was with me the other day." His mustache tilted to one side as he shrugged with his mouth. "What can I say? She hates it."

"And you never put it back? Why didn't you grab it before you came to the store?"

"I wasn't home, and I didn't *go* home because I got the impression from you that we were in a bit of a hurry."

Groaning in frustration, I leaned back against the seat. "*Now* what?"

"Now we try to find the bastard." Wyatt downshifted, and we moved slowly along the first row. I was not only looking for a black BMW but carefully checking each car we passed to make sure Miles wasn't about to steal another one.

We'd just started moving along the second row when a door in the middle of the lodge opened, and Miles stepped out into the night, suitcases in hand.

My breath caught, and I froze solid.

Wyatt was a little more clearheaded. He drove on as if we were two ordinary people doing ordinary things, backed into the first empty parking spot we came to, killed his headlights, and turned off the ignition.

Miles waited, head tilted, watching to see what we'd do next.

Muttering instructions for me to sit tight, Wyatt jumped out of the truck and began talking in a normal tone of voice. I don't know how he managed to sound so natural. My voice was locked up tight.

"Where'd you leave it?" Wyatt asked. He paused, pretended to get an answer from me, and then threw his arms in the air just like Dad does when he's irritated with Mom. "Honest to Pete, Meg. That means I've gotta go all the way back inside and *all the way* upstairs, all because you can't be bothered to pay attention."

He was good, I'll grant him that. Playing an insensitive jerk came quite naturally to him.

He slammed the door of the truck and plunged across the parking lot toward Miles. I could see him pretending to talk to himself, grumbling the whole way.

Miles must have decided Wyatt posed no threat because he picked up his bags and started away from the door. I don't know what Wyatt said to him. I was much too far away to hear. But Miles's head snapped up, and he stopped walking abruptly.

He turned to face Wyatt, and for the first time all evening I wondered how smart I'd been to bring my brother along.

I watched Miles walk slowly back toward my brother, and that empty, hard feeling took hold of my stomach again. Images flashed through my mind—those eyes, that sneer, the mocking smile—and the fear that had held me captive while I was with Miles earlier came back full force.

I spent about two minutes hoping the police would arrive before things got out of hand, but when I saw Miles lunge at Wyatt, I knew we didn't have time to wait. I hesitated half a heartbeat over whether to call Jawarski again or do something myself. But Jawarski could be anywhere, and I was here. That cut the debate short. I'd dragged Wyatt into this, I couldn't leave him alone over there.

Trying to ignore the searing pain in my knee and the tendrils of fire that were shooting up and down my leg, I hauled myself inch by inch across the truck's seat until I was behind the wheel. Thankfully, Wyatt had left the keys in the ignition. The only problem now was working the clutch with a leg that couldn't stand even the slightest pressure.

Gritting my teeth, I pressed the clutch as hard as I could. A cold sweat broke out on my face, and the muscles in my leg trembled as I cranked the engine to life. *Just get it into first gear,* I told myself. That's all I had to do.

Comforted by the solid purr of the engine, I worked the gearshift into place, pressed the accelerator, and slowly lifted my foot from the clutch. At least, I tried for slowly. My knee had reached its limit. The truck bucked and snorted, bolting out of the parking space with all the grace of a rodeo bull.

The engine nearly died, so I forced my foot onto the clutch again and, nearly crying now, finally got the truck running smoothly. In the sweep of headlights, I saw Miles land a solid right hook and Wyatt stagger backward, nearly losing his balance.

Wyatt probably had two inches on Miles and maybe twenty pounds, but Miles was crazy. That made up for a lot. I'd hurt my knee too badly to shift into second, so I got as much speed as I could out of first and finally pulled onto the row where Wyatt and Miles were fighting.

Miles must have realized that I was coming to help, because he bolted, weaving through the rows of cars until he came to a black BMW hidden in the shadow of the trees. He was inside and behind the wheel in a second, and his headlights flared to life.

I pulled up next to Wyatt and shouted, "Get in."

He mopped blood from his temple with the back of his hand. "Move over, I'll drive."

"Are you crazy? There's no time for that; he's getting away. Just get in."

He didn't argue, but it didn't take long for either of us to figure out that he should have. I didn't know which was worse—the engine revving higher and higher or Wyatt shouting at me to shift, shift, *shift*!

"I can't," I shouted back as I watched Miles's taillights disappear on the service road. "My leg."

Wyatt gaped at me—one whole second of blessed silence—before he started in again. "Then why in the hell didn't you let me drive?" he demanded, and even in the dim light of the truck, I could tell that his face was mottled with anger.

"Quit yelling at me and help!"

"How?"

"Get on the floor. Push the clutch for me." I could feel another argument coming, so I headed him off. "Come on, Wyatt, he's already too far ahead of us. Just do it."

I couldn't hear what he said as he slid to the floor and reached around my feet, and I was pretty sure I didn't want to. I focused instead on keeping the truck from sliding into the trees as we jounced along the rutted, ice-covered road. "Shift!" he shouted, and I did. A few seconds later, we repeated the process, and before long we were humming along in fourth gear. Another complicated maneuver later, we were in four-wheel drive, and Wyatt hoisted himself onto the seat again.

Only it wasn't as smooth as it sounds. I gripped the wheel so hard, my knuckles were probably white, and my fingers were losing feeling. Every now and then, I caught the reflection of Miles's taillights through the trees, but he had a big head start, and even with four-wheel drive I wasn't sure we could catch him.

"Call Nate," I snapped. "Tell him what's happened and find out where he is."

"Watch the—"

"I can *drive*," I shouted, cutting him off. "Make the phone call."

Glowering, Wyatt punched buttons while I steered past the spot where Savannah had died. I averted my eyes. Looking at it would have made the danger we were facing all too real, I guess. With my heart still in my throat, I steered through a series of S-shaped curves, and when we came out on the other end, I saw the BMW nosed into a snowbank, driver's door open. I couldn't see Miles anywhere.

I slammed on the brakes, and the truck went into a skid. I wrenched the wheel into the direction of the skid while Wyatt, by some miracle, managed not to scream at me. At the last second, the truck pulled out of its death slide, and I missed the BMW with inches to spare. Without the clutch depressed, the engine coughed and died.

Wyatt was out of the truck like a shot. He checked out the BMW to be sure Miles wasn't inside, shouted at me to stay where I was—as if I had a choice—and set off into the trees. In the sudden eerie silence, I felt alone and way too vulnerable. I reached across the seat to shut Wyatt's door. It closed with a satisfying click, but the effort wrenched my knee, and bright colors flashed in front of my eyes as the pain flamed again.

I dropped to the seat and lay there, breathing hard and trying to regain control. From outside, the muffled sound of footsteps reached me a split second before the driver's door opened.

"Why Abby," Miles said, his voice deceptively mild, "What a surprise. I guess this means you want to have dinner together after all."

Chapter 22

Miles didn't give me a chance to answer, he just leaned into the truck and shoved me aside like a rag doll. I scrambled for the door handle, but he had the truck moving before I could reach it. The movement threw me off balance, and the pain in my leg brought tears to my eyes.

Miles grabbed the back of my coat and hauled me onto the seat beside him. He kept one steel arm around my shoulders, pulling me in close so I couldn't move. I could hear sirens in the distance, but they weren't close enough to do me any good. I wondered where Wyatt was. Had Miles hurt him, or had he just beat him back to the truck? I couldn't let myself ask. It would only add to the power Miles was enjoying. So I consoled myself with the belief that if Miles *had* hurt Wyatt, he'd be bragging about it.

"I should have known better than to come back to this place," Miles said, jerking the wheel hard to bring us around a sharp curve in the road. "Nothing but bad things ever happened here."

The pain sliced through my leg with such fury it sucked my breath away, but it seemed like a good idea to keep him talking. "When were you ever here?"

"Doesn't matter, does it? I'm never coming back."

I hoped not, but not for the reasons he had in mind. My mind raced as I tried to figure out a way to save myself. I had no doubt he'd kill me if he got the chance, so I had to keep him from getting that chance.

But how?

My knee throbbed and burned, and he had me pinned against him so tightly, I couldn't move my arms. The only thing I could possibly use as a weapon was the window scraper on the seat behind my neck, and I couldn't even get to that. I cursed Wyatt a thousand different ways for leaving his rifle at home.

When I realized that I couldn't hear the sirens anymore, the tiny thread of hope I'd been holding onto snapped. I was on my own. "You'll never get away," I heard myself say.

He laughed. "Sure I will. You're going to help me."

Over my dead body!

That I would even think something like that under the circumstances told me I was in big trouble. "At least tell me why. What did Savannah do?"

He took his eyes from the road for a split second. "I thought you knew everything."

"I do. Most of it, anyway."

But I hadn't fooled him. His face puckered for a second, then he laughed as if I'd just told him a great joke. "You *were* bluffing. I knew it."

"Not completely." Everything had happened so quickly in front of the store, I was having trouble remembering what he'd said. "I know that Savannah was going to leave you," I told him. "And I know that she was planning to bring you down. She was going to tell Jason, remember? I know about that."

"She would never have told Jason. She wanted that job in New York as much as I did."

Now we were getting somewhere. "I don't know," I said, trying to sound relaxed and unafraid. "I think she would have. She was talking about staying here in Paradise, you know."

"Stupid bitch!" His face contorted, and his grip tightened around me. "She'd have gone crazy after two days."

Better than ending up dead. "So she was going to tell Jason, and that would have destroyed your chances in New York."

"In New York?" He laughed, but there was no humor in the sound. "If she'd told Jason about that file she put together, she'd have destroyed my *life*. And hers with it. That's the part she didn't understand. And for what? Huh? Everybody embellishes, don't they?"

Everybody embellishes? Maybe I was crazy, but I couldn't imagine Savannah getting worked up over a little embellishing. Not worked up enough to document everything in a file. I thought about the folder I'd knocked over in the hotel room. Was that it? Is that why Miles had started watching me so carefully? I'd seen the file and I'd taken the chocolates, and he'd seen both of those actions as a threat to his safety.

"Savannah obviously thought that what you did was a little more serious than stretching the truth," I said. It was a guess, but judging from the direction we seemed to be going, not really a long shot.

"I did what I had to do."

Yeah. We all think that.

"So where did you get the Elavil? Was it hers?"

He actually seemed pleased that I'd asked. "Naw, it's my sister's." His speech was changing, becoming less polished. "She's so damn dumb, she never did figure out what happened to it. Thought she'd thrown it away in the trash. Damn things cost her a fortune every month, and she's that careless."

We reached the end of the service road and pulled out onto Hillside Avenue. Unfortunately, there's not much along Hillside in that area of town. Lamps on the golf course, deserted at night, created spills of light at regular intervals, but nobody was going to help me, and we both knew it. I had to do something quickly. Miles would get rid of me before we got near people again.

Find a weapon, I ordered myself. *Find something. Anything.* But Wyatt kept his truck immaculate. I couldn't even find a straw from a fast-food drive-through on the seat. "So why poison Savannah and then hit her with the car?" I asked, "Why not just let the Elavil do its job?"

Miles seemed rattled for the first time all night. "Because it wasn't *doing* its job."

"It might have if you'd just waited."

"For what? For her to call for help?" I don't know what he had planned, but he seemed to make a spur-of-the-moment decision, veering off the road into the golf course parking lot. This was it. Now or never. I could save myself or end up a statistic.

He skidded to a stop in front of the clubhouse, and I waited breathlessly for him to let go of me. He'd have to at some point, if only for a second. I'd have to be ready to make my move.

But I was wrong. He left the truck running and dragged me behind him as he jumped from the seat. Frantic to save myself, I grabbed the steering wheel and held on with both hands. He was strong, but despair can work miracles. I created just enough resistance to loosen his grip, which gave me a split second to slither away from him. I was lying across the seat again with my head near the open door, so I used the only weapon I had.

Frantic to stay alive, I sank my teeth into the soft

flesh of his wrist and bit as hard as I could. He let out a roar of pain, but that only made me more determined. It meant I had a chance.

He jerked his arm away, and I thought he might pull my teeth out with it, but I managed to hang on. But only for one breath. With a bellow of rage, he hit me across the side of the face hard enough to make my nose bleed. Pain lanced through my temple, cheek, and jaw, but I refused to let go.

I turned loose of the steering wheel, but only so I could lay my hand across the horn. The noise echoed in the emptiness around us, and I prayed that Wyatt would hear it—that Wyatt *could* hear it.

Miles hit me again. This time, the pain seemed dull and far away. My bite loosened. There wasn't anything I could do to stop it. Miles grabbed my arm and hauled me out of the truck. I knew my knee hurt, and my leg wouldn't support my weight, but that pain, too, seemed almost disconnected from me somehow.

As my hand left the steering wheel, the horn stopped honking, and silence settled around us again. Miles took a couple of steps, but even if I'd wanted to keep up with him, my leg simply wouldn't let me. I sank to the ground, aware of a sickening pop and a burning sensation I hoped I'd be around to feel later.

Miles whipped back around and stared down at me. His eyes were glazed, his face contorted with fury. "Get up."

"I can't, Miles. My knee—"

"I don't care about your knee. *Get up.*" He jerked on my arm and moved me a couple of inches along the pavement. Just as I'd suspected, the more control he lost over the situation, the more vulnerable he seemed. "Get up, or I'll kill you right where we stand."

I had no doubt of that. This was it. I had to find a way to save myself, or I was going to die. One sharp image—

a maneuver I'd learned during a long-ago self-defense course—flashed through my head, and I knew it was the only chance I had. I held one hand up, beseeching. "Help me, Miles. I can't get up by myself."

He hesitated for so long, I thought he might refuse. Then, slowly, he reached for my hand.

I grabbed him by the upper arm and, using every bit of strength I had, pulled him toward me. He staggered, lost his balance, and landed on his knees beside me. While I still had the advantage, I wrapped my hands around his head and pressed on his eyes, hard, with my thumbs.

He reared back, dragging me upright as he went. In the distance, I caught the flash of light through the trees, and I knew help was on its way. Just a few minutes more. I had to hang on until them.

I pressed harder, refusing to let myself worry about the damage I might be doing. Let him sue me. That was the least of my worries.

Again he jerked back sharply, and this time I let go. Roaring in pain, he covered his eyes with his hands. I was too desperate to care about how much I hurt, and somehow managed to find solid footing with my good leg. My other leg was on fire as I pushed to my feet and hopped back to the truck. My face throbbed, but I got myself into the truck's cab and locked both doors. Exhausted, weeping with relief and fear, I leaned onto the horn and sent up my distress signal again.

As the horn blared into the silent winter night, my heart ached for Savannah. I'd suffered a horrible betrayal at my ex-husband's hands, but it didn't even begin to compare to what Miles had done to Savannah. She had to have known that Miles wanted her dead. Even if only for a minute, the hurt must have been more intense than anything I could imagine.

Even Savannah had deserved better than that.

Chapter 23

A week later, I sat behind a white-clothed table in the second-floor meeting room at Divinity. Wyatt, who had emerged from the forest that night just in time to see his truck and his baby sister disappearing around the bend, had carted me upstairs for the contest. Jawarski was there to make sure I got to my apartment when the judging was all over.

He caught me watching him, and concern creased his face. "You okay?"

Nearly dying can make even the most stoic kind of woman get a little emotional. I blinked rapidly, nodded, and readjusted my leg on its cushion of pillows. I'd only been wearing it a few days, but the leg brace the doctor had prescribed was driving me crazy. "I'm fine, just annoyed that I have to sit here, that's all."

Jawarski grinned and pulled up a chair so he could sit beside me. "Keep this in mind next time there's a murderer running loose in Paradise."

Like this was all *my* fault. "How 'bout you answer the

phone next time there's a murderer running loose in Paradise?"

His smile faded, and his expression grew serious. "Don't do anything like this again, Abby. It's too dangerous."

It was only about the hundredth time he'd said it, but I kind of liked the look on his face, so I nodded agreeably. "Deal." And I meant it. Really I did.

We fell silent and watched the activity around us for a few minutes. Karen, back on her medication and back at work, at least until my leg was better, was running the show with quiet efficiency. We still had issues to work out, but they were out in the open now, and I figured that would make it easier to find a resolution. I wouldn't be happy until she'd come back permanently, and I think she knew it.

Evie Rice, whose first-place win on the second night of competition hadn't surprised anybody, stood a few feet away, watching intently while Meena Driggs delivered her egg nog fudge to the judging table. I'd tasted Meena's fudge earlier, and I had a feeling Evie had some competition. I just prayed that we wouldn't have a repeat performance from the first night. A cook-off between the two contestants I could handle. I wasn't sure I'd survive another round of hysterics.

It seemed like a lifetime ago that we'd been here for the first night's judging of the contest, and for Savannah I guess it had been. I hadn't always liked her, but no one deserved to die simply because she'd stumbled across the truth.

It had taken a few days, but once Jawarski and the other investigators had started tugging at the threads of Miles Horne's life, they'd unraveled a whole nest of lies. In fact, his *entire* adult life had been one lie after another, from the Harvard education right down to the job he'd landed in New York.

How he'd faked the credentials well enough to pull that one off was beyond me, but he'd done it. I guess he'd had lots of practice. He'd been scamming people since he graduated from high school—maybe even before that. The police were still unraveling who knew what and when they knew it, but everyone connected to him seemed to be shocked and outraged. I wasn't sure we'd ever know the whole truth.

Even Savannah hadn't suspected the truth until a chance encounter with someone from Miles's past had opened her eyes. That's all any of us really knew at this point. Her biggest mistake had been in confronting her husband instead of going to the police.

Maybe she thought she owed him something, even if he had lied to her since the day they met. Love can make fools out of anybody, I guess.

Speaking of foolish hearts, mine thumped around a little when Jawarski reached past me for a Rocky Road Drop. He popped it into his mouth, closed his eyes, and moaned with pleasure. "These are great," he said. "Better than the ones my mom used to make."

I cocked an eyebrow at him. "You have a mother?"

The question dropped out of my mouth before I could stop it. I was all ready for him to give me that look and clam up the way he does, but one eye opened, and he gave me one of those lopsided grins of his. "Yeah I do, believe it or not."

"Is she still alive?"

He nodded slowly and looked away. Another silence fell between us, but this one didn't last as long. "Still alive."

"Does she live around here?"

He shook his head, still without looking at me. "She's in Montana. Lives about ten miles from my kids."

I nearly choked on my tongue. "You have kids?"

"Two." He did look at me then, and the question in his

eyes touched something I still wasn't completely sure I wanted touched. "They're fourteen and twelve."

It was my turn to sit silently, but that didn't last long either. I wasn't sure what this meant for us. Maybe nothing. "Are they boys or girls?"

"One of each. Ridge is the oldest. Cheyenne's in seventh grade." His gaze dropped to his fingertips, and he scraped at something on one finger. "I don't see them often enough, but I talk to them twice a week."

"Oh." A million different things were tumbling around in my head, but I wasn't sure how to react or what to say. He had kids. That meant he probably had an ex-wife out there somewhere. At least, I *hoped* she was an ex.

After a long time, I reached across the space between us and put my hand on his. He turned his over and laced his fingers through mine. Yeah, I wanted to know more, but I decided not to push. I'd asked, and even though it had taken a while, he'd answered.

For tonight, that was enough.

Candy Recipes

Divine Saltwater Taffy

Yields: 1 pound

- 2 *tablespoons butter (use real butter, not margarine)*
- 1 *cup sugar*
- ¾ *cup light corn syrup*
- 1 *teaspoon salt*
- ⅔ *cup water*
- 1 *tablespoon cornstarch*
- 1 *teaspoon flavoring of your choice*
- *food coloring*

Using the butter, grease a square 8 x 8 x 2-inch pan.

In a saucepan, mix together the sugar, corn syrup, salt, water, and cornstarch. Cook over medium heat, stirring occasionally until a candy thermometer reads 256°.

Remove from heat at once.

Stir in desired color and flavoring and pour into buttered pan. Allow candy to cool.

Pull taffy until it is light in color and stiff.

Pull into 2-inch strips, cut, and wrap in waxed paper.

Cappuccino Divinity

Yields: 20 Servings (1½ pounds)

- *2½ cups sugar*
- *½ cup dark Karo syrup*
- *½ cup water*
- *¼ teaspoon salt*
- *2 egg whites*
- *2 tablespoons dark rum*
- *1 teaspoon vanilla extract*
- *2 teaspoons instant coffee powder*
- *½ teaspoon ground cinnamon*
- *1 cup chopped walnuts or pecans (if desired)**

In a 2-quart saucepan, stir together the sugar, Karo syrup, water, and salt. Stirring constantly, bring to a boil over medium heat.

Reduce heat.

Stop stirring and cook to soft ball stage (candy thermometer registers 248°). Just before the candy temperature reaches 248°, beat egg whites in a large bowl with mixer at high speed. Beat until stiff peaks form. Keeping mixer at high speed, slowly pour about one-half of the hot mixture over the egg whites.

Cook remaining syrup to 272°, or until a small amount of mixture when dropped into very cold water separates into threads that are hard but not brittle.

Remove from heat and stir in the dark rum and vanilla. Beating constantly, slowly pour the hot syrup over the egg white mixture.

Beat in coffee powder and ground cinnamon. Continue beating until mixture begins to lose its gloss, and a small amount of mixture holds a soft peak when dropped from a spoon.

*Add 1 cup chopped walnuts or pecans to mixture with coffee powder and cinnamon if desired.

If the mixture becomes too stiff for the mixer, beat with a heavy wooden spoon.

Drop by teaspoonfuls onto waxed paper.

Let cool.

Store in a tightly covered container at room temperature.

Lady Slippers
(Butterscotch Drops)

Yields: about 4 dozen

2 cups sugar
¼ cup light corn syrup
½ cup (1 stick) real butter
2 tablespoons water
2 tablespoons white wine vinegar (don't substitute another kind)

Combine all ingredients in 2-quart heavy saucepan. Stir and cook mixture over medium heat until the sugar is dissolved.

Reduce heat and cook at a medium boil, stirring as needed to control foaming and avoid sticking as mixture thickens. If sugar crystals form on sides of pan, wipe down with a moistened pastry brush.

Cook to the hard crack stage (300° on a candy thermometer).

Remove from heat and let mixture stand for 1 minute.

Meanwhile, butter 2 sheets of aluminum foil and place on 2 baking sheets. Quickly drop teaspoonfuls of butterscotch onto foil, making patties about 1 inch in diameter. Space them at least 1/2 inch apart.

If the candy thickens and does not drop easily, set the pan in hot water until the mixture is again workable.

Strawberry Bonbons

Yields: 40 berries

1 can sweetened condensed milk
2 7-oz. packages flaked coconut
1 4-oz. package strawberry gelatin
1 cup blanched almonds
1 teaspoon almond extract
red food coloring
water

2¼ cups confectioners' sugar, sifted
2 tablespoons heavy cream
green food coloring
(You'll also need a pastry bag with an open star tip)

Combine the milk, coconut, 1/3 cup of the gelatin, almonds, and almond extract. Add red food coloring to tint the mix to the shade you want.

Chill for one hour.

Using 1/2 tablespoon–size drops of the mix, form into strawberry shapes. Sprinkle the remaining gelatin onto waxed paper and roll each strawberry to coat.

Using a pastry brush, lightly brush each strawberry with water.

In a small bowl, combine the confectioners' sugar, heavy cream, and green food coloring.

Using the pastry bag and open star tip, pipe leaves on top of each strawberry. Place bonbons on baking sheets lined with waxed paper. Chill berries for one hour.

Store covered at room temperature.

Rocky Road Drops

Yields: 5 dozen

1 11½ oz. package milk chocolate morsels
1 14-oz. can sweetened condensed milk
3 cups miniature marshmallows
2 cups dry roasted peanuts
1 cup raisins

In the top of a double boiler, over hot (but not boiling) water, melt chocolate morsels together with sweetened condensed milk; remove from heat.

In large bowl, combine the marshmallows, nuts, and raisins; stir in chocolate mixture.

Drop by teaspoonfuls onto baking sheets lined with waxed paper.

Chill for 2 hours or until firm.

Store loosely covered in cool, dry place.

Celestial Chocolate French Toast

Yields: 6 servings

3 1.55 oz. milk chocolate candy bars (no nuts)
3 eggs
1 cup milk
1 teaspoon sugar
1 teaspoon vanilla extract
¼ teaspoon salt
12 slices day-old bread
2 tablespoons real butter
confectioners' sugar (for dusting at the end)

Break each candy bar in half, the short way. Grate just a little chocolate (no more than 1/2 teaspoon off of each piece) and save in a small bowl for later.

In a medium bowl, beat the eggs with the milk, sugar, vanilla, and salt. Pour half of this mixture into a large (13 x 9-inch) ungreased baking dish.

Layer six slices of bread horizontally over the egg mixture. Place one piece of candy bar in the center of each piece of bread. Top each slice with remaining pieces of bread like sandwiches. Pour the remaining egg mixture over the sandwiches. Let this stand for at least 5 minutes so the bread can absorb the egg mixture.

On a griddle or in a large skillet, melt the butter over medium heat. Fry sandwiches until golden brown on both sides. Add an additional 2 teaspoons of butter midway, if cooking in batches.

To serve, cut each sandwich diagonally. Dust with confectioners' sugar and sprinkle with chocolate shavings.

The *Tea Shop* mystery series by

LAURA CHILDS

DEATH BY DARJEELING

0-425-17945-1

Meet Theodosia Browning, owner of Charleston's beloved Indigo Tea Shop. Theo enjoys the full-bodied flavor of a town steeped in history—and mystery.

GUNPOWDER GREEN

0-425-18405-6

Shop owner Theodosia Browning knows that something's brewing in the high society of Charleston—murder.

SHADES OF EARL GREY

0-425-18821-3

Theo is finally invited to a social event that she doesn't have to cater—but trouble is brewing at the engagement soiree of the season.

THE ENGLISH BREAKFAST MURDER

0-425-19129-X

Just as she's about to celebrate her work to help protect the sea turtles of Charleston, Theo spots a dead body bobbing in the waves.

THE JASMINE MOON MURDER

0-425-19986-X

Theo is catering a Charleston benefit, a "Ghost Crawl" through Jasmine Cemetery, when the organizer drops dead—and it looks like foul play.

Available wherever books are sold or at
penguin.com